Man Harvesting Man

By John P. Waters

A Virtual Publishing Group Edition
2000

For Information Address:
Virtual Publishing Group, Inc.
2817 Stanton Street
Berkeley, California 94702-2522
U.S.A.
Published and Printed in the United States of America

Virtual Publishing Group, Inc.

Man Harvesting Man

By John P. Waters

A Virtual Publishing Group Edition
2000

Virtual Publishing Group, Inc.

The mystery begins...

and ends with murder in the farming town of Lyons, Michigan. The townsfolk try to convince rookie M.B.I. Agent Kevin Sir that the victim Doug Richards was destroyed by drugs and alcohol, as well as by the murder weapon—a bloody pitchfork. They suggest that Kevin take a hard look at the "longhairs," the town's bad boys. Agent Sir is perturbed that a crime such as this has occurred in a farming community, a place that prides itself on growing and nurturing life, not extinguishing it. The longhairs have their own idea about who killed Doug Richards. They blame the worshippers of the Men's Episcopal Group. They claim this right-wing band of religious zealots are getting rid of the drugs by killing off their morally bankrupt users and distributors. Ultimately, Kevin confronts dark and dangerous resentment, not only within the townsfolk, but also within himself. It is a tough fight, but he vanquishes both.

Introduction

Ring!

"Hello, Waters residence."

"Yes, my name is Professor Hashimoto from Whitman College, may I speak to either Mary or James, please."

My mom nervously responds, "Yes, this is Mary."

She motions for my dad to come closer to the phone.

Professor Hashimoto says, "Mary, I'm your son's, John's, freshman English teacher and I have some serious concerns about his studies. He's a curious young man. He turns in some very creative pieces, but grammatically his writing is all over the map. He's failing."

"Oh."

Mom looks over at dad and whispers what the professor just said. My dad motions to mom for the phone.

"Jim Waters, here. Thanks for your call. What do you suggest that we do?"

"Well, the semester is almost over. I could give him a C minus or..."

"Yes?"

"Well, there are some students, every now and then, who need special attention because they really do deserve it. I'd like to out and out fail him and then allow him to retake my class next semester. He and I would meet in my office and I'd tutor him one on one. If he completes this program, he'd get an A."

Yes, this conversation really did take place. And the book that you're about to read is from me, a guy who flunked freshman English. My life can best be described as passionate. I really do well in the things that I like; and I really don't do well in the things that I hate. Also, it takes perseverance in life to make those things that you like an integral part of your life, in spite of many people's attempts to divert you from your goals. In short you have to have what Earnest Hemingway calls "intestinal fortitude" for the things in your life that you deem is worth fighting for (oops! ended a sentence with a preposition, sorry Prof. Hashimoto).

Life as depicted in this novel "Man Harvesting Man," is very complex. The human condition exists because we are constantly fighting for our place in society and often times our plight rubs someone the wrong way; be it religion, money or drugs.

I've fought my path through life much like a harvester swaths its way through a cornfield. I've attempted to harvest as much as I can from every situation. For instance, when I was in high school, I ran for class president and won. But I also took Latin and almost killed myself trying to learn this arcane language. Then in college, I started off poorly in my studies, as you just learned. But I fought off those negative experiences with positive ones: leading whitewater raft trips down the Deschutes River (Class IV rapids), hosting my own radio show on the college station, joining a fraternity, Beta Theta Pi, and writing for the college newspaper. I also started to take creative writing classes, my real love (in which I got As).

Remember my freshman English experience? Terrible. But it did teach me that if I wanted to write creatively, I had to learn to also write well. Thus, I discovered that anything I want in life is going to be fought for with my sweat. I remember a chemistry college professor saying to me: we are humans, we are not rocks, so we sweat.

Well, if you're going to be a success in life and you're not intellectually gifted, be it through studying the law or medicine, not only are you going to sweat, but you are going to be drenched in it because of all the battles that you have had to overcome.

In fact trying to get this novel published was a feat. When I first graduated from the University of Colorado in Boulder, I got into advertising as a copywriter and thought that writing print, radio and TV ads was going to be fulfilling. I had no desire to write fiction because I was creating award-winning headlines and fun spots that people in their cars and at home would laugh and marvel at.

Alas, that wasn't the case at all. I remember being so disillusioned by the process of taking a copywriter's and graphic artist's ideas and running them into the ground that in a burst of frustration, I imagined the account managers and clients being killed by a pitchfork, thus, the murder weapon of choice in this book.

I had no formal training in writing novels. Most M.F.A. programs introduce master's students to the format, but not undergrad, so having only completed my B.A., I was starting from scratch.

So I read some books about how to get published and attended adult-learning classes and writers' workshops. The only conclusion that I came up with was that this goal of getting published was insanely risky at best. Only after five years of writing and rewriting, did I get an agent.

And get this, she receives 3,000 unsolicited manuscripts a year, of which she agrees to represent only 20. Then only a handful out of the 20 make it into bookstores.

"Man Harvesting Man" is murder mystery. Its prime goal is to take you the reader on a suspenseful journey. But it's more than that as well. It's also an editorial of sorts about what I think is going on in our society. My voice resonates through the thoughts, actions and deeds of many of the characters, including the narrator. I'm truly not as judgmental as many of the characters are in the book.

I have strong feelings about religion, drugs and money. I can see many sides of the picture. I feel for how Dale Horton sees his life as being "good" and Doug Richards' life as being "bad." But I can also see how Doug was just experiencing youth. Don't we have a sitting President who has tried, albeit, not inhaled, marijuana?

Life is not simple, nor is it neat. Remember we're not rocks that can be assembled into orderly piles.

Life is not all bad, either. When I first started this project in my twenties, I was the typical angry, young man. I was in a profession, advertising, that was 1% creative and 99% kiss ass; and I hated it. But I wasn't smart enough to go into law school or medical school, my first two choices. So, my first drafts of "Man Harvesting Man" were painfully negative. None of the characters were likable, which to my readers is an important characteristic!

My life had to become better, itself, before the voices in my head that propel my fingers on the keyboard became better tempered. And it did and it has. Let's just say, I'm not dead, I haven't killed any body and I'm happy with the little things like, "It's a beautiful day," "This pop is really cold" and "I'm glad my brother and sister-in-law's new son just smiled at me."

The reason why this first novel about main character, Kevin Sir, is based on a farm is because I grew up on one very similar to the farm in the book. Born in Michigan, I grew up on one of the largest independent farms in the state. The four generation-owned family farm was lost during the grain embargo of the Carter Administration.

However, a lot of very good memories are with me today concerning how nature played an important role in my life:

I remember spending a half an hour, waiting for our school bus, throwing snowballs at a telephone pole across the street and loving it. I remember when after raking the leaves we'd pile them into the driveway and burn them. We'd jump over the flames while chestnuts exploded beneath our feet. I remember chiseling a tomato crop on a hot summer day. I had just finished lunch. The sun felt great. I took off my shirt, settled back and then promptly fell asleep on our John Deere tractor. I took out three rows of plants before I woke up! I remember seeing animals being born, raising them and seeing them die.

I guess I just remember how the outdoors always seemed wonderfully out of my control. Today, as our culture becomes increasingly more ordered and commercialized, I find it sad that to experience nature we need to max out our credit cards at R.E.I. so that we're "prepared" before the next big hike up Long's peak. I find it sad that we're so frickin' lazy that we cannot park our cars and sit down and have a nice meal, instead of angrily waiting in line for some anonymous teenager to take our order for lunch.

Our society is becoming increasingly more hostile because we're coming up with as many contraptions as possible to make our lives sweat-free. But we're not frickin' rocks, remember, we're humans. We need to interact with each other!

Enough said.

If you like my style of writing, my next book, also based upon Kevin Sir's adventures as a state agent take him to Utah where he meets many unusual characters, not unlike Sneakers in this book, and does battle against corporate greed in the telecommunications field, while off in the not too far distance Olympiads and the citizens of Beaver City gear themselves for the start of the pinnacle of winter sports, the 2002 Olympics.

Now, sit back, relax and enjoy "Man Harvesting Man."

If you have any questions, thoughts or ideas about
this piece, please e-mail me at johnpwaters99@yahoo.com.

P.S. Here's to all the supportive parents of writers, caring English teachers and of course bartenders in the world! Cheers.

Chapter 1

From within a small, brick silo, a scream breaks out. The murderer stabs at the prone, wriggling Doug Richards with a pitchfork. Its steel tines rip into the victim's soft, white body. Doug reaches up, as if to pray. But the killer's only blessing is another jab into Doug's bloodied torso. Again and again, the human threshing machine chops up the kid's crimson flesh. The end comes when one prong brakes through a rib and punctures the aorta.

The murderer hisses, "Take that longhair."

As Doug's blood spills onto the floor, the countryside's crickets sing louder. Sensing danger, farmer Snipes' only barn owl flies off into clear Michigan night. And so, tonight in Lyons, a town of 900 people, experiences its first murder in more than 20 years.

The next day, Doug's body is found by farmer Snipes' cat. While hunting for its breakfast of mice, the cat runs through a pool of human blood. The cat's bloody paws leave a trail, which the Snipes' grandchildren closely follow. The children, small brained but not totally inept, cry to their grandfather that they think they've seen a dead man. Snipes, more a poet of Jack Daniels than Mr. Keorac, downs some liquor in the hopes that his youngins are wrong.

"Shit, what's I's supposed to do? Bury him? Shit, I'm an old man. Supposed to be the other way around. Don't like lookin' at no dead kid. Specially not before I'm good and drunk."

After a half of bottle, Snipes stumbles to the door. He stamps his feet and grabs his trusty cane, which is wrapped in silver electric tape after he cracked it over the head of the last banker who tried to repossess his farm. He wipes his left h and across his unshaven face. His old eyes peer down the porch steps as if they're insurmountable boulders that would turn back an experienced Himalayan guide. Tap. Tap.

He concludes, "Ok, time to go."

He takes one last swig. The cheap juice burns its way down a blackened esophagus. He swaggers, but he still can walk. He climbs down the wooden "boulders" and makes his way to the silo. Silence. Darkness.

Every silo has its own character, much like people. Some silos are big, some small; some tall, some short; some full, some ain't. This one is short, broken down, small and full of something... Doug Richard's body.

The old man enters the silo and sees a curled up corpse. He ambles over and pokes at Doug Richards with his cane to confirm the boy's death. The old man's eyes roll over and he starts to shake.

The phone, he thinks, does it still work? For the first time since he needed help with his departed wife, he picks up the phone, shakes the dust off the spindle and calls Sheriff John Sackett.

"Sackett, here."

The old man manages to say four words: "Kid. Dead. Silo. Blood."

"Who is this?"

"Snipes on Devereux."

"You drunk again, Snipes."

"Not as drunk as I'm gonna get. Now, get this kid out of my silo."

Sheriff Sackett rushes to his cruiser and speeds through town. He confirms the boy's death and dispatches an ambulance from Madison, a much larger city only fifteen minutes away.

Word of Doug's death creates a flurry of activity. Farmers come in off their fields. Farmers' wives cry in disbelief. Churches fill with grieving members. The Café is busier than ever. Lou's Bar is packed. Lyons' town council has an emergency meeting to iron out the public relations' wrinkles.

The consensus: No one can believe it. Murder, in Lyons? No way. Not here. Maybe in Madison a town of a 100,000 where a few bad apples run around in gangs and are occasionally seen on TV for fighting, drinking, drugging, vandalizing and getting themselves pregnant outside of wedlock, but everyone in Lyons is good. Everyone in Lyons is decent, except as a few in town would call the "longhairs." But even the longhairs are mild compared to what most people would call your criminal element.

Doug was considered a freshman longhair, newly recruited into the world of an occasional joint and the obligatory chug-a-lug at weekend keg parties. Doug was eighteen: old enough to die for his country; old enough to drive. Doug was a man now. High school was getting boring, besides. Yea, he was a good student up until his junior year, but when you're a senior—and you're not going to college—what's the point of trying. It's time to party!

In fact, so caught up in this new world of getting high and drinking beer that Doug quit high school a month ago and got his first full-time adult job working as a tire salesman in another small farm town down the road. All he had to do was greet farmers at the door, show them the newest tread designs,

take a few orders from his midget boss and collect a paycheck. Then it was off to the bar. Life was good!

Doug also discovered that he could make a little extra money selling marijuana from some guys who drove down from Madison once a week. They'd show up at the bar, Doug never had to leave his barstool. They'd sell him a few dime bags for $100 and Doug would sell it to his friends, plus a small commission for himself.

Doug was feeling good about himself. In a month or so, he was going to have enough money saved to move out of his parents' home. All he needed was a girlfriend. She didn't need to be beautiful, either, just nice and faithful. Kind of like Mom.

But now, all of Doug's dreams are dead. And so is he, thanks to some pot he sold to the wrong person. He's dead, because he never thought that there are always two sides to everything: what's good for one person is bad for another—Yin and Yang. Doug was too young to know that someone could be so upset with a weed so harmless.

Doug's funeral occurs on Wednesday. Doug is buried next to a baby who died in 1953 from influenza. On the other side is a cornfield. Everybody in town shows up. Wealthy farmers, poor farmers, townsfolk, even Lou, who shut the bar and got sober enough to shave and make a Windsor knot with his only red tie that still has last Thanksgiving Day's gravy stain on it. Yes, everyone is here. Everyone, including the killer.

Lyons, representative of any body of people, is torn: People who want change and people who don't. Doug's killer is one who desperately wants change. He's a member of the next generation. He sees Lyons' potential. He sees all this land and sees money. He and his fellow entrepreneurs see empty cornfields filled with new homes, shops and high tech industrial campuses. He sees decent people with good jobs raising families during the week and doing the Lord's work on Sunday.

Doug was too young to know what he wanted. But the people who grew up like Doug and are now the town's working class fear change. They don't want to lose their town to yuppies and their fast way of life. These working class Joes and Janes like driving slowly, like low tax rates, like having no pressures, no problems and no real responsibilities, besides the occasional Teachers Conference.

There's another more side of Lyons who fears change: The landowners,

who have been farmers their whole lives. These industrious men not only make ends meet but have enough left over to buy nice things. These hardworking people want the community to stay exactly as it was when they inherited the land from their fathers, who in turn inherited the land from their fathers, who in turn either inherited their land from a previous generation or killed enough Indians to make it White Man's land.

Manifest destiny reborn with each new generation.

This melting pot of greedy go-getters, those getting by and great landowners, all here to attend the funeral of one insignificant kid, demonstrates that everyone regardless of who they are, are scared to lose what they have. Doug's funeral represents the final fear everyone must eventually face.

The minister in town, Maynard, addresses the crowd, "My flock, Sunday was a terrible day for us. One of our own, Doug Richards, was taken from us. Please Jesus take him into your arms and reunite his soul with The Father. Amen. Now, everyone, please if you something to say speak up."

Mayor John Tapestry raises his head and reflects, "Doug was a hard worker. He helped out on my farm over the past few summers. Hang in there kid. Heaven to me is rows and rows of golden corn, where a man can watch over his herd without fences. Take care young man, I pray you're in a better place. A place where every day is a bountiful harvest."

The crowd mumbles in unison, "Amen."

A longhair, known as Keith Spelling, speaks, "Hey man, like the old man just said. Hope you're in a better place. Except my Heaven is filled with babes and beer. Here's for you!"

Keith pulls a Budweiser from his jacket, pops the top and downs it. The others in his ragtag group do likewise. Tears collect near the sides of Keith's eyes. Keith, even though he's rough around the edges, means every word. Like every one of his peers, he doesn't expect much out of life except a fair wage for a good day's work and some time to blow off some steam.

Some well-dressed women in boiled wool overcoats and Chanel perfume mutter under their breath about the longhairs' total disregard for drinking in public. They whisper into their husbands' ears that they have never seen such a display before at a funeral.

Trying to steer the funeral back to a more traditional bent, one of the leaders of this well-healed crowd, Dale Horton, says, "I think what everyone is saying is that a terrible tragedy occurred. And no one is more sorry than me. Doug was a person. A person who could have chosen Christ.

"Now, most of you know that I didn't approve of Doug's lifestyle. But that doesn't mean I shouldn't forgive him for his misdeeds.

"Jesus says we're all sinners before him. I'm no better than Doug, even if I don't do the things Doug did. We're all no better than each other before God. I too have a vision of heaven. It's bright with the sun and my wife and son are with me.

"And, all of you are there, too, including Doug. He's happy. He's the old Doug. The Doug who got good grades. The Doug before finding…"

The crowd collectively breathes in, waiting for Dale's judgement.

"…sin."

The sound of beer cans being crushed under the longhairs' feet tell Dale where he can put his precious speech.

The mayor and Sheriff Sackett quickly walk over and calm the longhairs down.

Minister Maynard finishes the ceremony with a hymn.

Everyone stops briefly to say goodbye to Doug and to give their condolences to Mr. and Mrs. Richards, who are standing numbly next to a shiny, new headstone. The stone has Doug's name carved into it, along with a trombone, like the one he played in the school band, and a pair of running shoes, like the ones he wore when he ran the 800 meter dash.

Lyons' inhabitants stumble back towards their cars and trucks. Some climb into Mercedes, others into mud-covered pickups.

No question, Lyons is boiling over. The top is about to shoot to the moon. The three main ingredients of this melting pot are tired of sharing space with each other.

And no one is more ill prepared to handle the policing of this melt down than Sheriff John Sackett. Sackett is a one-man show whose job is to hand out speeding tickets, not to keep the town from ripping itself a part.

So, Sheriff Sackett, unaccustomed to much ado, spends the majority of Thursday and Friday calming down Lyons' citizenry. He feels that his first job is to restore order, rather than to further tear apart the farm town with a lot of insinuating questions pointed at people who he has grown up with, gone to school with, hunted with, gone to church with and lived next to for so many years. At the end of the week, he is exhausted from all the additional police-work.

The crux comes Saturday morning, when Mrs. Richards' a non-confrontational person by nature blasts the sheriff for sitting on his hands while her son's killer runs loose: "Sheriff John Sackett, if I wasn't a Christian, upholding God's will that everyone be forgiven, I'd curse you for not doing your best in finding Douggie's murderer!"

"Madame, don't blame me. What I'm I suppose to do? No one's talking. I haven't got a clue."

"Sheriff, what about those drugs he was taking. Have you questioned any of his friends, you know the ones with the long hair?"

She turns away and looks up at the ceiling, yelling, "Oh, Douggie, why did you have to quit school and run with their kind! You know liquor is bad. Look what it's done to your father!"

Mrs. Richards' mind goes blank and she walks like a confused marionette to the door. God is up in the heavens pulling the strings. Her arms jump at her sides. Her legs fall under her torso. Sackett wonders if she'll make it to the door before stumbling.

The sheriff takes Mrs. Richards' hand and steadies her, escorting her the rest of the way.

"Norma, if I can't solve this thing. We'll need to bring in some outside help. Don't worry, one way or another we'll get this guy. Ok?"

Mrs. Richards doesn't answer. She opens the door and leaves.

Sunday afternoon the Town Council holds its second emergency meeting of the week, Mayor John Tapestry moderates the council. The council is made up of the Mr. Tapestry, who's been mayor for the past 25 years and the county's largest landowner; his sister Jane Dubois, another large landowner and one of Michigan's finest antique dealers; Maynard Baynes, St. John's Episcopal Reverend; Sal Everett, co-owner of the grain elevator, and its newest member, Derrick Palmer, Mr. Tapestry's son-in-law and heir apparent to his three farms—The Chestnut Hills farm complex.

All of the members are Lyons' pick of the crop. And there's not one townsfolk among them. All these council members are landowners who have been gifted some of the best farm land in America.

Jane, the most vocal of the council, states, "John, Sackett is a mess. We all know that. We need help, but not an overwhelming force, either."

Sal adds, "No, F.B.I."

Mr. Tapestry concurs, "Right, no F.B.I."

Rev. Baynes, suggests, "How about the M.B.I. (Michigan's Bureau of Investigation). They're local, and good."

Sal agrees, "Yes, the M.B.I. Someone young too. Young enough that he won't try and take over our town and bull-headed enough not to be swayed by a bribe or a threat."

Mr. Tapestry concludes, "Good. Let's give 'em a call.

"Now, how about an early cocktail hour up at the house?"

Everybody agrees except Derrick, who stopped drinking years ago and knows he has three farms to run.

Derrick knowingly chides, "It's only 2:30 p.m."

John Tapestry smiles, puts his long arm around his son-in-law and together they walk out of the library, which doubles as Lyons' Town Hall and which used to be Lyons' train station.

Monday morning comes and the sun's rays wash over the Wolverine State, awakening Detroit assembly-line workers, small town farmers and big city policemen. Detective Kevin Sir and his new wife Peggy are asleep in the Ann Arbor townhouse they just bought. They paid only $180,000, which Kevin thought was rather expensive. The clock radio begins to blare. Kevin and Peg brake through each other's sleepy clutches. The young detective taps the alarm clock.

"Morning, beautiful."

He leans over and tenderly kisses Peg.

She winces.

At last, she smiles and says, "Good luck today. Call me at the office— after 3—when you hear the good news. Now, let me go back to sleep."

Peg rolls over; her arm rests down across her shapely figure. Kevin admires his beautiful bride. Kevin unconditionally adores his new wife Peg. He thinks of her as his soul mate.

Not so with Peg, who married Kevin because she thought the time was right in her life's "executive planner" to merge with a good-looking, controllable member of the opposite sex.

She feels that he is good enough in bed to satisfy her for many years. He doesn't make enough money, but she wants to bring home the bacon, anyway. Her goal: To become partner in three years; which is unheard of at most law firms, unless you're an attractive female at an all-male firm who intentionally wears short skirts, makes an effort to suggestively touch every guy in the office and works sixty hours a week in order to bill the most. And Peg is all that. She wants people to know she's got a body and a brain and that she knows how to use both.

Kevin turns away—oblivious of his wife's controlling ways—and jumps into the shower. He gets dressed, jogs to his Ford Contour and backs out of the uncluttered garage. As of yet, there's not a Hot Wheels car, nor a pink Barbie bike to impede Kevin Sir's trip backwards. He speeds through the city, hurrying through traffic.

The rookie parks the car, gets out and strides into the downtown office of the Michigan Bureau of Investigation at a speed and with the strength of young ambition. Life's smattering of troublesome minutiae has yet to touch Kevin, nor even land on him, where the weight would slow down the young man. At this juncture in his life, he is all arms and legs.

Inside the well-kept brick M.B.I. building, a buzz of organized chaos ensues. Agents, mostly young men, are busily filing reports, telling jokes, going over current cases and taking phone calls from concerned citizens about leads and new crimes.

One phone call is fielded by Sergeant Jim Caretaker, a successful black agent who fought his way through the "white ceiling" of corporate crime-fighting.

"M.B.I., Sergeant Caretaker."

"John Tapestry calling. I'm the mayor of Lyons. Ever hear of us?"

"No sir. Continue."

Chuckling, Mr. Tapestry continues, "Didn't think so. To most people, we're kind of off the beaten path. What many Michiganders don't realize is small farm towns are everywhere, like bitsy sentences in a Hemingway book. But like reading 'Old Man and The Sea," if you don't like Papa's style, you won't pick up 'For Whom the Bell Tolls." Similarly, if Alba, Michigan isn't to your liking, Lyons, Michigan probably won't be either. That's OK. We don't like most people anyhow. Sergeant, I won't waste anymore of your time. We're at a dead end here."

"Yes?"

"Doug Richards, a local boy was murdered two Sundays ago. Our sheriff isn't too bright if you know what I mean. I mean no disrespect to John. It's just that a murder case is a little over his head. We're a small farming town. John Sackett is good at handing out speeding tickets, but…"

The sergeant cuts in, "I hear you mayor. What can we do?"

"Send us one of your agents."

"Well, before I do that, tell me more about the case, tell me more about Lyons."

"Lyons, Michigan—Our inhabitants are predominately church-going folks. It's a town that wants to be left alone. It's a town where people leave each other alone. Before Doug Richards' murder, Lyons was relatively crime-free. It's a town of people who know that if someone commits a crime, eventually that person will get caught. Because, where else are they going to go? Farms are relatively illiquid. You can't just pack up a few hundred head of cattle over night and move to the next county.

"It's a town where if a crime is committed then the criminal is usually caught without much ado. Because after a few weeks, maybe a couple of months, the criminal blabs something to their neighbor or friend and that person gossips what he's heard to a new party, until the news of the crime reaches someone with authority.

"Some cityfolk call this internal justice system "the small town way." But, there is a lot to be said for mob justice. No lawyers. No trial. And, this system is usually right about who did what to whom."

Sergeant Caretaker argues, "Yeah, but isn't the 'the small town way' a potential powder keg. What if you have corrupt leaders? The American justice system grew out of this 'small town way' many years ago. Because, there is an inherent danger when the law-makers turn out to be the law-breakers. And when the law that is broken is murder—a ghastly one at that— and the victim seems like a normal farm kid out doing his chores, "the small town way" really seems small and inadequate. Wouldn't you agree mayor?"

Mr. Tapestry asks, "Where you from Sergeant Caretaker? I detect a Southern accent."

This time Caretaker chuckles, "Louisiana. Went to college at Florida State. Have spent the majority of my time in Michigan. It's been 25 years now. Hate the snow."

"Look Sergeant, I would really appreciate your help. How about sending a newer agent, so that you don't waste one of your veterans on a minor murder investigation."

Sergeant thinks that out of all his agents at his disposal, one, Kevin Sir, fits the bill perfectly for this type of mission. Kevin's young, book smart and has done very well at his team assignments. What Kevin needs now is his first solo assignment. Kevin needs to develop his street smarts; he needs to learn to tap into himself for help, he needs to discover who he is without relying on others.

"Mayor, I have a man—Agent Kevin Sir. He graduated top of his academy class. He played college ball at the University of Colorado. Ever hear of him?"

"Sorry sergeant. Really don't pay attention to those things anymore. So, when can we expect Agent Sir?"

"I'll send him this A.M."

"Thank you sergeant. Thank you very much."

"Take care mayor. Let me know if there's anything else the M.B.I. can do."

Sergeant Jim Caretaker hangs up and looks outside his office window and remembers his first solo assignment. The Feds were close to raiding a fringe paramilitary group called the White Knights. They were holed up in a series of cabins near the hunting town of Grayling, a town in upper Michigan that didn't have one black family. Needless to say, young agent Caretaker stood out like a sore thumb.

His job was to cause enough problems that the White Knights would come after him. His fellow agents, working undercover in various positions, including one inside the militia group, would then take the Knights down. It took what seemed like years for the Knights to act against the black agent. In the meantime, he had been beaten, spit on and shunned from every store in Grayling.

In Grayling, there was no gray line: you were either black or white; a nobody or a somebody. Even the ignorant criminals, the White Knights, were more respected than a college-educated black federal agent.

Caretaker had other similar assignments where he, the token black man, had to flush out prejudiced criminals.

It wasn't until he met his future wife, Marie, in a Detroit diner that he felt loved. They married and she made her new husband leave the F.B.I. to stay closer to home. Jim Caretaker has been with the M.B.I. ever since, focusing on major crimes in Michigan.

Twenty-five years later, the Caretakers now have a beautiful, bright daughter studying pre-med at University of Michigan and a son who's a star athlete and junior class president in high school. Jim is very happy and proud of how his life has turned out. Even though he had to take his lumps early on, he wouldn't trade The Bureau for anything.

Now, it's Kevin Sir's turn. Is Kevin ready to go it alone? Is he ready to spend lonely days by himself investigating people who hate him? And spend even lonelier nights sorting out the days heated events, dreading the next day's onslaught?

Jim has been impressed with Kevin's first year on the force. Kevin's been on some major drug busts, but Kevin has always been surrounded by his team members. The longest Kevin's been undercover or had to make major decisions alone was the night he spent with The Dragons. Even then, his cover was created by another agent, who has since transferred to Denver for a less stressful job as a Unite Us Airlines pilot.

Kevin walks past his best friends on the force, Ted and Tim. He smiles at them and takes a seat at his desk. Kevin's desk is located in the middle of a large open room, affectionately called "The Bull Pen." It's where the animals—the agents—assemble to sort out the state's biggest crimes. Kevin admires a stunning picture of Peg, who's dressed in a red Lycra ski suit that hugs every bit of her athletic body.

Kevin looks around the room and sees the brightest and best police officers in Michigan. He feels proud to be a part of the elite group. He looks over at Sergeant Caretaker's door. A large black man fills its doorframe. The black sergeant waves at the rookie.

"Kevin," Sergeant Jim Caretaker's voice booms across the bullpen, "I have a case for you."

Kevin confidently addresses his superior: "Yes, sir."

Kevin gets up and walks into the sergeant's office.

"Please, shut the door and sit down."

Kevin grabs the brass handle and firmly shuts the door. He sits down on a leather chair, adjusts his blue Brooks Brothers' suit and waits for orders.

"I've been going over this week's log and see a spot where you can do a lot of good. Ever hear of Lyons, Michigan?"

"No sir."

"It's a small farm town forty-five minutes southwest of here. A murder occurred there last week. The mayor just called me. Now, it's not a big case, but it's important. Lyons may only have 900 people, but to them a terrible thing has just happened to one of their own."

Kevin acknowledges, "I understand."

"Kevin, murder in a close-knit community is tough. Everyone becomes suspicious of everyone else, even though they've known each other their whole lives. Yet everyone is afraid to be the first one to point the finger at someone else.

"Kevin, what you must do is gain power over Lyons' watchers and in turn you'll gain their respect. Only then will one of them trust you enough to squeal. The rest of the case will fall into place, like dominoes."

Somewhat confused at his sergeant's recommendation, Kevin asks, "Sir?"

Sergeant Caretaker lets out a sigh and reiterates, "Kevin, you must be in a position of strength. You will have to force the issue. No one's going to come up and say, 'He did it.' In fact, even when their back is up against the wall, you still may have to rub their face across the bricks to make sure that they know you're serious. OK?"

"OK."

"Good. Here's the case file. I expect you to go out there this morning. Be sure to pack enough clothes in case you're there for a while. I first want you to interrogate a farmhand named Keith Spelling. He's the leader of this group called 'the longhairs.' Mrs. Richards blames them for her son's death."

Caretaker extends the file to Kevin.

Kevin takes hold of it.

The two men's eyes meet for an instant.

Momentarily, they cease their superior/underling stance.

Each man continues to hold onto the file: one having lived in harm's way and another about to be immersed into it.

Caretaker smiles and consoles: "Kevin, one more thing: You're about to discover that being a detective, especially in a seemingly pleasant, but very hostile and secretive environment, will take every fiber of your being to make the case stick.

"You'll be in a situation where having coffee in a small town's Rotary Club will be more deadly than being in a shootout in a big city's drug-infested alley."

"Why?"

"Because at least in the alley, the enemy is sticking the gun in your face, not in your back."

Caretaker releases the file.

The sergeant pats the rookie on the shoulder and sits back down.

Kevin leaves by saying he'll try his best.

Jim concludes the meeting by saying that he knows Kevin will and to check in by phone on a regular basis.

Kevin shuts the sergeant's door and strides through the bullpen to his desk. Ted and Tim are anxiously waiting the results of Kevin's meeting.

Ted chain smokes, he is skinny and not too athletic, but he is both book- and street-smart. He is a good guy to have in the background of a complex case. The guys at the office say he is incredibly mellow under fire.

Tim is a tiny man, who carries himself as if he is 6' 4". He is a real fireball. He is also detail-minded and a great sharpshooter. You would want him next to you anytime during a raid.

Ted jokes, "Hey rookie, whatcha get. Another by-the-book drug bust. You know we're thinking of trading you in for a German Shepherd. A drug dog costs a hell of a lot less and, like you, all they do is rush in head first. No college degree needed."

"Ha, very funny."

Tim asks, "Seriously, Kevin, what's your case?"

"Have to investigate a murder in farm town called Lyons. Ever hear of if?"

Both seasoned agents shake their heads no.

Tim asks, "What did the sergeant recommend?"

"Be careful because small towns can be deceptively sinister."

Ted says, "Caretaker should know. His first assignments as a rookie were based in small towns. Tell you what, when Tim and I were staking out this pot farmer last year, I pulled this interesting case study off the Internet, having to do with small town mentality. I printed it out. Hold on while I find it."

Tim and Kevin discuss Tim's family. He has three children: 7, 5 and 2 years old. Kevin thinks each one is adorable. It reminds him how great it will be when he and Peg decide to start a family. Peg promises that as soon as she makes partner, they'll have a serious talk about having kids. Tim says that he and Sally may have a fourth. They just love having a newborn around the house.

Ted comes back with the report, put together by the National Opinion Research Center, a 1994 General Social Survey. The three agents spend an hour or so perusing the report and helping Kevin map out his case.

Ted reads, "The report says that small-town people are proud to be Americans 52% over the 48% of the U.S. Small-town people say they feel safe walking around their neighborhood at night 65% versus 55% for the rest of America. They are predominately more Republican—37% versus 32% for all U.S."

Ted looks at Tim, who says, "So they respect law and order and they don't like big government."

Ted continues, "Yes, but the white paper also says that 65% of small-town people versus 45% of all U.S. have guns in their homes. That 80% of small-town people versus 67% don't want to share America with newcomers. And that small-town people disagree with the Supreme Court ruling that the Bible and the Lord's Prayer are not to be read in public schools 69% versus 59%."

Ted sets the report down.

Tim concludes, "And so folks in small towns like their guns, their space and their God."

Ted asks the rookie, "How many people live in Lyons?"

Kevin looks at the file the sergeant gave him and says, "Only 900 people."

Ted warns, "You see Kevin, I know what you're thinking. You saying to yourself, 'Lyons is small so it's going to be an easy case.' However, solving a murder in a small town is going to be much tougher than that. As the sergeant says and as this report details, small town people act as one. You can question them all, but no one will turn in the other because they risk being ostracized. Got it?"

The rookie says, "Look, I know you're trying to help me. Let me go out there and try. If I fall flat on my face then I'll dust myself off and try again. All I'm asking for is a chance. Ok?"

Ted says, "Kevin, you're like a butterfly with a life-span of nine months. Like your insect brethern, you live on the adrenolinous edge of things. Sugar is your day's staple. To maintain your energy, you hop from situation to situation, from flower to flower without thinking."

Tim holds out his hand and says, "Good luck. And call us if you need help."

Ted reiterates, "If you want to bounce ideas off us without the sergeant knowing, call us. We haven't been around here for a more than a decade for nothing. Ok?"

"Thanks guys. See you in a week or so."

The agent puts the file and report into his briefcase. He snaps the brass latches down and grabs the leather handle. The rookie puts on his Raybans and walks outside.

A tiny hand nudges Kevin's elbow. It's Tim's.

The veteran agent says, "One more thing, don't worry about Peg. Sally and I will take care of her. Sally is already cooking extra dinners to take over to your condo. Peg still likes Sally's cooking?"

"Of course."

"Great. Take care Kevin. And be safe."

Tim goes back inside.

The autumn sky is blue, which for Michigan is rare. The October sun blazes, but can't quite pierce the chill that is enveloping the state. The rookie gets into his Contour and drives back home to pack.

Chapter 2

The one, new, stick-of-a maple tree in front of Kevin and Peg's condo has already dropped its dozen or so leaves. The rookie pulls up to their condo, quickly packs suits and sundry toiletries for his trip and leaves a short love letter for Peg.

Kevin then consults his road map, picks up a Starblacks' coffee and hits the on-ramp to the highway. He settles back and stabs at his coffee. He turns on KBLU, University of Michigan's alternative radio station, and listens to the Dave Matthews Band croon away. Then a Honda Accord, with a Christian fish symbol screwed onto its trunk, unforgivingly cuts off the agent, causing him to spill hot coffee into his lap.

"Damn it," he pants.

He bolts up and wipes away the coffee from his pants. In a few minutes, he calms down. His two-week old Ford Contour easily keeps up with the speeding semis along Highway I-94. The drive is short. The farm town is only an hour from Ann Arbor.

Kevin's Ford pulls up behind an empty cattle truck. Cow shit stains the bottom half the metal trailer. Kevin and the cattle truck together bounce down the highway. KBLU's signal gets weaker; more static than music. He tries the other FM stations, but nothing. He turns the radio off and looks out across the fields.

Kevin thinks, Lyons, what kind of name is that? He remembers that French settlers inhabited this area early in Michigan's history. Maybe, they named the small hamlet to remind them of home across the Atlantic?

Lyons' exit approaches. Kevin gets off the highway and pulls onto broken pavement surrounding the Truck Stop. He parks in front of filmy, pane-glass windows speckled with small, black fly excrement.

Kevin leaves his spotless car and walks into the smoky cafe. Men with huge stomachs hunch over plates of pan-fried food. Their forks shovel up eggs, syrup and sausage bits.

The closer he walks into the Truck Stop, an air of dull hatred begins to seep into Kevin's consciousness. The rookie does not like this emotional transition.

Kevin stomps his feet on the linoleum to shake the dread. The men, hearing this challenge, stop eating. Their forks momentarily cease their upward flight. Mouths open, the men turn toward this interloper and wait for his next move.

Kevin eyes span the crowd looking for the source of their antagonism. He feels small. He tries to fight their looks. But the older men patiently wait for Kevin to give in.

A chubby waitress, stuffed into a pink uniform, confronts the M.B.I. agent. The waitress' head looks as if it is a battered weather balloon left up in the heavens much too long. The icy rain and howling winds have made her skin thick and red.

She squints through the smoke at Kevin.

The barrel of a lady remains mute.

Kevin asks, "Where I can find the Sheriff's Office?"

She retaliates, "Yeah, what for?"

"I'm the state agent here assigned to the Richards' killing."

The men's forks simultaneously drop on chipped China plates. Their heads drop lower as if they are positioning themselves to lunge forward to protect a known member of their cause—the waitress—from an unknown member of their clan—Kevin.

Kevin tries to pretend he is not intruding, keeping his facial muscles relaxed, his eyes glazed and unfocused, his mouth frowning and his jaws loose. He centers his anxiety towards his hands, which are conveniently located behind the counter. He stabs his fingernails into his palms and waits for her to serve him a few, choice words that will direct him to the Sheriff's Office.

She remains stubbornly quiet.The whole place has verbally shut down.

Then finally, an aged farmer, whose visage is blotchy from too much cheap Skol vodka, coughs, breaking the long silence.

The slug of a waitress moves into action.

From behind the beat-up, manual cash register she pushes a few, large buttons and spews, "Just go up the road. If it'd be any closer, it'd bite your ass."

Kevin glares at her. His athletic instincts take over, as if Colorado State's all-state middle linebacker, Jason McReady, is rushing him. Time to fight back.

"Hey, look, lose the attitude. I'm here because your mayor called for our help."

Kevin glares at her.

The waitress slams the cash register drawer and retreats behind the row of large stomachs.

She mumbles, "We don't want your help. Go home city boy!"

Kevin states, "Well, you're going to get it."

The men collectively pick up their forks again and begin the task of gorging themselves with lipid-based foodstuffs. The likes of which have been practically banned in today's health-conscious society. Long live LDL (the "bad" cholesterol) goes the cry!

The rookie angrily looks around the room for any sort of acknowledgement. But the men's eyes are focused on their next bites. Kevin exits the greasy spoon, fuming.

He jams the key into the ignition, jerks the car from park into drive and speeds through a canyon of oily tractor-trailers. Their massive engines continue to run. The sound tries to rumble through his tense body.

Kevin mulls, "What in the hell just happened?"

He slows the car down.

"No matter," he concludes, "because as Jim teaches, a good agent must work through it—on to the next interview."

Making his way on North Lyons Road, the rookie passes a number of commercial buildings made of inferior cinder blocks—the building material that drives today's more visionary architects to slit their wrists. He hops over worn railroad tracks and then motors onto Main Street.

The town looks deserted, as if someone pulled a fire alarm handle a few years ago and no one has given the go ahead for its people to come back home.

The sidewalks are clean, but the street's gutters are littered with empty potato chip bags. They are made of plastic, so they, along with cockroaches and old Sonny Bono records, will be here 10,000 years from now.

Kevin parallel parks outside the small storefront with a Sheriff's Office label stuck to a large, pane window. The label is cracked, faded and peeling. Flies buzz around it, as if they are trying to escape. Further inside the office sits a small girl. Down is her head, bowing to her secretarial pressures, i.e., fighting tedium and looking busy.

Kevin glides open the car's door. Unconsciously, he pulls out quarters from his front pocket to put into a parking meter, but Lyons has none. He surveys the sides of the street.

Across Main Street is a large, well-dressed man entering the town's insurance office. Kevin waves towards him. The man flicks his lit cigarette Kevin's way and barrels through his office's door. So far, Lyons' fierceness is living up to a trait it shares with its homophone, Lions.

Kevin enters the Sheriff's Office. He gives the door a firm push and steps into the lobby. Inside, the secretary blinks, similar to cheap, plastic blinds that you "custom order" in one day. They snap shut and bounce back open. Her eyes roll around in their sockets. Finally, her gaze meets the rookie.

"Hello, I'm Kevin Sir from the Michigan Bureau of Investigation. It's nice to meet you."

The thin, bespectacled woman says, "Hi, the sheriff will be out in a few minutes. Would you like a cup of coffee?

"Yes, thanks."

She pops up, fetches the coffee and runs back behind her desk. She moves with the efficiency of a human vending machine.

She blurts, "What do you think of our fair town so far?"

Kevin thinks, he could bring up the Truck Stop incident to her, but she probably wouldn't understand. Better to keep things conversational.

"Fine."

She fires out another question: "How long did it take you?"

"An hour"

"Heavens, you must have been driving fast."

Trying to stay in sync with her, Kevin hastily responds, "Oh, traffic was light. Got here in no time."

She stops pouring the coffee, looks up at Kevin and snaps her gum.

He continues, "Looks like you don't have a rush hour problem here, though."

The secretary asks, "Cream, sugar?"

"No thanks."

She takes quick baby steps towards Kevin and places the Styrofoam cup on the table.

She leans over to Kevin, smiles and announces "Name's Starla."

She adjusts her glasses, turns her back to Kevin and says to the wall, "We don't have many cars in these parts, mostly trucks and tractors. But I've seen highways full of cars on reruns of C.H.I.P.S., you know the cop show with Eric Estrada. He's such a... hunk."

She returns to her chair and smiles again. A two-pack a day smoking habit has left her teeth black around the edges. Kevin politely smiles back at her. He settles further into the tweed couch and stabs at his coffee.

Kevin surveys the sheriff's beige-on-beige office. The tan couch that he's sitting on is next to a brown, wood table. On the table is a brownish brass lamp with a burlap lampshade. The walls are covered with chestnut and white wallpaper. Even the framed art is of reddish-brown deer standing in front of trees with yellow and brown leaves. The secretary sits behind a partition of flimsy brown paneling.

Her brown hair, brown eyes and beige skin are perfect camouflage for the similarly colored surroundings. If it were not for her quick, movements, as those of a house fly evading a plastic swatter, Kevin would swear she was a part of the furnishings.

Minutes go by.

Then ten.

Then fifteen.

The sheriff doesn't appear.

Kevin drains the rest of his coffee.

Starla hums to herself while reading the horoscopes.

Kevin stands up and clears his throat.

He says, "You said the sheriff would see me after a few minutes. But he's still in his office. Madame, I mean Starla, you know this case is important. Can you tell him it's urgent?"

Starla smiles at the handsome agent and soothes, "Honey, the sheriff has his own timetable. If I try to hurry him, he'll only get mad at both of us. Relax, he'll be out in a few minutes."

Kevin sits back down and flips through the magazines on the table. None of them are newer than April of '91 and most of them have covers of new combines or dead deer. Kevin turns around to face Main Street. From behind the large pane window, he scans Lyons. Main Street is deserted—a sad fact, which according to the case file was not always so.

In its heyday, Lyons was on the brink of becoming a thriving metropolis. There was excitement here. People did not think about murder, nor about having their farms taken over. Instead they thought about life, of making it rich and of creating a city that their children would gladly inherit. Less than one hundred years ago, gentlemen farmers on sturdy carriages once rolled through town and the place bustled with excitement and commerce.

But ever since the railroad company re-routed the tracks in the 20's and ever since President Carter enacted a grain embargo bill on the Russians twenty years ago, the town has been dying. All the original buildings still stand from their pre-Civil War era, but today none is worth saving, except Jane Dubois' antique store. However, as it was a long time ago, Lyons' lay-out remains wondrously simple.

Directly across from the Sheriff's Office is the Cafe. Next to the Cafe is the Antique Store, with a newly painted green and maize sign. Next to the antique store is State Farm Insurance. Behind the Cafe, antique store and insurance company is Lyons' biggest business, the grain elevator. The elevator's swollen metal pipes, which connect the huge storage bins together, disrupt the town's skyline, arcing over the town's shops, and in the sunshine create a false, metallic rainbow.

To the right of the Sheriff's Office is an Amoco gas station, the post office and the town's Episcopal Church. A white plastic banner hangs over the church's doors. Its bright red letters read: "Jesus Saves."

To the left of the Sheriff's Office is the printer and then the bank. The street deadends at a bar, Lou's Place, and the Library-slash-Town Council Hall. Every building is comprised of two stories, an awning or sign and double wooden doors. Except, of course, for Lou's, which is a flat one-story hovel, built out of charmless cinder blocks.

The sheriff quietly opens his inner door and walks past Starla. He sees the tall M.B.I. agent leaning on the window-frame. He's wearing a rather expensive suit and three-hundred dollar shoes. His leather briefcase is open. "Lyons/Richards" in big, red letters marks the case file. Inside is a cell phone, some pens and a tape recorder. Sheriff Sackett remembers watching this kid quarterback the CU Buffaloes and beating the University of Michigan with a Hail Mary pass with the time clock running out. He had an arm of gold and nerves of steel.

Sackett taps Kevin's shoulder.

Kevin turns, straightens his tie and holds out his muscular hand. The tiny sheriff shuffles back, not saying a peep. His eyes focus on his small, shiny, black shoes. He detects Kevin's hand using sonar.

Kevin thinks that the sheriff looks pleasant enough, but watery. He is the grown-up version of every shy kid who silently passed through Kevin's elementary school, virtually unnoticed, but almost always remembered as being nice. The kind of child who with flushed cheeks sat silently in the back of the room, solemnly staring at the black board.

The sheriff softly spins on one heel and retreats to his office. He expects Kevin to follow, which the rookie—out of respect for all those shy kids he never harassed—hushedly does. They sit down in his small office.

Starla yells, "Want me to hold your calls?"

On Sheriff Sackett's walls are photos of fat kids, a fatter wife and a nearly empty gun rack. The air is clear of smoke. Kevin thinks that it is probably no big leap in judgment to assume that this guy does not drink, either.

Sheriff Sackett says yes and asks his receptionist to close the door.

When it's shut, the sheriff's demeanor shifts. He becomes edgy and frustrated. For the first time, the sheriff's tiny eyes focus in on the rookie. His pupils shrink. They look like little black marbles. They're glassy and vaguely self-confident. This little office is his world. It's the only place he feels omnipotent.

He curtly says, "My name is John Sackett. I'm the sheriff here. The business at hand is to find out why Doug Richards was murdered. Obviously, I'm having trouble, which is why the Town Council voted to call your boss, Jim Caretaker, of the M.B.I. What do you think?"

For a second, Kevin is stunned by the sheriff's directness, given how nonchalant the sheriff was when he first met him.

Kevin states, "First, I'd like to go over the details with you."

Sackett responds, "Sure, but I thought you would have already gone over the file I sent you. We really need to bounce on this case. The trail already is as cold as a gold digger's ass."

Kevin, now cognizant of the sheriff's change in temperament and still a little hot from the Truck Stop, warns, "Sheriff, I have to be thorough. You and I both know that case files reveal about half of what really happened!"

The sheriff retreats back into his chair.

The rookie continues, "Now, Doug Richards' body was found at the bottom of Snipes' silo. Doug died from puncture wounds in the chest. He had lacerations on his head and buttocks. The weapon hasn't been recovered, but it's clear to Lyons' doctor, Dr. Barbara Fortune, that the weapon was a pitchfork. What I'm confused about is the motive. Was it money? Revenge? A girl?"

John's body jiggles, and his rolling desk chair moves forward an inch. He gently takes a sip from his coffee mug that jokes, "One more speeding ticket and my wife gets a new toaster."

The sheriff says, "It's true, Doug experienced an awful death. He was viciously stabbed with a pitchfork. It is a horror that this whole town has to live with. To be honest, I'm not sure why the Richards' boy was killed. He seemed nice enough to me. Well, except for..."

Kevin induces, "Yes, except for..."

"Drugs... unfortunately, the kids in this town smoke marijuana and snort cocaine. Every year around Halloween, I give a speech to all the parents about drug abuse, and I tell them to discourage their kids about using them. I also tell the parents about the warning signs, such as secretiveness and depression.

"I do the speech in the fall. Because as soon as it gets colder, kids—or the as we call 'em 'longhairs'—start using more of the contraband substances. I should start preparing for my talk soon because October 31st is only a few days away. Doug Richards, well, it was rumored that he may have dealt a few ounces of marijuana every now and then."

Kevin taps his Mont Blanc pen, which his parents gave him from graduating from the academy, on his leather-bound notebook, waiting to see if the sheriff has more information.

Silence.

The sheriff concedes: "So, Agent Sir, what are you going to do?"

"First, I want to talk to Keith Spelling, the longhair whom Mrs. Richards spoke of in your report. Then I need to see with my own eyes where Doug was killed. Finally, I will need to confirm some things with his family and then interview his employers, co-workers, friends and of course Dr. Fortune."

Sheriff Sackett frowns, warning, "Young man, it's nothing personal, but you've got your work cut out for you. People around here don't warm up to city folk nosing around. This is farm country. Our residents think that your kind has turned their back on America's heartland in order to fight for riches in the concrete jungle. They know city people have all the money and have gone to fancy colleges.

"Lyons is from a different time. We know and accept that. We only care about our farms, each other and our families. We're proud of having stayed here and keeping up our fathers' rural traditions.

"People here don't trust city folk because the only ones we are used to seeing are the bankers who come to Lyons to foreclose on our neighbors. On top of Doug Richards getting killed, no one around here is getting rich. It seems every other Saturday, another farmer is having his tractors, combines, plows and prized land auctioned off by the banks."

Frustrated, Kevin says, "When I first drove into Lyons, the lady at the Truck Stop practically ripped my head off. Even you seem unappreciative that I've shown up to help. Is this the kind of treatment I'm in for?"

"Yes."

Kevin slowly gets up.

He shakes his head in disbelief.

Kevin holds out his hand and says, "Thank you for your time. Anything else?"

Sheriff Sackett shakes Kevin's hand and responds, "Possibly, what has me really buffaloed is that no one is talking about his death. I would've thought by now that we'd have some finger-pointing. But nothing. Either this town is happy that Doug has been killed, or they don't have a clue about who killed Doug. It's very odd. Sorry, that's it."

The rookie asks a final question, "In the case file, Doug's Mom mentioned that her son recently befriended a "longhair," as you call 'em. Name's Keith Spelling. Where can I find him?"

"When you drove into town, 'member passing a grain elevator, just over yonder, passed the other side of Main Street?"

"Yes."

"Saw him getting supplies just before you drove up. But Agent Sir…"

"Yes?"

"I don't think Keith could have done it."

Kevin thanks the sheriff and leaves the inner office.

The rookie smiles at Starla and exits the Sheriff's Office. He then walks through an alley that connects the grain elevator and hardware store with Main Street.

Kevin walks up to the grain elevator/hardware store's counter and asks, "Where can I find Keith Spelling?"

A portly man behind the counter looks up from reading last January's issue of "People." The man has to squint to see Kevin. His appearance looks as if God cut two narrow strips into a piece of cardboard, gave it to the man and said, "Here, look through this."

The man behind the counter, seeing that he doesn't recognize this stranger, sarcastically rephrases Kevin's question, "Where can you find Keith Spelling?"

"Yes, where is he? The sheriff said that Keith's over here."

The rookie pulls out his M.B.I. badge to emphasize the importance of his question.

The man behind the counter sees it and shouts, "Yer that agent!"

"Yes."

He laughs.

"You city dicks are sure amusing."

"What do you mean?"

"All your guns, badges and college degrees don't scare us none."

Rather than getting riled, Kevin takes control of the discussion.

"I'm sorry sir, I didn't catch your name?"

"I'm Sven, co-owner of SalSven Elevator and Hardware. My brother Sal is over at the elevator loading up feed bags. He thinks more of you than I do. Sal is on the town's council."

"I may not be from around here, but at least I'm trying to help you folks out. Right?"

"I don't mind you being here. I know after your job's done, you'll pack up your suits and leave. It's funny. That's all, like 'The Tonight Show.'"

"Sorry, I don't see the humor in murder."

Kevin leans over and grabs the magazine out of the hands of the businessman.

Sven stops laughing.

Sven warns, "Hey, boy, don't get cocky. We brought you here. We can ask you to get the hell out. Now, you must have been blind because you passed Keith when you walked over here. He's out loading up his truck. Good day."

Kevin snaps his leather badge protector shut and hits the door hard, as if it is a blocking dummy, or an Oklahoma Sooner. What clannishness!

As Kevin storms out, he runs into Keith. The farmhand does not notice the upset rookie, instead he balances two sacks of feed, one on each shoulder. The rookie quickly follows Keith. The farmhand throws the sacks into the back of his pickup. A flash of steel catches Kevin's eye. The rookie focuses on it... a new pitchfork.

Keith turns around. He is wearing a black Harley Davidson T-shirt and ripped jeans. His long hair has recently been washed. He flicks it back as if to challenge Kevin, but at the same time his wide eyes connote he is scared.

Keith asks, "What'd you want, mister?"

"Agent Kevin Sir, M.B.I., here to investigate your 'friend's' death."

Keith leans over and covers the tines of the new pitchfork with an empty feed sack. The farmhand opens the door of his truck and gets in. He starts the truck and starts to back away.

Agent Sir grabs the doorframe and demands, "Stop this truck!"

Keith does so, sitting there fuming, helpless.

Agent Sir asks, "What about your drug connection to Doug?"

"You can bust me for having dope. But, I ain't no killer, man. You must of have sucked up too much car exhaust from all those automobiles in your big city because it's affected your brain. Later, pig."

Keith drives away, not caring whether he's dragging the M.B.I. agent with him.

Kevin releases the doorframe and angrily watches the longhair evade his interrogation.

Kevin purposefully jogs across Main Street and heads caddy corner to Sackett's official abode. He pushes open the door. The force of the rookie's entry shakes the deer paintings on the walls. The secretary's mouth opens wide, as if she is a baby robin stretching open its beak for worms from its mother.

She quickly maintains her composure and squeals, "Agent Sir, please, do you have to be so rough? You almost knocked John's paintings off the wall!"

"I'm sorry."

Out steps the skinny sheriff, frowning and scared to come any closer. He slips back into his office. Kevin walks past the secretary into John's office.

The rookie asks, "Why don't you think Keith killed Doug?"

"Agent Sir, I just told you. He's just a good ol' boy who has some substance abuse problems."

"Well, wasn't it Keith who introduced Doug to drugs?"

"Yes."

"And just now, I saw a new pitchfork in the back of Keith's pickup. What did he do with the old one? I'll tell you what he did with it: After he stabbed Doug, he broke off the handle and burned it. Then he buried the metal spokes behind his barn, or something like that."

"He just couldn't do it. He likes to act tough, but he's a good guy in his own way."

"Well, what about his lifestyle? He probably gets drunk all the time and smokes pot. You, yourself, are about to give a lecture to kids about drugs. You hate them. And yet, you don't hate that Keith is taking them? That Doug Richards took them? That Keith and Doug probably got into some kind of drug war... in your town? And Doug Richards lost—with his life?"

"You're right I hate drugs and, personally, I don't drink. But all things considered, I don't think Keith could kill someone. I've known Keith since he was a baby. Sure, he drinks and does drugs. He needs counseling for that. But, I've seen him work hard his whole life. He loves farming. He loves his ma and pa. He loves Chestnut Hills Farm for giving him a chance to make something of himself.

"Just before you came, some cattle broke loose through a hole in a fence and scattered all throughout the woods. The whole town helped round up the animals. But no one, I mean no one, searched harder than Keith. He organized everyone. He stayed out all day and all night for a week to round up every animal.

"Anyone who cares about cattle like he does, certainly cares more about people. He's a good ol' boy who just has some vices. I don't think killing is one."

"Fine. But just to be on the safe side, I'm going to check out Keith's story about the pitchfork."

"It's your investigation."

"Where's he working at today?"

"Chestnut II. My nephew, Stick, and Keith are out there workin' the fields. Here are the directions. Also, Mayor Tapestry knows you're here. He's on his way over."

Sheriff Sackett writes down directions to Chestnut II and Snipes farm on a yellow pad. The rookie walks out of the Sheriff's Office towards his shiny, white Ford Contour. He sets his briefcase on top of the car, grabs the rain-gutter with his other hand and lets out a sigh. He picks his head up and feels for the keys in his pant's pocket. He takes out the keys and unlocks the driver's side door.

Just as he's about to get in, a large hand grabs his shoulder and turns him around. Kevin, standing 6' 3", meets another similarly tall man, Mayor John Tapestry. They stand eye to eye.

"Agent Sir?"

"Yes."

"John Tapestry, I'm the mayor here."

"Yes, sir. I know who you are. The sheriff said that you wanted to see me. Sorry about the Richards' killing."

"Glad to see your boss Jim Caretaker works as quickly as he says he would. People in town already talking about you. What do think about our sheriff."

"Looks like he had his hands full."

"Nonsense. Sheriff Sackett is a cream puff."

"Sir?"

"But he's our cream puff, if that makes sense."

"I still don't understand."

"Sackett does a good job of being this town's only cop to these people who work hard, love their families and go to church. However, it would seem out of character if he tore this place apart looking for Doug's killer. People would get jumpy.

"That's why I called you here. Lyons needs someone like you, an outsider, to catch this killer. And I pray to God that you can. This way when you leave and you take the killer away, the grandmother down the street, who makes extra spending money mending clothes, goes to bed at night thinking her safe town is being run by Sheriff Sackett, a nice man with a shiny badge and a clean, but never fired gun. Don't you see?"

"I guess so."

"Your boss is smart. Told me that he thinks you have a lot of promise and guts. So use 'em kid. Good luck."

"OK, then. Before you go, do you have any ideas? What about Keith Spelling?"

"Just bully your way through the case. And Keith is no more a killer than I am."

"That's what the sergeant said."

"Well, he's right."

"But what about the new pitchfork laying in the back of Keith's pickup? And what about Norma Richards saying that Keith's group, the longhairs, killed her son? You must have seen Keith and Doug together…"

"Look, son, I don't mean to interrupt. But my son-in-law, Derrick, handles all the men, now. I'm semi-retired. Go see him about Keith and Doug. Now, good luck Agent Sir. And when you've solved this thing, come by the house for some cocktails."

Mr. Tapestry smiles and turns away to go and then thinks of one last point: "Oh, and one more thing: People here can see you've got city slicker written with a big, black marker across your forehead, so don't try and fit in. They'll see right through it."

Mayor Tapestry drives away in an old, red Ford pickup, which looks more auburn with years of sun, rain and snow fading its color. Kevin opens his Ford Contour and gets in. He tries his cell phone to talk to the sergeant, but the display says, "Out of reach."

Kevin's alone.

He rests back and thinks that this case will either make him or break him. Now that he knows that the sheriff is more milquetoast than Muhammad Ali and the mayor's only tip is to hit the beach running, he believes that this case will be much more challenging than putting on a bulletproof vest and running head first into some drug den. Today could be Kevin Sir's first real day of being an M.B.I. agent.

Chapter 3

Kevin starts the car and drives back through Lyons, passing by the Truck Stop and underneath Highway I-94, which would take him home. For the first time, Kevin drives into Michigan's grand countryside. Ripe fields of corn stretch out to the horizon. Huge maple trees—planted over 200 years ago—rise up next to North Lyons Road, creating a natural passageway through the fields. With autumn in full swing, the land is bright with oranges, dark greens, reds and yellows.

The rookie wonders, what did Doug Richards do to deserve to die? He was only eighteen years old. He lived in this quiet, farming community, which even Ralph Waldo Emerson would admire. Farmers are unlikely suspects for murder. They grow and nurture things.

Kevin looks out through the window. He hits a button on the armrest and the window silently slides into the doorframe. The cool air rushes in. Big farms and open fields pass by through the spaces between the skyscraping maple trees. He tries to experience what the farmers see, hear and smell. It looks and sounds so peaceful. Neither bright lights, nor big city noise, just fluttering maple leaves and the constant hum of crickets. The corn, at its peak, fills the air with a slight sugary smell.

The Indians had similar thoughts. They knew their gods would not tolerate man's inventions. The Indians did not have to worry about trading money for groceries. They just grew, or pierced what they needed. They did not need check guarantee cards, or even social security numbers in order to collect carrots and mushrooms. Even small towns, inhabited by peaceful settlers, seemed too ambitious for their tastes.

From what Kevin has heard about farming, farmers' long, sweat-filled days are in the past. Today's farming is different from planting behind a horse and harvesting with a sickle. Experts call '90s farms, agribusinesses, and they come with all the newest accruements: air-conditioned tractors, self-cleaning barns and all sorts of drugs to enhance growth and ward off diseases and bugs for safer, leaner meat.

Kevin comes up to Belleview Street and almost misses the turnoff. The bright October sun makes it difficult to read the fading green sign. According to the sheriff's map, Kevin should turn left. The rookie straightens himself up and puts on his game face. Time to confront, for real, Keith Spelling.

In a few minutes, Kevin approaches Chestnut II. Next to the farm, Kevin makes out some shadowy workers doing something in the middle of the field. Kevin does not see an access road, so he continues to drive along side the field.

At last, he sees an opening in the trees. It is a dirt entrance that has been packed down by tractor tires. Kevin turns left. Over the bumps, he cautiously drives, kicking up dust, which clings to the new auto. The frame of the car bangs down on the tires. Kevin's briefcase opens and the contents fall on the floor. This pathway parallels the workers in the field. After a half a mile, he is even with the workers.

He opens the door and steps out into the autumn sun. His leather shoes sink into the soft Michigan dirt. He walks across the field towards the workers. As he gets nearer, Kevin notices two guys with their shirts off, slumping over and picking up objects. The men drop these objects into the tractor's bucket. The tractor driver is a tall man sitting stiffly upright.

Kevin looks back. His car is a small dot near the trees. The tractor and its team of men grow larger. Soon, Kevin can hear the whine of a tractor's engine.

The tractor driver is a handsome gentleman with gray, slicked-back hair. His back is arrow-straight. He is wearing a clean, blue denim shirt and blue jeans. He is preoccupied and does not see Kevin approaching.

To this older man, this tractor is his steed; this land, his charge. He feels that he is one of Lyons' last, great kings. And as such, he has been chosen to guard and protect her from intruders.

The rookie sees, now, what the two youths are picking up—rocks. He read that if they are not removed, they will damage farm machinery. The youths backs are flour white. The whiteness continues down their arms and stops in the middle of their biceps.

To the old gentleman, Kevin shouts, "Hello."

The ruler slowly looks Kevin's way and soberly nods his head. He is visibly disturbed. He doesn't like talking when there's work to be done. He especially doesn't like talking when a beautiful day is taking shape on a field that he manages.

Over the sound of the running tractor, Kevin loudly asks, "Can you stop this thing for a moment? I need to talk to one of these guys, Keith Spelling."

At the sound of his name being mentioned, the bigger youth turns the rookie's way. The moment Keith sees Kevin, he throws down his twenty-pound rock and glares. Kevin looks back at the old man.

The king of the cornfield obeys Kevin, albeit for now, waiting for Keith, his knight, to defend the Lyons' land.

Kevin sensing the tension, grasping that now, more than ever, he must be strong. He pushes back his shoulders. He clears his throat.

Kevin waits for the tractor's engine to die.

Silence.

The smell of diesel fuel surrounds the men.

Kevin walks forward.

"Keith, I'm back. And this time you're not protected by your truck."

Keith mutely stands there.

Kevin's adversary has long brown hair, which is now matted down by sweat and dust. His pudgy face continues to scowl. His puny chest and small white arms sit on top of a large stomach. His torso looks similar to a cheap vase from a flea market. His pants rest low on his hips. His filthy jeans are weighed down by dirt and collect at his ankles like a sagging curtain. His boots have disappeared into the soft earth from the weight of the rocks.

The tractor driver taps his boot.

Finally, Keith says, "If you know what's good for ya, you'll leave Lyons."

"I'm not going any where until I've caught Doug's killer. Now, the word is that you two partied together. And that possibly, Doug was selling drugs. Is there someone else who sells drugs in this town that didn't like sharing the profits with Doug?"

Keith's face turns red and puffy.

Kevin continues, "When you two drank together, which I hear was a lot, did he ever say he was scared of anyone? Was he frightened of you? Did you want to hurt him?"

"Yea, we used to party together, but I didn't poke any holes into him with a pitchfork, if that's what you're trying to get at."

"Why the new pitchfork in the back of your truck?"

"You saw that?"

"Yes, before you tried covering it up."

The old man on the tractor says, "Keith?"

"I dunno. We lost one at the big farm. We needed to buy a new one to bed down those sheep for Derrick's boys. It's their 4-H project, or something.

Man, just take a chill pill. Leave me alone."

"Did you kill Doug with the old one?"

"Are you crazy? Everyone knows he was my friend. This is bullshit."

The rookie shouts, "Look, I know that you know more than that!"

Keith picks up another rock and throws it at Kevin. It lands on Kevin's toes. The heavy object does not break any bones, but it causes the agent to fall forward. His knee strikes the rock. His hands brace for the fall and are cut by smaller, sharper rocks in the field. His face lands in Lyons' rich loam.

Accustomed to 300 lbs. of defensive linemen using him for a tackling dummy, Kevin takes the blow and then jumps to his feet. He brushes the stone away and strikes Keith.

The distinguished old man turns to face the rookie. The glow from the October sun makes the old man's silver hair glisten bright red. His eyes snap away from the horizon and target Kevin as if they are lasers from a sniper's rifle.

While Kevin and Keith roll on the ground, the old man pontificates, "You, have a lot of balls, not taking a man's word as gospel. If Keith says he didn't do it, then he didn't do it. Agent Sir this ain't no goddamn kangaroo court. Now, go!"

Kevin stops fighting. The old man sounds like a coach he once knew. Out of respect for him, Kevin gets up.

Kevin addresses the old man, "You're right, this isn't a kangaroo court. So, can you either confirm or deny about the truth of Keith's story concerning the new pitchfork?'"

"No. You'll have to speak with Derrick Palmer. He approves all the purchases."

Keith, wiping blood from the corner of his mouth, reiterates, "Get the hell out of here."

Mr. Tapestry says to Keith, "Spelling, bury the hatchet. It's over. Now, we have a lot of work ahead of us. Let's go."

Kevin looks back at the old man. The old man looks satisfied with the outcome. He starts the tractor. Black smoke shoots up from the tractor's exhaust pipe.

Kevin struggles forward, upset that so far, nothing has been accomplished. He languishingly makes the trek back to his once-clean car. His head his bowed. He feels sick. Kevin stumbles on a rock and falls to the earth. He picks himself up again and continues walking.

He reaches his car. Sweat runs down his cheeks. His hands are bleeding. His suit is ripped at the knee. Kevin opens the door. He falls onto the seat and looks at his reflection in the rear view mirror. His face is covered with dirt. Kevin rests his head against the steering wheel. After a few minutes, he starts the car and carefully backs out of the field. He drives to the scene of the murder—Snipes' farm.

The sheriff wrote down that the Snipes' farm is five miles, or so, north of town and that Kevin should turn left onto Devereux Road. Kevin, after traveling two miles to reach Chestnut II off of Belleview, comes to the intersection of North Lyons Road and Devereux Road after three miles and takes a left. He passes a sign. It reads: Fresh Apple Cider. Orchard Farm. According to Sheriff John Sackett, the first farm on the right is supposed to be Snipes'.

The Snipes' farm hugs the road. It is in terrible shape. None of the buildings are painted. The barn's concave roof droops down like melted plastic. Two dirty, bug-eyed kids play in the long grass out front. The people are not in much better shape than the buildings.

Kevin stops the car and gets out. The screen door screeches open and a weathered man steps out on the porch. His gray hair is greasy and his jeans are faded and stained. He does not greet the rookie; instead, he stands there with his hands tucked into his back pockets. He looks similar to a sullied Roman statue without its arms.

The rookie wipes his bloody hand on his pants and offers it to the farm owner, saying, "Hello, I'm from Ann Arbor. I'm with the M.B.I. to investigate the murder of Doug Richards."

The statue does not speak.

"What can you tell me about the killing?"

Mr. Snipes only grits his decaying, dark teeth.

Kevin raises his voice, as if yelling might jar some long forgotten brain cells into action: "OK, then. You don't want to talk. I understand. Just tell me what day and time you discovered the body. Then I leave you alone. You have my word."

Mr. Snipes kicks the dusty, wood planks and then points over to the brick silo, saying, "Over in there. The kid was lying dead in there. Day? Time? Phooey on those things. One day is the same as the next. This minute here is the same as the one to come. The only difference is that the surroundings tend to change a bit."

The old man walks down the steps, as if his joints are made of rusty metal hinges that have been left out in the rain. He stands there achingly erect. As the sheriff warned, this small town farmer is challenging Kevin's big city investigation.

Kevin takes in a deep breath and says, "Sir, I know you don't trust me. But you have to understand that I'm just doing my job. Let me investigate your silo. Then I'll leave. OK?"

Snipes harshly screws his shoulders all the way around. His legs, arms and head snap like rubber bands in pursuit. The old man disappears into his shack.

Kevin walks across the thick grass towards the crime scene. With Maglite in hand, he walks into the silo. Inside, there is a musty smell. A cat bolts past him.

A big shadow hides half the floor, the part where Doug lay. Kevin adjusts the flashlight and flicks on its powerful beam, searching the dark half. The blood has dried. It looks as if the cat had been rolling in it. The rest of the floor looks undisturbed. With a pair of tweezers, Kevin extracts some of the reddish straw and places it into a clear plastic bag.

Kevin saw pictures of the victim from the thin case file that Sackett forwarded to him in Ann Arbor. Doug was a good-looking kid, some acne. His shoulder-length hair was parted down the middle. There was a kindness in his brown eyes. He probably trusted his killer.

The are many questions about his death. Was Doug killed here, or was he brought here after? Does that matter? What did he do to deserve to be murdered? He must have done something, known about something, or seen something he was not supposed to see.

In any case, someone must have an idea about why this kid was killed. His family will have an opinion. It is time to talk to the Richards and get an insider's point of view.

Walking outside the silo, Kevin takes a gulp of fresh air. He sees the cat squatting besides a dead maple tree. It is taking a shit.

Kevin thinks, Snipes should know where the Richards live. However, the rookie hates to bother him—considering he seems so distraught. But in the interest of saving time, Kevin thinks that he should.

Walking up the dirt path to the screen door, Kevin sees a rusty razor

                                    Virtual Publishing Group, Inc.

blade and a garter snake that slithers next to his shoe. Kevin looks up, concentrating on the shack. The wood porch looks deteriorated and dusty. It looks as if he steps on it, the unsound structure will break into a thousand pieces and the dust will rise up into a mushroom-shaped cloud. When he gets to the landing, he gingerly treads onto the porch.

Floorboards creak.

Snipes violently swings open the screen door and emerges from the dark house. The squeaky wood is a crude, but effective alarm system.

Mr. Snipes snaps, "Look mister, get off my porch, now. 'Cause I'm gettin' my gun."

Instead of getting upset, Kevin remains calm.

"Mr. Snipes, I'm not here to harm you. I'm here to help you, and your town. All I want to know is 'Where do the Richards live?'"

Snipes' small shoulders dip. He suddenly looks dispirited.

Then one of his bug-eyed grandkids comes running up the porch and gawks at the rookie. The kid is holding the thin garter snake. The snake coils around his pudgy, little fingers. The kid puts the thing in Kevin's face. Kevin backs away and almost falls off the porch.

Kevin puts a hand on the boy's head and says, "I'm talking to your dad, son. Please give me a minute with him."

The kid stomps away, holding the snake close to his chest, squeezing the life out of it.

He turns around, and yells, "He ain't my Pa. He's my Gran Pappy."

Kevin looks back at Snipes and asks, "Sir, please tell me where the Richards live?"

Snipes sunken cheeks quake.

He says, "The Richards live north of town a ways, just off of North Lyons Rd. It's the first house passed the pond."

Kevin does not remember passing a pond on the way here.

"Thank you. I'm sorry you had to find the dead Richards boy. If you know about anything else, I'm staying at the Best Western, Room 105. Call me anytime."

The poor, old farmer—whose gun was never loaded and its hammer has long since locked up—sighs. He takes leave of Kevin and retreats into his dark shack. Back inside, he crumples onto a wood chair and remembers when his wife used to bake biscuits in the morning and the smell used to pull him in from the fields.

Why has he been dealt such a lousy hand of cards? He looks down at his own hand and sees where a combine removed two of his fingers; he was only 25 years old. He saw that as an omen. Ever since then, God has been steadily removing other parts of his life—his son, his wife and now his farm. The bank people say they are coming for his farm next week.

He is done fighting.

He yells up at the yellow, cracked ceiling, "Dammit! Those men ain't gonna take my last possession. I'm gonna see it to that I'm the one givin' it to them. Time's up here. Time to be with my wife and son."

Snipes struggles to get up and fights through his home's clutter. In the kitchen, he bends down and grabs the rat poison underneath the sink. He pours the white powder into a jelly glass and mixes the last of his bourbon into the lethal cocktail. He says a quick prayer to Jesus and then downs it.

Blood erupts from his mouth and nose. He falls onto the linoleum. Mr. Snipes is a husband, father and farmer no more.

The rookie, unaware of Snipes' suicide, starts the car and slowly backs out of Mr. Snipes' farm. He takes one last look back. Snipes' house is truly shameful, even the trees are in poor condition. The bark looks sick; the dead, sharp branches cut through the sky in disorganized fashion, as if they are dirty kitchen knives all jumbled in a drawer.

Once the car is on Devereux Road's pavement, he taps the accelerator, so as not to further annoy old man Snipes. He brakes at the stop sign, looks up and down North Lyons Road and takes a left towards the Richards'. Kevin winds his way through smaller and smaller fields until there are none. He enters some woods with a swamp. Kevin wonders if this is Snipes' version of a pond.

It is a dirty, shallow-looking swamp. A place where only frogs and snakes live, no fish. It is the perfect place for a serial killer to hang out and chop up pretty young girls with a large, shiny ax.

The country road coils along side the quagmire and rises up above it. A long, black power line droops over the road, dangerously close to the roof of the car. The power line looks as if it is a licorice whip that has been left on the dashboard of a car on a hot August day. The Richards' home is on the right.

Kevin pulls into the paved driveway and steps out of the car. Cats greet him. He steps through the Maginot line of felines and continues toward the house. A sheep dog, chained to a tree, begins to furiously bark at him.

On the other side of the driveway, a tractor and a plow rest inside a metal barn. Stacked next to the barn are some huge rubber tractor tires. There is a three-wheeled motorcycle parked next to a tree. Clothes hang on a line stretched between two unpainted metal poles.

An uncoiled garden hose and a chewed up gardener's glove obstruct the path to the front door. The Richards' lawn is mowed to the road and to the sides of the woods where bushes and ivy dominate. The bushes are not trimmed. The house is covered in cheap aluminum siding. There are many piles of dog shit scattered throughout the premises. These stinky land mines fill the air with a sweet/sour smell, much different than how the corn smelled.

The garage door is open and inside Kevin can see a maroon Chevy Caprice up on cinder blocks, old toys and a stack of newspapers. There is also an orange hunter's suit, a BB gun and an old refrigerator that holds the old man's beer. It is the kind of icebox that cannot be opened from the inside. The kind that suffocates little boys who play around them and who get accidentally locked inside.

Kevin decides these people regularly use the garage entrance. He heads for the garage. As he gets nearer to it, the dog's noises get louder. It is not just barking, now, it is trying to pull up the tree by its roots.

Mrs. Richards, in a flowered smock and pulled back peppered black and gray hair, peers through the screen door.

As Kevin walks closer to her, he can see that the dog has clawed the door she is looking through. The deep scars look as if a werewolf on LSD made them.

Above the din of the dog, the rookie yells, "Mrs. Richards? Mrs. Richards?"

She whines, "Yes?"

"I'm so sorry about your son. Please believe me."

She squints into the dark garage, and asks, "Who might you be?"

"I'm Kevin Sir. I'm the M.B.I. agent from Ann Arbor who the Sheriff sent for.

"May I come in? I really need to ask you some questions about your son's case and accident, OK?"

She does not move. Kevin's eyes adjust to the dark garage. He can see into the room where Mrs. Richards is standing. It is the wash room, and heaps of clothes lie waiting to be cleaned. There are many sets of muddy boots near the door. The gray concrete is stained by the dog. It smells of Tide detergent and a pair of old sneakers.

Mrs. Richards finally backs away and says, "Yes, let's go up to the kitchen and talk."

Kevin walks into her home. Dodging piles of laundry, they make their way across the room. They walk up worn stairs, which have been made by workmen's boots.

In the kitchen, she invites the rookie to sit down at the kitchen table. He politely sits on a plastic covered chair with a pattern of indescribable plants that possess weed-like properties. He rests his hands on the table. One of his palms gets caught in a small pool of syrup left over from this morning's breakfast of pancakes.

Outside the kitchen window there is a hummingbird feeder filled with a thick, red fluid. The birds suck at this liquid through a red and yellow plastic flower. Next to the kitchen table is a wooden credenza filled with many porcelain miniatures of hummingbirds.

She asks, "Some coffee?"

Kevin looks over at the stained, empty coffee pot.

"No thanks."

She sadly looks back at him.

She asks, "Were you in a fight?"

"Yes ma'am."

"How about some soap and water?"

"Yes, ma'am. That would be appreciated."

"Help yourself to the kitchen sink."

Kevin cleans himself up and sits back down.

Kevin says, "Again, I'm sorry about your son. Let me complete my questioning as quickly as possible for your sake. Putting it bluntly, 'Is there anyone you know of who wanted to injure your son?'"

No answer.

She is upset.

She is scared.

She wonders if it is morally right to put someone in jail for the rest of their life, even though they killed her only son. Does not God want her to forgive and forget? God will punish the killer. It is not up to us. And besides, what if Doug and the killer were just fighting, as boys always do, and the killer made a mistake? What if this young policeman here does not understand an older woman's fears?

Kevin consoles, "Look, Mrs. Richards, I understand you're experiencing a lot of pain. If I had a son and lost him at such a young age, I'd be devastated. Children are supposed to bury their parents, not the other way around. I just tied the knot with the most beautiful woman in the world not too long ago. We plan on having our own kids some day. I want them to be safe. I want this whole world to be secure. That's why I'm an M.B.I. agent.

"So, you can see why I need to know what you know? It is up to me to make this world a more sheltered place for all the children now and to come. Will you help me?"

His face strains for a response. Mrs. Richards' eyes seem to briefly light up, as an old cat that has just realized it has a couple lives left.

She confesses, "Doug drank a lot. He went to parties where they served a lot of liquor: 'Keggers,' I think, he called them."

She pauses then continues, "He used to come in here acting crazy, sometimes. He didn't smell drunk. I think he was smoking marijuana. He used to go down to the barn. After a half-hour or so past, he'd come back and start talking non-stop. His eyes would be red and swollen, and he'd squint at me with this mean smile. I never told his father."

"Madame, it's the times. Kids are doing all kinds of things to get their kicks. In Detroit, it's crack cocaine. In Ann Arbor, it's 'shrooms washed down with Johnny Walker Red. Heck, even I got high once, or twice when I was Doug's age. Many kids do. They're bored."

Mrs. Richards sadly looks at Kevin as if she has had enough of him and his questions. She does not say anything.

Kevin thinks, he should have kept his mouth shut. Instead, he had to make a case supporting substance use. He needs to remedy this mistake.

So he says, "Well, anyway, that was a long time ago. I've since seen the errors of my youth. Just as Doug would've!

"You see, that's the point: he was just undergoing growing pains. You would've been very proud of him."

The woman faintly smiles and nods her head.

Kevin asks, "Why do you think booze and drugs killed your son?"

"It's the only thing he ever did wrong in his whole life. Before he dropped out of school, he got real good marks. He did a lot of after-school activities, too. He always cleaned his room. He even would carry my husband up to bed after he had too many beers watching ESPN. The drugs killed Doug. I know it."

"And Keith Spelling?"

"Maybe, oh, I don't know. Keith has always been wild, but not mean. Doug really liked Keith. I just don't know, before he met Keith, my son was an angel. Then when he started hanging out with Keith, all the bad began."

The kitchen becomes very quiet. Outside, the dog faintly whines. Downstairs, the washing machine is spinning the family's clothes. Kevin looks at Mrs. Richards, who is facing the stove. She does not cry.

She has never cried in her whole life. She lives as if every day will be the same. She tries to keep chugging along at the same speed, occasionally slowing down when her troubles get the better of her. Her Puritan pride will not let her completely break down.

Kevin gets up and gives Mrs. Richards a brief hug. She does not move. He slowly walks to the door.

"Good-bye."

She resignedly responds, "Good-bye."

Then, she urgently adds, "Doug wasn't all bad. He was going to get his GED in the spring, and then he wanted to go to college. He was a good musician. He could carry the nicest tune."

Kevin politely smiles. He opens the front door, forgetting to leave through the garage. The front door is stuck. He gives it a yank, and the aluminum door pops off its warped frame. Between the front door and the screen door lie a two-year old newspaper and lots of dead bugs. The screen door is likewise hard to open. He quietly closes both of them and leaves.

Mrs. Richards watches Kevin leave. She thinks that Agent Sir seems so sure of himself. So proud of what he is doing. If only Doug could have had a role model like Agent Sir. If only Doug had not dabbled in drugs. If...

Mrs. Richards feels her cheeks becoming wet. She raises her hand to see if she is bleeding. But when she pulls her hand away to see, she is astonished to see her own tears. The wetness continues to build. The salty liquid collects in the corners of her mouth. So this is what happens when you cry. It feels strange, sad, a relief and natural. Why did her mother insist that crying is bad? These tears are for Doug, for her life and for the times she and her son will never have together.

Outside the Richards' home, Kevin looks at his watch and it reads 12:30 p.m. Even though he isn't the least bit hungry, his stomach in knots with the adrenaline of the case pumping through his body, he knows that keeping up his strength requires food. He quickly enters the car, steps on the gas and speeds to The Café for lunch.

Chapter 4

The fields rush by. Kevin flies underneath the I-94 overpass. Lyons' buildings are a blur. At the Cafe, he pulls up besides a truck with mud flaps that read "Back Off" with a cartoon of Yosemite Sam. On the truck's bumper screams a sticker, "Buy American!" He screeches into a spot.

The rookie gets out, walks over and surveys the Yosemite Sam truck: Its gun rack is filled with pump-action shot guns. The floor of the cabin is littered with empty Red Man chewing tobacco bags and spent shotgun shells. A rebel flag emblem that doubles as an air-freshener hangs on the rear view mirror. The bed of the truck serves as a recycling bin for spent Budweiser cans.

Kevin turns his attention away from the truck and enters the crowded Cafe. There are many men busy eating, smoking and chatting. The dining area smells of sweat and day-old goulash. The rustic restaurant becomes quiet when the rookie closes the door behind him. The customers give him one, big angry stare.

Kevin looks around the room. As in the Truck Stop, Kevin has to fight their dark looks.

Kevin thinks, "Damn, this town."

He straightens his shoulders and says to the men, "OK, I'm the agent from Ann Arbor. You can either help me or get in my way. I hope you choose to help me…

"…for Doug's Mom's sake."

He looks around for a reaction. A majority of the men nod their heads in agreement. Others stare blankly through Kevin, as if he's a ghost. A few men angrily clamp onto their utensils, but sensing they're out-numbered, decide to keep their thoughts to themselves… for now.

The men who disagree with Kevin aren't against what he just said, per se, because they, too, feel sorry for Mrs. Richards. However, these men are against Kevin's mission because it affects their bosses' paychecks.

What Kevin will learn is there are two sides to Lyons: the winners and the losers—the winners, who own or want to own most of the land, and the losers, whose only position in town is to maintain the land, kind of like serfs or white migrant workers. The winners don't like Kevin because he might rock the boat and show the losers what scoundrels—and killers—the landowners really are. The winners don't want Kevin to awaken the losers from their poverty-induced comas.

The rookie, satisfied with the majority's response, walks through the dining room and sits down at the counter, which is located at the far end of The Cafe. He

glances at a worn plastic menu and drinks lukewarm water from a small glass. Table by table, people begin to talk, again. The buzz around the room seems to be about the cattle that everyone helped round up last weekend at a farm called Chestnut Hills.

Sitting next to Kevin is a good-looking farmer, about five years older than the rookie. He is talking passionately about something to an old farmer in his seventies. Kevin leans in closer to hear.

The young farmer says, "Poor Snipes. He can kiss his farm good-bye."

The old farmer says, "It ain't right."

The young farmer says, "A man lives and works on the same stretch of land his whole life and some guy in a Lincoln Town Car takes it away in a couple hours."

The old farmer asks, "You live near Snipes. What is he doin'? Has started packin', yet? Or, is he going to hold 'em off with his shotgun?"

The young farmer says, "I don't honestly know. It has been quiet over there, lately. I hope he doesn't, you know, put that gun in his mouth and end it."

The old farmer says, "That's what I'd do."

The old farmer gets up and lays down five dollars. He waits for his change and tips the girl fifty cents.

The old farmer says, "Well, see ya tomorrow Abe."

The waitress comes over to Kevin. The waitress is a stick of a woman with breasts the size of quarters. Her stringy blond hair is pulled back off her forehead. She once was attractive. She still carries laugh-lines. However, time has not been kind. She has deep wrinkles under her eyes, on her fore-head and around her mouth.

Kevin orders a hamburger. This woman is still quick. His hamburger arrives within minutes. It's deliciously greasy. Kevin devours it. The food placates Kevin, putting him into a better frame of mind.

Abe looks over at Kevin and smiles.

Abe jokes, "That went fast."

"Hi, name's Kevin. I'm the agent."

"I'm Abe. I already know who you are. I saw you poking around Snipes' farm. I think you're doing a good job. My wife and I are both glad you're here. Not that the sheriff doesn't try. He just has to keep up his image to the old folks."

Kevin sets down his fork and asks, "Thanks. So, who do you think killed Doug?"

Abe laughs, "Shit Kevin. I've got a farm to run. I work my butt off every day. I'm too busy to even know what year it is. The last time I read a newspaper was when Bush was President."

Kevin laughs with him.

Kevin asks, "Why is Snipes out to get the world? What happened to him that has made him angrily hole up inside his farm and distrust every visitor?"

Abe lets out a sigh and says, "A long time ago, my wife guesses about 23 years, he lost his wife. She had a brain tumor. After that, his farm has gone to pot and he's kind of waiting—hoping—to die so that he can be with her. I heard he used to have a nice, profitable, little farm back in the '60s, but around here if you let your farm go by the wayside even for a couple days, the weeds, bugs and the weather take it over and destroy what you've built.

"He hasn't touched his fields since his wife past away. His house is a wreck. He just doesn't care any more. Finally, I guess, the I.R.S. is tired of him not paying taxes, so they're auctioning off what's left. I got to tell you, there are a lot of people who like Snipes, not because of what he has become, but because of what he used to be, and the fact that he's still a small farmer getting the shaft by men in business suits and expensive cars.

"I personally can't stand the guy. But since he's lived here longer than I have, I can't say a bad thing about him. Around here, unless you've grown up with a person, and your folks went to elementary school with their folks, there's an unwritten law saying you can't judge them."

"I don't follow."

Abe continues, "Snipes may be the world's biggest jerk, but to the people of Lyons, he's our jerk. Does that make sense? He belongs to us; his bitterness is our grief. And he's not the only one. There are many others who I must steer clear from because their troubles came before I did. In short, even though it's none of my business, I must still respect it."

Kevin says, "Snipes, he's one poor fellow."

As Kevin's words end, one of the guys eating at a table nearby loudly throws his fork against plate.

He shouts, "Snipes is a good man. Abe, you have no business talking about him."

As this guy is barking, Kevin thinks, remember what Jim said: words are bullets. This guy just fired a round. It is Kevin's job, as a peace officer, to stand up to him and return fire.

Maybe, this is why Sheriff John Sackett walks around Lyons with his tail between his legs. If a person stands for law and order, they have to make a speech every ten seconds to defend himself.

Kevin walks up to the table and looks down at the muscular man with grease all over his body. He is a good-looking guy with a large, smooth forehead, big, brown eyes, a small nose and a mouth that somewhat droops. He cannot be much older than Kevin.

The troublemaker, Jerod, is a good four inches shorter than Kevin but easily outweighs the rookie. And there's not an ounce of fat on him. The loudmouth wears a green NIKE tank top that he has been cut off near the bottom. His stomach muscles pop out. He is wearing black shorts. His face and arms are brown underneath the dirt, but his legs are snow white.

"Look, no one wants any trouble."

The muscles in Jerod's enormous neck bulge. His face turns red. It looks as if his words are being formed deep inside. His neck muscles flex. His esophagus channels the words from his gut to his mouth. The sentences are simply constructed, but very powerful.

He passionately says, "No, but Snipes is my uncle. I think that gives me the right to defend him."

Kevin asks, "Fine, how do you want to resolve this? Outside. C'mon I'll fight ya. Then I throw your ass in jail."

The troublemaker's chest heaves.

His eyes bulge.

As Jerod rises up to tackle Kevin, Mayor Tapestry steps between the two men.

He confronts Jerod, "Look, you both can fight somewhere's else. But, not here. Not now. If you pick a public place Jerod then Agent Sir's right, he can toss your ass in jail. And my hands will be tied. Be smart and let it go."

Jerod swings his arm across the table. Plates explode. Five men, two of whom are Jerod's brothers, the other three men employed by Jerod's father, who owns the McMurtry Farm, jump up and restrain him.

The gorilla is ushered out into the street, but not before Jerod warns, "You son of a bitch. This ain't over. Your ass is mine, college puke."

The mayor sits down.

Kevin returns to his seat.

Abe has left.

Kevin pays for his meal and leaves The Café in a huff, swinging the door almost off its hinges. He storms over to his car. The truck with the Yosemite Sam mudflaps is gone; Jerod McMurtry drove off in it minutes ago.

Dale Horton walks out of his insurance store, takes a drag on his cigarette and waves at the rookie. Kevin stops. Dale, wearing a gray suit, red tie and his omnipresent Rotary pin, casually, almost neighborly walks towards Agent Sir. It's the kind of slow, relaxed walk that overtakes someone when they see a good friend. But in this case, Dale has practiced it to include anyone he's trying to win over. When Dale reaches Kevin, he smoothly brings the cigarette to his puffy lips and inhales.

As he exhales, he asks, "I hear you met with Keith Spelling. Is he your number one suspect?"

"So far, yes."

"God bless you, Agent Sir."

Dale holds out his big, smooth hand and says, "Dale Horton. I run this little business here. I'm very glad that you're serving our small community. Jesus will reward you.

"In honor of your Christian diligence, my wife, Helen, and I are having a pot roast tonight that is bigger than the premiums Tapestry pays on his farms. It's a celebration of sorts."

Kevin swallows hard, trying to rid his mind of Jerod's threat and still being polite to Mr. Horton. Kevin puts out his hand. He expects to be greeted with a firm handshake. But Mr. Horton only softly squeezes Kevin's hand. It feels similar to a slice of clammy bologna.

Kevin forces, "Dale that would be a treat."

"Good. Come by at six."

Dale slaps Kevin on the shoulder as if they're now lifelong friends.

Before Dale leaves, Kevin naively asks, "Should I bring anything? Bottle of wine?"

Dale's pale, plump face wrinkles up. He stomps his cigarette to bits.

Dale shouts, "Agent Sir we don't drink in the Horton household! The Bible forbids it."

Seeing the insurance man loose his cool so quickly takes Kevin by surprise. The rookie takes a step back.

Seeing the peace officer startled at his temper, Dale quickly makes amends, as if he was meeting sales resistance from a potential client buying an expensive whole life policy: "No, just bring your appetite. You'll see, my wife is a great cook. Call my secretary for directions."

Dale pulls out another cigarette and chuckles, glad that he averted Kevin's mistrust. He turns around and goes back into his office.

Kevin shrugs his shoulders, upset with himself that he brought up the wine. He should have realized by Dale's wording that drinking is a no-no. Dale seems like an honest, family man who's relieved that the M.B.I. is here to quell Lyons' anxiety about a murderer running around and to restore the town's peace. Besides Kevin could use a sit-down dinner around a real kitchen table. Peg's idea of cooking is adding grated cheese to Wolfgang Puck's wood-fired shrimp and eggplant pizza. According to their credit cards, they're on course to spend more than $6,000 this year eating out.

Kevin enters his car and pulls the case file off of the car's floor. He flips through it and finds that the victim, Doug Richards, worked at a farm implement store ten miles west of Lyons near another farm community, Alma, Michigan. The rookie consults his map and reaches Doug's workplace in fifteen minutes.

The bland storefront of Rich's Tractor & Tire is decorated with a faded wooden sign hanging over the warped front door. The picture windows facing the street show off huge tractor tires.

Kevin gets out of the car and assuredly walks into the store. His once-polished Florsheim shoes stir up dust from the broken linoleum. There are a couple of young workers behind a worn, greasy counter staring down this strange-looking customer.

Kevin, a little tired of being polite, announces, "I'm with the M.B.I. What do you guys know about the Doug Richards' murder."

The workers look at one another.

Their bloodshot eyes narrow.

The big one chomps on his chewing tobacco.

He spits a long stream of brown juice onto the floor near Kevin's shoes.

The little one crosses his arms.

Neither says a word.

"Get me your boss, or I start to tear this place apart."

The big one turns on his heels and goes to the back office. In a few seconds, the worker returns with a small, fat man, who could easily fit inside one of his store's swollen tractor tires.

The owner disgorges, "Rich Tremble here. Yes, Doug Richards worked at my store. He punched in over at that time clock almost every day at 5:30 a.m., and he left around 3 p.m. Some days he'd call in sick, but I could tell he was faking it, probably... oh, well. That's all I'm going to say mister. Now, get the hell out of here. Unless of course you've got some real business!"

Kevin walks across the tobacco juice and up to the counter. He grabs the little owner by the throat and slowly picks him off the floor. Kevin a "gym rat" in college, still manages to lift weights almost every day, and picking up this smart ass by the jugular feels good.

He demands, "To hell with you fella. Now, what do you mean Richards was faking it."

Rich Tremble, turning blue, points to his mouth because he can't answer the question in that Kevin's squeezing the life out of him.

Kevin releases his grip.

The owner falls to the floor, gasps for air and begins to rub his neck.

Mr. Tremble pleads, "OK look. What I just told you is the truth. The only thing I might of left out is that Doug missed a lot of work because he was too hung-over. His Mom used to call in sick for him. That's it."

"That's better. Now, what about you two?"

Kevin points at Tremble's counter help.

The little worker says, "Yeah, like the boss just said. Doug was a drunk. Hell, even when he was here, he couldn't sell a set of tires to save his life."

The big worker nods in agreement.

Still not satisfied, Kevin presses, "Yeah, and what about after work? Didn't you two pal around with Doug at Lou's? Maybe you two killed him for his drugs?"

The big worker says, "No. No. Fred and I don't take drugs. We may have gone to Lou's with Doug on occasion, but only to scope out girls. I've been dry for six months now."

The big worker pulls out a prescription of Antabuse, the drug that makes a person vomit if they take it along with drinking alcohol.

The little worker nervously bobs his head up and down.

Kevin takes their confession down on paper.

He tells the three of them that he may be back and that they should not discuss the Richards' case with anyone. Kevin leaves the tire store with a small chip on his shoulder. He got his first real answers by himself, by using what some people would call, moxie.

With Kevin's confidence returning, he thinks that it is an opportune time to report to his boss. Kevin drives back to Lyons and pulls up to the town's only pay phone, which is located in front of the gas station next to the Sheriff's Office. Using his calling card, he tells the operator the number of his office in Ann Arbor.

"Sergeant Caketaker."

"Sergeant, Agent Sir, checking in."

"Thanks, I appreciate that. I don't want anything to go wrong on your first case. So, what's happened?"

"Well, a lot. You read in the file that Doug quit high school."

"Yes?"

"Ever since then, the kid's life has been going downhill, culminating in his murder. After he quit high school, he started drinking a lot, selling marijuana and hanging out with a crowd called the "longhairs." The sheriff, his Mom and his co-workers all will corroborate this. It seems, like you said this morning, playing it straight and a little rough is the best approach down here.

"Finally, it's as if I've stepped back into time. My cell phone won't work. There are no radio stations out here. And when I toured the Sheriff's Office this morning, believe it or not but they still use rotary phones, you know the kind of phone you use by spinning the dial with your finger. They don't even have a fax machine. And, there's not one computer in sight..."

Jim interrupts, "I get the picture. Now, where you off to this afternoon?"

"I need to get a blood sample from Dr. Fortune and then FedEx it, along with some bloody straw I collected at the murder scene, to the lab. Then I want to drive out to Chestnut Hills Farm to check on Keith Spelling's alibi about buying a new pitchfork."

"Keep up the good work agent. Keep calling me. Remember, I spent almost three years in towns like Lyons. I know how they think. Good-bye."

Both peace officers hang up.

Agent Sir walks over to the Sheriff's Office. Outside, Starla's sitting on a curb, smoking a cigarette.

She jokes, "Catch the killer yet?"

"Gimme a break, Starla."

"C'mon, can't you take some ribbing?"

"Yeah."

She exhales and smiles up at the handsome agent. He has to be the best-looking guy she has ever seen in real life.

"Pull up a curb and take a load off."

Kevin sits next to the sheriff's secretary.

Kevin asks, "So, how long have you lived in Lyons?"

"Whole stinkin' life. Hate it. But I've got my own house and a good job. The men here, though, have a lot to be desired."

Starla sets her hand down on top of Kevin's.

Kevin smiles, slides his hand away from Starla and says, "Well, I'm sure the right guy will come along."

"I guess."

"So tell me, can you tell me where Chestnut Hills is?"

"Which one?"

"How many are there?"

"Three."

"Three!"

"Yeah, three."

OK, the main one."

"You've already passed it."

"Come again."

"It's on North Lyons road. You passed it when you went out to see old man Snipes."

"I remember passing by what I thought was a subdivision."

"No. That's Chestnut Hills. It belongs Mayor Tapestry. It's the largest independent farm in Michigan. He and his daughter's family live there."

"What do you mean by 'independent'?"

"Privately-owned. Most of the big farms nowadays are owned by corporations and their shareholders."

"Thanks, Starla. You're a big help."

"You can buy me a drink."

Kevin holds up his ring finger and shows off his gold band.

Starla crushes her cigarette against the side of the curb and gets up.

"Yeah, I saw that. But what's one drink between co-workers?"

Kevin laughs and asks, "How about some flowers instead?"

"Yeah, those will do, too."

"One more thing."

"Yes?"

"Where's Dr. Fortune's office?"

"Two blocks up the street, 150 South Lyons Road. But she's closed on Mondays."

"Oh, OK. Thanks again, Starla."

Kevin walks back to his car.

Starla shouts, "Daisies."

Kevin waves back to her and gets into his car.

He thinks, boy, she's a real pistol.

Chapter 5

Kevin travels the three miles on North Lyons Road and slows down when he reaches the handsome, hand-carved oak sign, reading: "Chestnut Hills Farm." Vast fields, green lawns and lush gardens surround the compound that is made up of grand houses, towering silos, solid barns, numerous sheds, and more sturdy barns. Miles of whitewashed fencing border and define the agribusiness.

Thousands of heads of cattle and hogs make this business profitable, but horses, sheep, goats, chickens, rabbits, dogs and cats give it its personality. Tens of men on the newest John Deere tractors race around. Teams of combines and trucks harvest this year's crops. Machines whirl, men yell and animals bawl.

The main house—the Palmer Mansion—is tremendous. Three thick pillars stretch to the sky. Two large hanging, gold lamps swing behind the pillars. Four huge maple trees, with their 200-year old trunks, proudly stand guard in the front yard. Two long driveways partition the mansion. Behind the house, dozens of metal barns gleam. They backlight this scene of country opulence, as if the main house is a priceless gem being displayed in a jeweler's showcase.

Kevin flicks on his left-hand signal and turns onto the second driveway that is just used for family members and their guests. Along the stretch of grass that runs parallel to the driveway, a child rides a new, red dirt bike. Two other youths dressed in Michigan Wolverines' T-shirts intermittently watch the rider and throw a leather football. Kevin waves at them. They politely wave back.

After a few minutes, Kevin passes the front of the house and drives to the back. He pulls up to what used to be a carriage house, but is now a comely four-car garage. One bay is open. In it is a yellow Mercedes convertible. The plate reads "Em's."

To the left of the remodeled carriage house is a red-brick patio filled with vivid geraniums in red, clay pots. The door is open. Through Kevin's open car window he can hear two women talking about tonight's dinner.

Reaching down, Kevin grabs a pad of paper and a pen. He exits the car and walks up to the open door. He knocks on the door's frame, patiently standing next to a large, glass jar of sun-tea that is steeping. Emily Palmer comes to the door.

Em is lovely. Her faded blue Levi's and midnight blue turtleneck hug her 28-year-old body. Her silky, black hair is pulled back, exposing a wide forehead and full eyebrows. A silver charm bracelet dangles from her wrist. Her wedding ring is filled with emeralds and diamonds. She shuffles in her blue Norwegian clogs. Her green eyes sparkle.

She cheerfully says, "Hello."

Kevin cordially introduces himself: "Hi, my name is Kevin Sir, the M.B.I. agent from Ann Arbor, here to look into the case of Doug Richards."

She holds out her hand and says, "I'm Emily Palmer. But please call me Em. Our children playing on the side yard are Steven, Scott and P.J. This is Anna."

Kevin happily takes Em's hand and smiles at Anna.

"Please come in Agent Sir. Do you want something to drink?"

"No, thanks."

Kevin enters the service entrance of the Palmer Mansion.

In the center of the enormous kitchen is a gorgeous Bernhardt table. Linen mats with subtly different shades of khaki rest on the wood. A strip of palomino-pale cashmere runs down the center of the table. Simple Russel Wright plates, black and gold Wedgwood, Victorian silver luster bowls and vintage crystal sit on top of the linen. A medium sized glass chandelier tinkles above the table set for ten.

Among all this luxury, there is a simple, black Franklin stove to the right. Festooning above the stove are tiny birds handmade out of wrought iron. A small inlaid wood table sits in the corner. A blue and white Mottahedeh ginger jar lamp rests on the table. Em has managed to combine both rustic woods and irons with rich-looking silvers and golds to perfection.

Towards the back of the dinningroom/kitchen is the cooking area and back farther towards the porch is a breakfast nook, complete with a small French provincial table and a couple of Louis XV chairs. Fresh golden pears rest in white porcelain compotes.

The kitchen floor is pegged pine. Tufts of herbs and chili peppers suspend over the multi-porcelain sinks. In the back right corner is an antique gold and black Baroque cupboard. Next to it a golden retriever takes a nap in a large maroon L.L. Bean pillow.

"Let's go into the living room."

Kevin and Em walk through the kitchen into the living room; again luxury is married to both the charms of farmlife and to the practicality of having three grown boys running around.

There are many dark oil paintings framed in gold-leaf: They are of Emily's parents and grandparents. They have stern expressions on their faces. To the left is a set of cognac-colored leather chairs. Against the wall is a mohair couch. A large refurbished Indian door serves as the table. An Indian candlestick lamp rests on the table. Under the table is a ruby and deep pine Tufenkian Tibetan carpet.

To the far left is an 18th century grandfather clock from Germany. In the back left corner is an 80-year-old Steinway grand piano. It sits in an alcove looking out towards the front yard. Em's grandparents bought it when they visited New York City. To the right is the bar. Vintage Baccarat decanters sit on silver trays.

Four doorways break up the living room, the framed entrances go into the foyer, the TV room, the library and to the formal dining room. Kevin thinks that

what makes this mansion so big are its twenty-four-feet ceilings.

"You have a very beautiful home."

"Thank Agent Sir. Please, sit down."

"Have you lived in this house long?"

"After my mother died of breast cancer and I graduated from college, my Dad moved into the little white house and gave Derrick and me this place as a wedding present."

"Tell me more about your father, Mr. Tapestry. My boss, Jim Caretaker says he's quite persuasive."

"My Dad owns all this land. I know that I'm biased, but John Tapestry is the finest man around here. He's a legend. My grandfather, his father, farmed here. But it was really my Dad who turned this land into profits. When John Tapestry was a kid, his steer always placed first at the Madison State Fair. He went to Harvard on a football scholarship. He played the game back when they wore leather helmets. And when he feels good, he can still work harder on his farms than a man who is thirty years younger. The people of Lyons voted him mayor because they respect him."

Kevin asks matter-of-factly, "They voted him mayor because they respect him, or because they are scared to death of him?"

Em blushes a little, but continues to state: "I know Dad can be intimidating, but he's not mean. He loves life. When Mom, her name was Marion, died of cancer, Dad wept for weeks. He couldn't work for a long time. Now, he's happy, again. He's a very caring gentleman."

"Look Em, I'm sorry to trouble you, but I read that Doug Richards used to work here. Can you tell me about him?"

"Derrick dealt with Doug. I never go out into the compound. I did see Mrs. Richards at the funeral. Derrick and I sent her a fruit basket. Odd woman, though."

"Why's that?"

"When they were burying Doug, she never once shed a tear. And yet Doug was her only boy. Funny, she just stood there, scared like. As if she had seen a ghost."

She smiles and finishes by saying, "My husband Derrick is down the lane. You should really talk to him about Doug. Derrick will fill you in."

"Where's the lane?"

"Once you drive in the compound, just ask one of the farmhands. They'll be happy to the point the way."

"Thanks."

Kevin thinks, here is a bright, attractive woman, just like Peg. She could fit in at Saks Fifth Avenue any day of the week. So how can she possibly be happy without city entertainment: ballet, museums, outdoor fairs, good restaurants and of course shopping? Peg would not last more than a couple of days out here. Peg's idea of the country is being pampered at a bed-and-breakfast inn. If Kevin brought Peg to live out here, he knows that Peg would go crazy.

Kevin hesitantly asks, "Em, may I ask you a personal question?"

Em smiles, "Of course. Us country girls, are nothing but up front."

"I think I know the answer, but why do you and Derrick like living out here?"

"Peace of mind.

"This land offers us the best place to raise a family. The space gives our children freedom. They couldn't fly a kite in the suburbs unless they went to some park filled with gangs, violence and drugs. Here, they can not only fly kites whenever they want, but they can grow up with animals, ride dirt bikes—with helmets—run through corn fields, listen to birds sing and, most importantly, naturally discover themselves.

"They also have access to their history, to their relatives and to their grandparents. My family is the most important thing in my life.

"I feel at home out here.

She smiles at Kevin and continues, as if she knows that Kevin is about to interrupt because she's not answering the question, "But, when I do miss the city, I tell Derrick and the kids to mind after the house and then I leave. I'm not tied here at all. Derrick, on the other hand, hates the city. He rarely leaves Lyons.

"In fact, Saturday night we have tickets to attend Gilbert and Sullivan's 'Pirates of Penzance' and I already know that I will have to drag Derrick to it. It's in Madison."

Kevin smiles at Em's honesty, while relishing the love she displays for her family.

"That's a very nice sentiment, Em."

Kevin slowly gets up, because he could have sat in the leather chair all day. He thanks her and leaves the Palmer Mansion for his car. He backs up and then slowly drives forward, passing through rows of hedges and two concrete fountains that separate the house from the main compound.

In a few minutes, he enters the working section. Men scurry back and forth. Some are carrying pales of water. Others are carrying bales of hay, or tools, but everyone is carrying something. On Kevin's right, there are dozens of pens of sheep and a giant garage filled with a few Sears' stores worth of Craftsman tools. To his left are a row of gas and diesel pumps, another tool shed and a huge barn filled with fertilizer and seed bags.

A mammoth cattle lot makes up the majority of the compound. Thousands of heavy-breathing cattle slog ankle-deep in mud and manure. The thousand-pound animals are stopped in the front by thick, wooden feed troughs that were once the sides of French sailing ships.

The animals are imprisoned on the sides by electrified, barbed wire. A football field-long, ancient, gray barn keeps the cattle from backing out of their outdoor cellblock. The beasts seem to move as one big cow. Each one adjusts to the animal next to it, no matter how small the movement.

Out of tens of men in the compound, one of the older guys with a dark tan, wiry legs and slight paunch comes bounding up to Kevin's car. He pokes in his head covered with a red, Mack Truck cap.

He asks, "Need something, mister?"

Kevin takes his hand off the steering wheel and holds it out for him to shake.

As they make contact, Kevin asks, "Quite a place you got here. How many cattle?"

He proudly exclaims, "2,000 in front of you. We got another 1,000 in a lot behind this one, 1,000 down by the lane, and another 3,000 on our new farm."

"That's a lot of Big Macs."

"You're right. This bunch, right here, is market-ready. They get butchered tomorrow."

The worker eyes this newcomer. He's driving a new car. Doesn't seem to know much about cattle. Wonder what he wants?

Kevin says, "You may have heard, I'm Agent Kevin Sir from the Michigan Bureau of Investigation."

The worker steps back.

"Oh yea, I heard you was in town. You're going to get Doug Richards' killer. Right?"

Kevin gets out of the car.

The worker yanks at his cap and says, "When you first pulled up, I thought you were a feed salesman. They hit us up almost everyday."

Kevin cuts to the chase, "I heard Doug used to work here."

"He sure did. Worked here on and off for almost five years. Left last summer. Personally, I liked the kid. He called me, 'the jet,' because I'm still real fast for my age and my real name is pretty close. It's Jed. Full name is Jed Spelling.

"One time, we broke up concrete together. He'd hold the spike, and then I'd hit it with the sledgehammer. After a while, we'd switch off. We broke up all the concrete in this whole yard. It takes a lot of trust to hold a metal spike when the other guy could easily miss and take off your fingers. I've seen him sober. He was a good worker."

"Have you seen him when he wasn't sober? The sheriff said he was into drugs, too."

"Well, three weeks ago, Doug Richards, his sister, Naomi and one of her friends came over to my house to visit my son Keith. I'm telling you this because I care about Norma Richards."

"Then what happened?"

"They drank with us. We were drinking bottles of Boone's Farm straw-
berry

wine. They seemed adult enough to me. Keith, my son, wanted to play
Monopoly. They didn't want to play and left for home.

"Keith was plenty pissed. I think he likes Naomi's friend, she's tall with
dark hair. Naomi's small and skinny. She was the drunkest and a wild one
from what I've seen. My son didn't do anything wrong, though. He's a good
kid. He can lift bales of hay all day. In fact, we're going to become partners
in my truckin' business..."

Kevin tries to interrupt because Jed's answer is becoming a soliloquy,
but to no avail: "Yes, but..."

Jed continues, "Every farmer around here needs a truck driver to take
their produce to the mill, or their cattle to the slaughter house. In fact, this
farm, Chestnut Hills, needs truckers to drive grain to the Ohio River drop-
off. And there's another farm that needs truckers to haul produce out West.
So, I know there's work. That's why I've put two rigs on order—big, sons of
bitches, too—Mack trucks!"

Before Jed can catch his breath, Kevin says, "Sir, I believe your son
Keith is involved. I spoke with him this morning. It's a known fact that your
son was the primary reason that Doug Richards dropped out of school and
started drinking and drugging. On top of all that, he was buying a new pitchfork."

The older man lifts his cap off, scratches his head and then tucks his hair
back underneath the red cap.

"Agent Sir, my boy ain't in trouble is he?"

Kevin, seeing that Jed has been trying to help, consoles, "Possibly. Now,
how do I find Derrick? I hear he runs this farm."

"Follow the driveway as it winds around these buildings. You'll pass
through some silos and Mr. Tapestry's spread. The lane divides a cornfield,
dead-ending at a feedlot. Take a left and drive to where we store the cattle
feed. Derrick's working in the woods. You should be able to hear him."

"Thanks."

Kevin gets back into the car, puts it into drive and starts to step on the
gas.

Jed runs up to the car window and says, "Mr. Sir, I need to tell you something... important."

Kevin brakes.

Jed continues, "If I was you, I'd take a good, hard look at them Hortons. They're an uppity bunch. Dale Horton had it in for Doug. Why? I don't know, but, boy, there was bad blood between 'em."

He slaps his knee.

Kevin puts the car into park.

"Bad blood?"

"Yeah, the last few weeks, Mr. Horton was swearin' up a storm about Doug. Tellin' everybody within earshot that 'Doug Richards was a no good loser, who was trying to corrupt Lyons with his vile weed.'"

"Dale seems like a good man to me. Met him after lunch today. In fact, I'm going to his house for pot-roast tonight."

"Just keep an open mind. That's all. Oh, and one more thing: my boy ain't no saint, but he's no killer either."

"Yeah, that seems to be the consensus around here."

Kevin nods that he understands this father's love for his son. He puts the car into drive and steps harder on the accelerator. As Kevin drives by the cattle lot, he sees one bovine move its hooves slightly. Its tail sways back and forth. The cow's head swings up and looks directly towards him. Its big, brown eyes study Kevin. Its ears twitch. There is an orange tag in one ear. Kevin's never seen a cow so close before. It seems very gentle and kind of sad.

Kevin read that they slaughter these beasts by hitting them over the head with a metal weight. Kevin thinks that maybe that is how humanity should deal with Doug Richards' killer. Then, the guards could finish off the other hard-core criminals and clear out Michigan's prisons.

The rookie blindly follows Jed's directions. At the far end of the compound, some cattle are being moved into a semi-trailer to be taken to the butcher's. The metal trailer has holes all along its sides for the animals to breathe through, and it is stained with cowshit. Kevin hears shuffling hooves, barking men and cows grunting and mooing. It is hamburger time for these beasts.

There is a series of metal gates directing the cattle from the pen. A cow journeying through this maze must first step onto a metal scale before it can enter the trailer. If it slows down, or skittishly steps onto the slippery ramp, a huge man, the size of a piano, jams the cow in the rear with electric prongs. The animal has no choice but to leap forward.

The huge man has gray hair shaved almost to his skull. His face is lumpy, as if his features had been created using a ball-peen hammer, pounding away from the inside out. The jowls below his cheeks sway back and forth like dirty sea foam lapping at a beach. A baseball-sized wad of tobacco is crammed into in his lower lip.

His taught overalls help keep his frame erect. If it were not for his sturdy, brass clasps holding the denim suit together, the huge man would explode and large terra-cotta chunks of lipids would rain down and bury Lyons. After a few hot summers, these bacon drippings would melt, soak into the ground and release Lyons from its fatty grave. In short, this man is a cow that has been given the power to walk on two feet.

There is a strong smell of ammonia, cut corn and cow shit in the air. Kevin's ears become filled with the sound of bellowing cattle: "Moo, moo, moo." These beasts are extremely active right now. They must know.

Kevin wonders, if he was a cow being cared after by these men, he would say to his fellow cows, "Hey boys, get a load of this: See that lifeform with two legs over there fixing that tractor by trying to put those little, metal nuts on those screws? I bet he loses one in the dirt and cusses. Then, I bet he bangs his finger trying to make that metal shaft fit onto its case. This a riot!

"Boys, I know we are going to die soon and end up a pot roast on some kid's plate, but let us live it up now: 'Moo, moo, moo.'"

Maybe, all those "moos" are just cows' way of laughing at us humans.

The main compound ends at five silos. On the right, there are three tall blue ones and two larger white ones. They could easily house MX missiles. Across from the silos is a modest white house and an attached garage. It's where Mayor John Tapestry now lives.

Farther left are more silos and a corn dryer. Trucks are streaming into the corn dryer and dumping their loads of corn into it and leaving. These empty trucks turn around and go back out into the fields for more corn from the combines.

When Kevin passes the silos on the right, he sees another large cattle lot filled with slow-moving brown hunks of meat, all wearing orange ear tags. The stench of their manure wafts in through the car's passenger window.

The road widens near this cattle lot. Kevin takes a left onto a narrow gravel lane that cuts through two cornfields. He goes down the hill, looking at the fields. The corn is brown and very dry. It is past the time when it should be harvested. It looks as if a big wind came down from the sky, the whole, wrinkled field would blow away.

The road dead-ends at another cattle lot filled to capacity. He gets out of the car and looks around. The cattle lot butts up against some woods. The woods' perimeter is dead. Cows' manure and urine have seeped into and saturated the ground, killing the trees' life-supporting roots. The dead pine trees have lost their bark closest to the ground, as these cows have rubbed up against their trunks. The dead trees are like those depicted in choppy, black and white newsreels, standing broken and black in the battlefields of turn-of-the-century Europe while tanks coldly rumble by them.

Off in the distance, a small engine whines. Over the hill of the lane comes the small motorcycle that Kevin saw in Em's side yard. It is coming at the rookie fast. The cattle behind Kevin back up and nudge each other to move. Kevin grabs his car door that is jutting out into the road and slams it shut. The young driver starts to make the turn left right in front of Kevin, but the gravel gives out underneath the knobby tires. He and the mini-bike slide into two taut strands of barbed wire.

Kevin runs to him, but the child is already on his feet.

"You OK son?"

The kid smiles up at Kevin with small cuts on his arms and banged up knees and says, "Yea, thanks."

He turns around and looks over his bike. He rubs his fingers over the metal and then quickly draws back his hand.

He cries, "Oh, no."

Even though Kevin has a feeling that the child has damaged the bike, he kindly asks, "What's wrong?"

"The bike is scratched. Stephen's going to kill me."

Kevin kneels down and says, "It's only metal. It could be worse—that could be your head."

The kid instantaneously looks up at Kevin with scrunched up eyebrows. His small round face and puffy cheeks are dotted with freckles and framed by bright blonde hair. P.J. is a scrappy, no-nonsense child. He is wearing denim cut-offs, a yellow-striped, short-sleeved polo shirt and new Nike shoes, which are already muddied and grass-stained.

He cries, "I'm OK! I have to get back to the house. If you see Dad, tell him that supper will ready in an hour."

Smiling at the tough youngster, Kevin says, "I'll tell your Dad."

The rookie returns to his car and heads towards the silage pit. The air is an inexplicable mixture of pungent pine needles and putrid cow manure. The lane to the pit is edged on one side with dried-up corn stalks and confined to the other side by skinny, dead pine trees.

The gravel lane goes up a steep hill towards a long concrete floor. Kevin drives over this slab, which runs into the side of a mountain of cattle feed. Kevin parks and gets out of the Contour.

There is a large red feed-truck with a conveyor belt attached its side parked near the enormous mound of silage. Kevin ambles up to the feed-truck and pokes his head into the cab. But, no one is in there.

Kevin walks around and sees an opening into the woods. There is a muddy path made by large tires. Now, there is a very different smell; it is an unpleasant odor coming from out of the woods. Kevin creeps off the concrete onto the path of mud and dead pine needles. The reek becomes stronger.

The rookie hears metal scrape against metal and a sputtering engine. Through the pine trees, he spies a man on top of a tractor with a front loader. The farmer is lowering a dead cow into a hole. Kevin walks over to him.

The man sees Kevin and smiles. Kevin attempts to smile back, but his face is knotted up by the terrible foulness. The man shuts off the engine. A bloated cow lies in the tractor's bucket. Its bony legs and hooves extend out from underneath the cow's belly at odd angles.

Kevin cannot make out its head. But, the sight of this puffy dead cow with its skinny legs poking out looks similar to a perverse pin cushion or a depraved game of real-life pin-the-tail-on-the-donkey, where gremlins have skewered the animal with its own legs many times but at all the wrong places.

Flies buzz around everywhere.

Kevin can barely breathe.

"Hi, what may I do for you?"

"I'm Kevin Sir from the M.B.I. on the Doug Richards' case. I need to ask you a few questions."

The man cocks his head sideways.

Kevin waves his hand in front of his face to make room for fresh air.

They both study each other for a few minutes.

Kevin looks into the pit of rotting carcasses and lime, into which the farmer is adding another.

Pointing at the dead cow, Kevin asks, "How did this one die?"

"He got tangled up in some barbed wire and choked himself. I have to bury them immediately, or else they'll spread disease. My name is Derrick Palmer. I help Mr. Tapestry run this place."

"Glad to meet you. I met your wife this afternoon. You have a very nice family."

"Yes, thank you. The Lord has been good to us."

"Mr. Palmer, how long have you been the manager here?"

"Ever since I married Em."

Kevin points to the dead cow grave and asks, "And what did you do before this?"

"Advertising in Chicago."

"OK, Mr. Palmer, I'll get to the point: Jed says Doug worked summers here and left last year."

"Yes?"

"Why did he quit?"

"He didn't. I fired him."

"Why?"

"It's a long story."

"Have anything to do with Keith, Jed's son?"

"Sort of. Keith has a drinking problem too, but Mr. Tapestry loves the guy."

"Mr. Palmer…"

"Call me Derrick."

"Derrick, what are your thoughts about the killing?"

"My personal feeling is that his murder was an unfortunate happening."

"What do you mean? The kid was basically tortured. Why would someone kill him by happenstance and then stab him twenty more times?"

Derrick longingly searches Kevin's face for a sign that he can trust him. Then, Derrick shakes his big head no. The proud farmer thinks that it won't be him who breaks first. His family has the right to protect themselves. Someone else, with less to lose, must come out of the closet before he does. Besides, this young agent looks smart and brave enough to find out by himself.

Kevin continues, "I caught Keith buying a new pitchfork today. He protests that it was for you. Is this true? If so, what happened to the old one?"

"Yea, we lost the old one."

"Well, what do think about Keith stealing your old one and using it to make a human sprinkler out of Doug Richards?"

Derrick shakes his head no.

"OK. So, who do you think killed Doug Richards? Could it have been Dale Horton? Jed tells me that there was bad blood between Dale and Doug."

"Dale Horton? Absolutely not. We're very good friends. We're in the same men's Christian group. Dale is a big teddy bear. He's a wonderful person. Dale has his own business and loves his family."

Kevin circles back to a previous question, "OK. Tell me more about Doug Richards. What did his drinking have to do with you firing him?"

"Sometimes I let the men drink beer after work. When Doug drank, he'd go crazy. Then he'd skip work because he'd be too hungover. I would have to do my job and Doug's. It wasn't fair.

"To his credit, though, when Doug was here, he was a good worker. All the guys liked him, too. But I couldn't rely on him because he got pickled so much.

"You know, if Doug Richards had been as good at avoiding booze as he was at breaking rock, he'd be alive today. Plus, when you handle our machinery, and you don't have your wits about you, you get hurt."

"What do you mean?"

"Have you met Snipes yet?"

"Yes, just this morning."

"Snipes' son, Marty, was out plowing. He was drunk or high or both. Anyway, he fell asleep and tipped over backwards. The plow rip him to shreds."

Kevin responds, "Ouch."

Derrick looks at the cow's soon-to-be grave.

There's a moment of silence when the agent has run out of questions to ask and Derrick feels like he's told as much as he's willing to tell.

Derrick says, "Got to get back to work."

Derrick starts the tractor's engine and lowers the cow in with his fellow lifeless mates.

Agent Sir, seeing that Derrick can't be persuaded to share anymore, hikes out of the woods.

He walks up to his dirty Contour. It badly needs to be washed. The grill and the headlights are the final resting spots for hundreds of dead bugs. Kevin gets in. The dashboard is covered with dust. Kevin starts the car and speeds away, forgetting to tell Derrick about supper.

Going back, Kevin drives quicker along the lane. Looking in his rear view mirror, he sees that the car is kicking up a cloud of dust. Pebbles ping and ricochet off the car's bottom. Coming in from the open windows, crickets and katydids screech in the weeds next to the cornfields. The last of the day's sun burns through the rear window.

Squinting into his dashboard's clock the rookie sees: 4:00 p.m.

Shit, he thinks, his cell phone doesn't work.

He really must call Peg.

Kevin speeds passed the cattle lot and the small, white house. As he rounds the silos, he makes a right onto the workers' driveway. To the left is a mighty metal barn filled with an army of plows, planters and huge tractors shaped like tanks. In front of the imposing implements, two men in filthy overalls tear into a tractor's engine.

Just past the barn stands the other side of the Palmer Mansion. There is a kidney-shaped swimming pool with yellow flowers running around it, another charming red brick patio with iron-wrought furniture, two long dog runs and a screen porch with bright yellow and white awnings. A whitewashed fence runs alongside the road, separating the grounds from the compound.

Kevin hits the road and speeds towards Lyons. Even though he's in a hurry, the drive back to town is splendid. Nature calls to him. The huge maple trees on both sides of the road stretch their strong limbs over the moving car, as a row of English soldiers raising their arms over their victorious general strutting underneath their shiny swords and past their swollen chests.

It is as if these big trees are putting on a show just for him. As if throughout the many seasons of rain and sun they were readying themselves for this moment. Now, they are standing as tall as they can in the last of today's October sun.

Kevin thinks that he never feels like this when he drives around Ann Arbor. Sure, there is that stretch of road near the campus of U. of M. that he enjoys. Many days he purposely drives out of his way to take in the sloping green grass, healthy trees, fountains and well-watered flower beds. However, he always had to share that beauty with others.

Thinking back, he felt rushed, too. Just as he was becoming one with that idyllic scene, Honda Accords and Jeep Cherokees would race up behind him inches away from his bumper. The busy drivers would stomp on their accelerators and anti-lock brakes simultaneously. The cars would violently jerk, pushing Kevin past that picturesque scene. Right now, though, he does not feel he has to share this beauty with anyone.

Just as Em said, Kevin thinks that is a picture-perfect setting far from the noisy city, nosy neighbors, cracked sidewalks, crack dealers, and all of obnoxious human beings' pointless activities, monuments and obstacles.

Out here, people do not have to bear the construction delays of the newest light rail system, or the widest eight-lane turnpike. They do not have to become upset when a city's water mains break and the flooding re-routes traffic. They do not have to get perturbed when taxes go up to pay for all that construction.

Country people do not have to cross under dark, underground parking lots to get to their cars where mumbling bums with bloodshot eyes would kill them for the change in their pockets.

People in Lyons do not have to cry to themselves at night when the news reports that another black eight year old from the "other-side" of the city was killed by gang crossfire as he played in the street. The city's crime means nothing to these farmers.

Just as Em said.

But, Kevin rationalizes that Derrick and Em do have crime here. A murder was just committed. They and the rest of Lyons must face up to the fact that evil has erupted in their small, once-quiet farming community.

Chapter 6

After a few miles on North Lyons Road, Kevin takes the on-ramp for I-94. Kevin drives to the Best Western for a quick shower before dinner with the Horton's. The motel is located half-way between Lyons and Madison. Madison is a rather large town that is home to the State Penitentiary.

Once in the motel's parking lot, he sighs. He collects all the material that fell out of his briefcase off the floor. He slowly rolls out of the car. His knee becoming stiff from the fall earlier in the cornfield makes Kevin stumble a bit up the steps to the Manager's Office. Once inside, he taps a little silver bell to announce his arrival.

A stooped, older woman with dark, black hair comes out to greet him.

"Hello, may I help you?"

"Yes, my name is Agent Kevin Sir, with the M.B.I. I have a reservation."

She checks the registry and finds the M.B.I. agent's name.

The motel manager reads, "Kevin. I like to call all my customers by their first names. I hope that is OK with you?"

"That's fine."

She smiles and gives Kevin the keys to his room.

"Looks like you've been fighting."

"I'm not hurt. Just a little scratched up."

The manager chastises Kevin: "You be careful young man. You're too good-looking to be walkin' into punches."

Kevin relaxes and smiles back at this perpetual grandmother.

"What's your name?"

"Donna."

"That's a pretty name."

The old woman blushes.

She says, "Thank you. Are you here to solve that Lyons' murder?"

"Yes, I am. Do you know anything about it?"

"Sorry, I'm too busy here to know anything besides changing sheets, who's checking in and out and between two and three o'clock watching my favorite soap—'The Young and the Restful.' You look a lot like Jake, he is my favorite. Besides, I do all my shopping in Madison. I haven't been to Lyons in years."

"Thanks, Donna. If you ever hear of anything, please let me know."

"OK."

Kevin thanks the kind woman and shuffles outside. He opens the trunk of his car and grabs a couple of large, blue duffel bags. Almost in front of where he parked, Kevin locates his room, #105. He fumbles with the keys, unlocks the door and throws the duffel bags on the spare bed.

Kevin gets undressed, tossing his torn Brooks Brothers suit over a chair. He unbuttons his wet shirt and peels off his socks. He reaches for the phonebook and looks up Dale Horton's business number. He dials it.

"Farmer's Insurance," a woman answers.

"Yes, ma'am. Agent Kevin Sir."

"Agent Sir I'm very glad you called. I hear you're joining the Horton's for dinner. Need directions?"

"Yes, please."

"They're at the corner of N. Lyons and Belleview. On the right-hand side."

"Thank you."

"Good-bye."

"Yes, good-bye."

Kevin hangs up and dials Peg's law firm.

Her secretary answers: "Bowman, Burgess, Ehnes, Hanes & Watkins. Margaret Brace's office."

"Hey, Susan. Is Peggy in?"

"Oh, hi Kevin. Hold on."

Even though Peg has been told that it's her husband, she still answers very business-like, ending her name with a downward inflexion, "Margaret Brace."

"Hi honey. I miss you."

Peg brightens up, "Oh, what a beautiful thing to say. Thank you. I love you, too. How's it going?"

"OK. Do you want to know the details?"

"Of course I do," Peg lies, while she rests the phone on the desk to proof-read a brief she's putting together against Marriott for not having handicap ramps.

Kevin confesses to the empty receiver, "The mistake that most outsiders', in other words me, make is in thinking that farmers' minds are of small scope—*Today is hot. This summer is humid. This winter is bitter. I'm hun-*

gry. I need to feed to the livestock. I need to fight the elements. I need to make sure the roof is dry, etc.

"Which simply isn't the case. Yes, farmers think about these things, but much of their thoughts are hidden. They lie buried deep. I cannot only read their thoughts, but I have the almost impossible task of digging below their innate, Puritan apprehension. Farmers, after hundreds of years of defending their lands, have been taught to bury their real emotions. That's the main problem: getting people to open up.

"In terms of the victim, Doug Richards, I believe the kid just got in the way of someone's vision of what Lyons should be. Doug Richards stepped into the middle of a war, of sorts."

Kevin finishes.

Silence.

"Peg?"

Peg hears the end of her husband's speech and quickly picks up the phone, responding, "I see your point. How are you going to handle it?"

"Like the sergeant says, 'Bully my way through it. Get these bastards to open up."

"Good for you. Now, when do you think you'll be home?"

"Don't know. Could be a few days."

"Well, hurry back. I miss you."

"I miss you too."

After the young attorney hangs up, she drops her elbows onto her mahogany desk and rests her chin onto her freshly manicured hands.

Peg thinks that men are such a pain. Except for sex and moving around furniture, what good are they? Kevin is a dear, but he is still a man.

She remembers that the only real reason she decided to marry him was that, biologically and socially speaking, it was the right time in her executive planner to become a partner with a member of the opposite sex. Kevin seemed harmless and controllable six months ago. Lately, though, he is becoming less malleable.

Kevin thinks that Peg seemed preoccupied.

It's obvious that she's upset at his being away on this case.

Kevin dials Campus Flowers, a shop in Ann Arbor. He orders a dozen long-stem roses to be delivered to her law firm.

He tells the young man at the flower shop to put this saying on the card:

"Dearest Peg, This is a tale of two cities. Your husband is on assignment in a rural village surrounded by yellow cornfields, proud maple trees and thick woods.

"You are living in a big town surrounded by bright lights, high rises and people, people, people, whose daily hustle makes the mundane almost magical.

"Our love must bridge this gap, as Romeo and Juliet's love did when they found a way to speak to each other through a crack in the garden wall. Imagine me with you, please. Two cities. One love. Kevin."

On the other end of the phone, the clerk taking Kevin's order asks, "Did you just make that up?"

"Well, sort of, I've been thinking those thoughts all day, but yes, those are my words."

The person says, "Well, mister, you should call Hallmarck Cards, and see if they'd buy it. That was a beautiful sentiment. Now, how are you going to pay?"

Kevin gives the worker his Visa card number and also tells the clerk to send a bouquet of daises to the Sheriff's Office in Lyons, Michigan; Attention: Starla; From: Agent Sir; Message: "Thanks for all your help. If only I wasn't married…"

The rookie smiles at thought of those daises being delivered to Starla and the look in her eyes as she reads the card.

Kevin hops into the shower, dries off and dresses into some khakis, a white turtleneck, an almond-colored cotton crewneck sweater and Cole Hahn loafers.

At 5:15, Kevin leaves his motel and drives to the Horton's. The Horton's home is a long, one-story, ranch house that is one of Lyons' nicer and newer homes. In fact, they just completed building an indoor swimming pool. The addition is in the back.

Kevin parks the car in front of a large black satellite dish mounted into a cement square. He gets out and walks up the asphalt driveway. Stepping on their plastic grass Welcome mat, he pushes the doorbell and waits for a Horton to unlock the irongate in front of him. Inside, Kevin hears music.

Kevin pushes the button again, but no answer. He pounds the glass behind the irongate. At last, a young man comes to the door. Gus is wearing a wool Detroit Tigers cap, a Cambridge T-shirt and shorts. The high school athlete swings open the fortified glass door for the rookie to catch. The home smells of cigarettes.

Gus takes Agent Sir into the living room. Kevin follows the young jock across a parquet wood floor. They step into a sunken, carpeted family room with a big screen TV. Behind the living room are the eating area and kitchen. The open layout allows for no walls. The space is defined by different styles of furniture. Way in the back, in the kitchen, Mrs. Horton is putting the finishing touches on dinner.

Kevin politely waves to her.

She holds up a gravy-soaked wooden spoon in acknowledgement.

Dale says, "Hello, Agent Sir. It's nice of you to come by. This young man is one of Lyons' finest, my son, Gus."

Kevin greets both men and sits down.

Dale asks, while getting up, "Would you like some coffee?"

"Sure."

Dale exits.

Mrs. Horton comes out, as if the couple is playing tag team with Kevin.

She says, "Dinner will be a few minutes."

"Mrs. Horton that sounds great."

"Oh, please, call me Gail."

Kevin jokes, "Dale and Gail. You rhyme."

"Yes, believe it or not, Dale and I sometimes wear matching outfits when we go to the mall. I guess marriage does that to some couples. It makes them one and the same."

Gail is attractive for forty-something. She still has light blond hair and a good figure. She walks over to the stereo and raises the volume of Elvis Presley to ear-bursting levels. She moves her hips and sings with him. She turns around and laughs with Kevin, who is sitting there enjoying the moment. Just above the entertainment center and a gold cross is a painting of the King.

She turns the volume down and says, "There's no one like Elvis. If only he was alive today. In my day, he was the guy to die for. I have every one of his records."

She exits the room softly humming along to Elvis Presley's crooning. Kevin smiles as she leaves. Gail seems to be a likeable character who probably spends way too much time playing house while big, bad Dale is off battling deductibles, liabilities and annuities.

In fact, if prodded, Dale will tell a person that he is a male chauvinist who enjoys the fact that his wife is held prisoner inside his home, whose cellmates include Mr. Clean, Mr. Tidy Bowl and the Dow Scrubbing Bubbles.

Kevin and Gus are alone.

Gus is a strong, good-looking kid. His chiseled features and tan suggest he is a good sport. His Cambridge cigarette T-shirt hides a strong chest and smooth muscles. He sits behind a coffee table littered with Pepsi cans, M&Ms, chip bags and ashtrays.

Kevin clears his throat and says, "Gus, as you're probably aware, I'm in town to get Doug Richards' killer. I'm not here to hassle you, or your family. I'm just following up on a lead. A gentleman told me, today, that your family had something against the murder victim. Can you tell me what was your beef?"

Gus studies the shag carpet.

Finally, his handsome, young face looks up and says, "You'll have to ask my Dad about Doug. I'm not supposed to talk about it."

Kevin knows that he must now take control, but he does not want to be too pushy and hurt Gus. Unlike the others he has questioned, Gus seems sincere.

Kevin weakly argues, "But, this is important son. You can't have people talking badly about your family. If you've done nothing wrong then you should want to clear your family's name. Right?"

Gus shrugs his square shoulders.

Maybe, Kevin thinks that he can goad Gus into talking, rather than confronting the young man.

"Why are you wearing Cambridge T-shirt? You don't look like you smoke. You look like you play sports."

"It's my Dad. He smokes. I've tried to make him quit. I've even hidden them. But he just buys more. Oh, well, he's hooked. Even though I hate for him to smoke, I love him.

"So, we've worked out a deal. He can continue to smoke, as long as he gives me his cigarette tabs. Right now, I have 200. I only need 25 more."

"What do you get for 225 tabs?"

"A new windbreaker and sweat pants."

Seeing that Kevin has Gus' attention, the detective continues, "What sports do you play?"

"Football and track."

"How's your football team this year?"

"Fine. We got a game tomorrow night. You should come by. Did you play football?"

"Yea, I was a quarterback. I went to college on a scholarship. I even played with the Raiders. Lots of good quarterbacks out there, though. More than I ever thought. So, after I got hurt, I became a cop. Next best thing!"

Gus nods approvingly.

Kevin says, "I bet you're a running back. You look like one."

Gus vigorously shakes his head up and down.

"Yup."

Seeing that Kevin has Gus back on his side, he asks one more time, "Gus, are you sure that you can't tell me anything about Doug? It's very important."

"I'm sorry. The only thing I can tell you is Doug and I were once friends. For the whole story, you will have to talk to my Dad."

Dale comes back in carrying both of their coffees. A cigarette dangles from his mouth. Kevin thanks him, and Dale sits down.

He takes a long puff and asks, "Did you hear Rush Limbaugh today? Boy, he was right on target about our school system. We pander to kids too much nowadays. I'll tell you what, we got to do something about this drug problem and quick. This whole world is turning into Sodom and Gomorrah. Jesus will fix things though."

Kevin asks, "How so?"

Dale picks up his coffee and takes a loud sip, puffs at his cigarette and says, "It says in the Bible that wasting one's time drinking and taking drugs is a sin. You'll go to hell for that mister."

Gus says, "Dad, please don't start that again."

Dale shoots his son an angry look, and continues, "It's true. And another thing, we as God-fearing American citizens have the right to exact punishment against those who do sinful things."

Kevin asks, "Like what kind of punishments?"

Dale blusters, "If I see a youngster drinking, or smoking wacky tobacky then it says in Michigan's constitution that I can hold that youngster against his will until the cops come. It also says that if that drunk, or druggie steps one foot on my land with the intent to steal something to feed his evil habits then I can shoot the bastard!"

Kevin says, "I read in *Time* magazine that drugs are on the rise in high schools after a steady decline for ten years."

Dale screams, "That leftwing rag doesn't impress me at all. I see things more black and white. I say once you start down the path of substance abuse, you're headed for destruction. It's a one-way street to Hell. And there are no exit ramps!"

"So you hate drugs."

"Yes sir."

"You hate drug dealers."

"You betcha."

"Enough to kill one?"

"I see where you're headed. No sir, not enough to kill one."

Agent Sir prods, "Go on then. Who do you think killed Doug?"

"I think Doug's own kind killed him. I think his other dirty, soul-stealin', no-good drug hooligans murdered him for his take. Heck, you hear about it all the time on the news. Drug dealers are a bunch of wolves. They kill the weakest one so that the pack stays strong."

"Well, I agree that does happen. But are you saying that Lyons has that big of a drug problem here?"

"Of course. The Devil is alive and well in Lyons. Just ask Keith, he runs a regular drug cartel from here."

Gail yells from the kitchen, "Dinner's ready. Come on guys, before it gets cold."

The men walk into the spotless kitchen with all the newest appliances.

Kevin says, "Mmmm, smells great. As I was telling your husband, this dinner is a treat."

Gail blushes. She unties her apron and neatly hangs it on a duck's bill. The family holds their hands in a small circle in the kitchen. Kevin includes his.

Before Dale speaks, he yanks out his cigarette and slams the butt onto a stack of many others in the ashtray. The ashtray looks as if it is a mass burial site for Jews in a Nazi concentration camp. The skinny, white objects are twisted this way and that in a pile of ashes.

Dale grabs his son and wife's hand and proclaims, "Lord, thank you for bringing Agent Sir to us. We're most grateful. Lord douse the flames of injustice by sending drugs and booze to the depths of hell. Give the M.B.I. the power to make it so.

"Let my son score enough touchdowns in tomorrow night's game so that they might win. Thank you for giving his team their last victory. Let my business grow so that I might buy Gail nice things for our beautiful home. We love you Jesus. We need you. Amen."

Gus walks to the front of the pot roast and cuts off a huge slab. He fills his plate with many spoonfuls of carrots, onions and gravy. Kevin takes half as much.

As Kevin walks over to the table, Gail whines, "Agent Sir, you must take more."

"Madame, a long time ago when I was Gus' age, I would have piled my plate from here to the ceiling, but you know, things change."

Kevin pats his stomach to reinforce his argument.

Dale shouts, "You M.B.I. guys kill me. Always trying to stay in shape. Trying to stay fit and chasing after important criminals. I wish I could stay in shape. But Gail cooks too good."

Gail blushes again. Dale sits down and dives into his plate of food. He has even more meat and vegetables than Gus. Dale lights a cigarette and smokes in between bites of food. He finishes drinking all the coffee halfway through dinner. He gets up and makes another pot. Meanwhile, Elvis plays in the background.

Kevin tries to concentrate on his pot roast, which is very good and tender. The meat falls onto his fork. The vegetables, which had been soaking in the meat's juice, melt into his mouth.

Dale says, "Kevin, you should come by and address our Christian organization."

Kevin shakes his head yes.

Dale continues, "We're having a meeting at Johnson's house Thursday night. He's in real estate."

"Yes, that might help."

Dinner finishes.

Gail clears the table and starts stacking the dishes into the dishwasher. She shuts off the water and wipes her clean hands on an embroidered towel. She says goodnight to Kevin, turns off the stereo and walks down the hallway towards the bedroom.

Dale thanks Kevin for coming by. He walks the rookie to the door.

He asks, "So, we'll see you Thursday night at 6 p.m. then?"

"Sure. I'm not very religious, but my folks are, though. Maybe my talking to your group may bring about a lead."

"You know Agent Sir, you're a strange duck. I can't figure you out. You're smart enough to be a law enforcement type, but the way you talk makes me think you're a liberal. I'll pray for you. Be careful driving home. And one more thing: John Tapestry may run this town right now, but you can bet the farm that Dale Horton is the man who this town really needs!"

Before Kevin can argue, Dale closes the thick wooden door.

Kevin shuts the metal security door behind him.

The entrance light goes on, and he walks to his car, grateful to escape the clutches of stale Dale and his Stepfordesque wife. Kevin wonders how Gus lives through it all. He is going to have quite an awakening at college. When Gus comes home for the first time for Thanksgiving break, boy is Dale going to blow a major conservative cog.

The drive home is tranquil. He passes through Lyons. The town is asleep. The quiet streets and dark storefronts mean night is here. In Ann Arbor, the night is does not mean the end of the business day; rather, it is the chance for stores to show off their neon signs and flashing sale signs. In Lyons, the night is a time for refreshment. In Ann Arbor, the night is a time for attainment.

Kevin bets that in Lyons when the snow falls, people slow down and take what nature has given it in stride. In Ann Arbor, the plows are cleaning the streets as soon as the first flake appears. People grumble if they cannot get to work on time. They yell at their councilpeople to put more sand on the roads.

Time does not stop, or even slow down in Ann Arbor for nature. The city people will not allow it. Snow to them is not a glistening wonder, it is a slushy hassle that makes a trip to the car wash inevitable.

Kevin parks the car in front of his motel room. He opens the door and flicks on the light. He locks the door and gets undressed. In the bathroom, he unwraps a plastic cup, takes a couple gulps of water and dials Peggy. He lets it ring three times and, after hearing his own voice on the recorder, hangs up.

Kevin wonders where Peg could be; it's 8:00 p.m.

Peg, having bought a new outfit at Saks and downing her fifth Bloody Mary, could care less where her husband is. Surrounded by good-looking men, pounding music and swirling lights, Peg and her girlfriend Amanda only care about having a good time. Peg sips her drink and lets a man smile at her. He comes over and places a hand on her thigh.

Kevin sets the alarm for six, gets into bed and drifts off to sleep.

Tonight, Kevin dreams about Indians running through the forest with bright, red holes in their stomachs. They are chasing the rookie with shiny pitchforks. He bursts through the trees until he reaches a cliff. Off the precipice he runs. Kevin awakes, looks at the clock that reads 2 a.m. and falls back to sleep.

At 2:30 am, on the other end of town, a young farmer, Abe, is in real trouble. Abe Jenkins, the man who earlier in the day talked to Agent Sir about old man Snipes, only wishes he were dreaming.

Earlier tonight around 9 p.m., after drying the dishes, Abe turned off the kitchen lights. After a long day, he walked into the living room and collapsed on his Lazy-Boy. He turned on the TV and saw Vanna Whitehead turn one letter. After that, he fell asleep. His wife Sarah threw a brown and yellow afghan around her hardworking husband and retired to their bedroom.

Now, it's around 2:30 a.m. and a truck with Yosemite Sam mud-flaps creeps up to Abe's humble home. The driver and his brother turn off the truck's engine and coast into the driveway. They get out of the truck and don burlap sacks over their heads. Earlier, they had cut out two holes for their eyes.

The driver grabs one of his Remington .30 pump shotguns.

The two masked men walk up to Abe's home.

Fortunately for any criminal in Lyons, no one bothers to lock their homes, so these two men enter the home by simply turning the front door knob. The two men stop for a second to let their eyes adjust to the darker living room. The driver of the truck sees Abe resting on a chair. He places his strong hand over Abe's mouth while his brother grabs the poor man's legs. The pair carries Abe out to his barn.

Abe tries to wiggle free, but the brothers are much stronger.

The driver of the truck throws Abe to barn floor and demands, "No more squealin' to the M.B.I. Got it Abe?"

Abe warns, "I know who you are. You don't scare me."

The driver cocks the shotgun.

The driver says, "Sorry I can't come up with something more creative, but this will have to do."

The other brother steps on Abe's shoulder, pinning the poor farmer to the ground. The driver aims at Abe's arm and shoots the poor farmer's hand off.

Abe screams.

Lights go on in Jenkins' home.

The driver says, "Next time, I'll aim at your head, or maybe at your pretty wife's. Now, leave well enough alone and mind your own business."

The bad brothers run to the truck, start it and get away before Sarah Jenkins can see who maimed her precious husband, Abe.

Dawn comes, and with it a new day to catch criminals.

Chapter 7

Tuesday morning, Kevin feels good. He jumps in the shower, dries off and dresses into a pressed Ralph Loren suit, a lightly-starched white oxford shirt, a yellow and cornflower blue paisley tie and shiny, brown penny loafers.

He walks out onto the iridescent parking lot. Its crushed gravel, tar and sand shatter the rays of light into pea-sized rainbows. He puts on his Ray-Bans. He locks his motel room's balsa-wood-feeling door.

He walks towards the Manager's Office. His wet hair in the cool morning air rouses him. The only thing he needs now to complete the process of awakening is coffee.

Ever since attending The University of Colorado, he has had to have a few cups of coffee to get his heart going. He got hooked on the stuff up in the granola-capital-of-the-world, Boulder, CO. He remembers Boulder's cafe's serving coffee that was thick and rich, like a hot chocolate malted, only stronger.

He walks into the lobby of his twenty-nine-dollar-a-night motel, picks up a copy of "USA Today" and says to the manager, "Good morning! And how are you on this fine day?"

Without waiting for an answer, he walks over to the coffee machine and sees light brown water. Even though he must opt for Best Western's complimentary cup of anemic Java, he shrugs his shoulders as if it is no big deal and pours the tan liquid into a small, white Styrofoam cup.

She smiles and says, "Good. Are we feeling better after yesterday?"

"Yeah."

Kevin exits the lobby into the day. The sun has risen up into the sky. Today, the sky is clear, which for Michigan is rare. Usually, every day exhibits endless clouds. Ordinarily, the sky looks as if God—playing street punk—has spray-painted the heavens with a matte gray, leaving not a seam of blue or a dot of yellow sunshine to enjoy.

The rookie gets into his dirty Contour and drives to the Cafe for coffee, which is not served in a Styrofoam cup, and waffles the size of hubcaps.

The Cafe is packed, so Kevin sits down at the counter on a plastic covered seat that swivels. The stool is bolted to the ground.

Glancing next to him, Kevin sees an old man with bumps all over his face. He is wearing a green, dusty Pioneer Seed hat. His hands resting on the counter are brown and wrinkled like tree bark. The skin is just as hard. His fingernails are black and chipped.

Kevin asks him, "How's the coffee?"

Without looking at the rookie, he says, "Ain't bad."

"Where's your farm?"

He growls, "Don't have one. I'm a worker at Chestnut Hills."

"Must be nice working on a farm, even if it isn't yours. I mean, all that clean air. It's not as if you're cooped up in a office like a sardine."

He frowns and places his coffee cup on the counter.

"Mister, driving a smoky diesel tractor all day long ain't no picnic."

"Sorry, I just thought that working outdoors has its moments."

"Right now, I'm draggin' a harvester behind it to reap corn. It ain't as if I'm physically holding a sickle and doing it myself. Farmers nowadays are basically truckers who travel up and down countless rows of plants... boring. Farmers' 'highways' are big dirt fields with no truck stops.

"What's more: There is nothing excitin' to look at. Haven't seen animals run through the fields for some twenty years now. There aren't no more rabbits to eat a carrot crop. They're all dead. There aren't no more crows to scare away with a few well-placed scarecrows. They've all been killed off. All those chemicals made from 3M has done in all of God's little critters."

"Sorry, I didn't know things were that bad."

He intones, "Welcome to Lyons!"

The bitter old farmer next to Kevin slurps his coffee.

Kevin coffee turns cold. The waitress, an overweight girl with black tights and brown, puffed-up hair that is dyed with silver streaks, ignores the rookie.

After breakfast, the rookie walks over to the sheriff's office. He's not in, so Kevin chats with Starla.

"Where's the sheriff?"

"Over at Doc's office. Someone got hurt last night. John's just checking it out."

"Who got hurt?"

"Oh, I believe it was Abe Jenkins. Too bad. He's a real sweetheart. His arm got caught in some machinery. That's what I heard."

"Dammit!"

"What's wrong?"

"I was talking to him yesterday at The Café about old man Snipes. Then this big guy Jerod McMurtry started threatening both of us."

"Yeah, I'd stay away from Jerod. That boy's no good. I went out on a date with him once and had to run through the woods to get away. He tried to rape me! The whole town is afraid of him. Well except, for Mr. Tapestry and maybe Mr. Horton. Makes sense, though, that Jerod came unglued. Grandkids found his Uncle Snipes dead yesterday after you left. Suicide."

"I'm going over to Dr. Fortune's office. Pronto."

Kevin grabs some things out his car and quickly walks to the intersection of Main and Lyons. He turns right and jogs the block and a half to a large, white three-story home that doubles as Dr. Fortune's office. He bounces up the steps. A white, wood sign with black hand-painted letters announces: Barbara Fortune, M.D. Hours: Tues. through Sat. 9am-5pm. Emergencies: Call Madison City Hospital at (517) 756-7777.

The rookie opens the screen door and scans the waiting room for any signs of trouble. Sitting on a white, wicker chair, Sarah Jenkins sobs. She has two small children in her lap. Blood is spattered on her yellow cotton flower dress.

Kevin is too upset to comfort her now. He struts past her and opens one of the two examining rooms. A patient, Abe, lies unconscious, but no sign of a doctor or the sheriff. Kevin checks the next room and a motionless body lies covered up. It's Snipes' dead body.

The rookie walks past the reception desk and opens a third door. It's the coffee room. Sackett is in here sitting at a round table, staring blankly out the window at a leafless maple tree. Kevin enters and shuts the door behind him.

"Sheriff Sackett what happened?"

The skinny peace officer turns to face Kevin. As he does, Sackett's oversized wire-rimmed glasses slip down his pointed nose. His finger catches the falling glasses and he jabs the bridge into his forehead. He looks different. He looks upset. He has temporarily come out of his shell.

Sheriff Sackett spouts, "Combine accident, my foot. Abe was shot!"

"Well, let me at the guy!"

"No, Abe won't confess. He's scared. He's got a young family. He finally got around to getting his life together and now this!

"If the Town Council didn't have me hog-tied to their notion that I can never upset the apple cart, I would go after 'em. Abe is my friend. We went to elementary school together. Dammit!"

"Sheriff, I don't understand."

"If I start showing my gun around, Tapestry will have my badge for sure and then my family will be on welfare. I don't know what to do."

Kevin walks over to the sheriff and puts his hand on his shoulder.

Sackett continues, "I know some people around here think that I'm just a showpiece. But, hell, that's the way it is. That's the way the council wants it."

"Yeah, so Mayor Tapestry can run the show. Right?"

"Exactly."

"It seems, though, that maybe some people are getting tired of John Tapestry running things. Could that be, also, right?"

The sheriff confesses, "I've heard talk that Horton wants to run for mayor next month. He wants to rezone most of the farm land into a business park and housing developments."

"Could Jerod McMurtry be the one who hurt Abe and possibly killed Doug? Do you think Jerod is Dale's muscle?"

Sheriff Sackett nods his head yes.

"OK, I'm going to go see him. You may have a guest in your jail cell tonight."

"Fine with me. I'll have to make sure the toilet still works. Haven't had to use the cell for quite some time."

"Here, I don't have time to talk to the doctor. I will later. But give her this bag of bloody straw and ask her to match it with the Richards' DNA. OK?"

"Will do."

"Thanks."

"Oh, and Agent Sir?"

"Yes?"

"Even though this case is yours, you can't work alone. You're on the right track, but you still need a conductor. Go see Mayor Tapestry before you arrest Jerod. The mayor is a fair man, but nothing will get accomplished without his help, but more importantly without his consent. He speaks for the people."

Kevin says he will and closes the door to the coffee room.

Kevin looks at his watch: 8:30 a.m. He needs to check in. He walks over to the doctor's phone and dials his sergeant's direct line.

"Caretaker!"

"Boss, it's Agent Sir. What's wrong?"

"We got a real mess around here with two gangs coming in from Detroit. We're swamped. And one of your classmates, Meyers, was killed last night in a shootout."

"Do you want me to come back to Ann Arbor?"

"No stay where you are."

Jim hangs up.

Obviously, Mr. Horton wants Agent Sir to nail Keith Spelling. Sheriff Sackett thinks Jerod McMurtry should be strapped to the electric chair. Mr. Tapestry just wants Agent Sir to get the job done and to "get out of Dodge." Agent Sir is somewhat confused about the how Keith fits into the picture. It's time to get grounded: See the mayor and ask him about the case, as well as about Jerod McMurtry.

Kevin gets into his Ford and drives out to Chestnut Hills Farm. He drives to the first driveway, the one for the workers. He turns onto the gravel road. The normally reddish brown road is now black, having been freshly oiled in order to keep the dust down.

He enters the compound. Younger cattle now mill about in the massive feedlot. The older ones were shipped to the slaughterhouse late yesterday. Kevin pulls up next to a red feed-truck that he saw yesterday at the silage pit. The truck's conveyor belt lifts feed into the trough. In the truck is Mr. Tapestry, concentrating on his driving so that feed will not spill onto the ground.

Kevin rolls down the window, and yells, "Hey, Mr. Tapestry! Can I talk to you for a second?"

The gentleman farmer puts a cupped hand to his ear and makes a face as if he cannot hear Kevin above the truck's clanking conveyor belt and noisy engine. Kevin hops out of his car and runs over to the passenger side of the red truck, climbing on top of its siderail.

The rookie pokes his head into the truck and asks, "Can I talk to you for a second?"

"Sure, as soon as I'm done feeding the animals."

The smell of the cattle feed shoots into Kevin's nostrils. It reminds him of the burnt cornflakes that he smelled when his fifth grade class took a tour of the Kellogg's cereal plant in Battle Creek.

Corn shells fly into the truck's cab. Mr. Tapestry's clothes are covered

Virtual Publishing Group, Inc.

with corn dust. Kevin jumps off the sideboard and waits for the gentleman farmer to finish. Mr. Tapestry completes his pass and drives the red truck back to the pit. Kevin follows him in his Contour.

The gray haired gentleman parks the red truck. He walks up to Kevin's Contour. He leans down within inches of Kevin's face. His bushy eyebrows rise up a little.

"Agent Sir, this is my town. In a way, I'm responsible for its people. You could say I'm Lyons' biggest admirer. I love this place."

"Yes, I know that."

Mr. Tapestry stands up straight. He has a tall frame and still has a barrel of a chest.

He commands, "Agent Sir, Kevin, let's go for a ride. I think there are some things we need to talk about."

They get into Mr. Tapestry's beat-up auburn Ford pickup. Kevin opens the passenger side door. It creaks. He plops down on the plastic seat. Corn dust flies up. Kevin wedges his loafers between some empty feed sacks on the floor. Mr. Tapestry elegantly leans into his truck as if he was Lou Gehrig leaning into a fastball, or Cary Grant leaning over a polished bar to ask for a martini. Very smoothly, effortlessly.

They drive up the lane. The two men exit Chestnut Hills Farm and drive down North Lyons Road. They pass the first of his many fields.

Tapestry says, "Heard you played some college ball."

"Yes, sir."

"Did you ever go onto another team's field without first preparing for them?"

Kevin says, "No."

He says, "Of course not. So, since your here in Lyons, you might as well know as much about farming as there is. Wasn't the kid murdered with a pitchfork? See where I'm going?"

"Yes sir, please continue."

He says, "Good. Farming in my day was part working the land and part loving it. What used to make farming so special was when you cleared the land—which was what Keith was doing yesterday, picking up rocks from the soil so that they don't damage the machinery—you picked up every one in sight and would even dig for the ones half buried. It was your land, your machinery and your livelihood.

"Not so, today. When you work on a farm owned by stockholders, you'll skip some rocks, maybe even secretly hoping a stray will break a chisel, or get sucked up into the combine where it bounces all around like a pinball, tearing apart the machine, so that you can spend a few days lying around the shop trying to fix it."

They hit the intersection with Devereux Road. They take a left and soon pass Snipes' farm. In the front yard is a new sign saying, "Auction. Monday."

Mr. Tapestry, seeing the sign, says, "In spite of my dislike for the crusty guy, I feel sorry for him. He's another farmer who's lost his homestead to the bank.

"Anyway, Kevin, nowadays, farming is taking on a mechanical life of its own. Now, it's all work and no love. The stockholders are cutting up the land into little shares of acres.

"Today's farms are made up of huge corporate conglomerates, such as ConAgra, General Mills, Monfort and IBP, Inc. These are the ones dominating America's agribusiness. They make it impossible for an independent farm to earn a living.

"These big companies do not even call it farming, anymore, either. They call it food-processing; harvesting corn is called grain processing. To mass-market their products, today's farmers are reduced to hired help who simply feed the chickens and fatten the calves. The animals are simply products that move on down the assembly line, from piglets to bacon.

"But a real farmer's life isn't bought or sold, like a share of stock. It's a gift. And Keith understands this. Doug Richards' killer doesn't."

"Is this why Keith means so much to you?"

"Keith's a farmer's farmer. My daughter's husband, Derrick, seems to like farming, but he's just going through the motions of farming. I can tell it's not in his blood.

"At first I was very excited about Derrick's coming. But after watching him, I've decided he's just using farming to escape society. It's not farming he loves. It's not being around people that matters to him. He figures as long as he works hard, which he does, he'll have a safe place to stay, which he will.

"But Keith, that boy, loves to farm. He crawls around the dirt like a worm. He can tear apart a tractor engine and put it back together blindfolded. And most importantly, he can get the cattle and hogs to move any direction he wants. He's stern with them. The kid is gentle, too, caring for and raising rabbits and chickens. He's not a bully, he's a farmer. And he's certainly no killer."

The rookie confesses, "Well sir, I must say I'm appreciative of your candor and reflections, but I'm not convinced. Not yet."

"You'll be wastin' your time chasin' after him."

"OK then, sir, who do you think killed Doug Richards? I mean, Doug used to work for you."

He turns his strong, square head towards Kevin and says, "That's your job. I will tell you, though, that I believe the killer wants this land for other purposes."

The truck rattles down the road.

Kevin asks, "Can you tell me how you got started in farming?"

Mr. Tapestry smiles and says, "Sure, son. My father was a farmer. My father wanted me to be a farmer, too. But he also wanted me to have an education, so he sent me to Harvard. I majored in biology and wanted more than anything to become a doctor.

"But once my undergrad was completed, Dad called me back home to take over the farm. At first I hated him for it. I always loved farming when I was a kid, but when I was away at college I thought that being a doctor was more important. I don't know. Over time, I gave up the notion of going to med school. Farming became my life, again. Do you know on a warm summer's night, I can hear the corn grow?"

Kevin smiles at the simple pleasure.

"It's true. I can. I haven't told many people because they'd think I was crazy, so don't start spreading any gossip."

"Where are we going?"

He smiles and asks, "Ever been to a slaughterhouse?"

The rookie frowns and say, "No."

"Well, son, as long as you're in Lyons, you might as well see who the real killers are—the butchers."

"Why are we going there?"

"Those cattle we shipped last night are being slaughtered today. I just want to see how it's going."

They arrive at the Baum's Meat Packing Facility. To the right of the slaughterhouse is a large penned-in field with cattle milling about, unaware of their soon-to-be deaths. There is a strong smell of blood and manure in the air. Trucks and trailers are everywhere, taking animals to and fro.

The rookie and the old farmer get out of the auburn pickup. A v-shaped gaggle of geese squawks over head. The two men walk into the front of the low-lying processing plant. There are some retail customers inside shopping for fresh meat. Mr. Tapestry nods to the clerk behind the counter. The clerk lets them pass.

Mr. Tapestry and Agent Sir walk through a rubber curtain. Instantly, the sound of small metal blades whiz in Kevin's ears. The white, vinyl-coated walls are splattered with bone chips, blood, fat and chunks of meat. On the cement floor are piles of fat and grooves to let the blood flow into drains. Mr. Tapestry and Kevin walk past the cutting room into a large locker with headless animal carcasses stripped to the muscle hanging on large metal hooks.

Kevin thinks that this all resembles Ann Arbor's city morgue, except these creatures are being slaughtered on purpose, where as most of the dead in the morgue met their untimely deaths by accident, or at the hands of un-known killers. It is funny, people rarely choose to die, but people have no problem with choosing the deaths of billions of animals.

They go to the back, where the animals are actually killed.

Mr. Tapestry walks up to a huge man watching over the executions, "Hello, Arlo. How're my cattle doing?"

Arlo looks at Mr. Tapestry with a smile.

Then he sees Kevin.

The huge man snorts, "Fine. We're almost done."

The two other men are dressed in hip waiters. Outside the slaughter-house, in the pen, they round up one of Mr. Tapestry's cows. The cow goes into the shoot. As soon as the animal is ushered in and prodded inside the final cage, a huge metal block comes screaming down on top of the animal's head—crushing it.

Mr. Tapestry looks at Kevin and says, "This is a dangerous contraption, but very humane. This machine doesn't care what's inside, it'll kill it. The animal never feels a thing. You see the floor? As soon as the animal steps on it, the floor falls a little and kicks off the counter weights. In a few seconds, that two-ton hammer falls down. It's instant death. Better than how we use to slaughter animals. I don't get too close to this machine though. It scares the living daylights out of me. Let's go talk to the bean counter."

They walk through the cooler again and back into the cutting room. To the right is a small room with glass. They walk in and talk to the manager. He says that Mr. Tapestry will get his check Monday. They walk out the employee's entrance.

"Where does all your meat go? Madison?"

"All over. Baum's slaughterhouse bids it out and sells it to whomever will pay the most. My cut is whatever Wall Street thinks is fair for a pound. This should be a good year for beef, better than the last five years, anyway. With NAFTA and all the other trade agreements, more countries will be able to afford American meat.

"Son, this country produces the best beef in the world. You and I are so lucky to walk into any grocery store and get a T-bone steak for a few bucks. Other countries' people save up for months to bring home a cut like that to their families."

"Aren't people buying less beef and more chicken? Peg, my wife, rarely eats red meat. She says it's not healthy. And all that fat."

"Well, we're trying to raise our stock without supplements. There's this guy Coleman in Colorado who's been real successful with natural meats. At first I thought it was a fad, you know like sushi, or something, but there's some merit in what he's doing.

"Now the government is getting into the picture, as if they don't have their fingers in everything else a farmer does. Uncle Sam is giving cattle ranchers more cents to a pound for natural meat. They think it's healthier. I don't really give a shit one way or another. A cow's a cow."

They get into his truck and drive back to Chestnut Hills Farm. On the way, Mr. Tapestry again talks about his love of farming. He points out some pheasants hiding behind some corn stubble.

At first the rookie cannot see them. Then one of the birds moves, ever so slightly, and Kevin can pick out three of them foraging about for errant kernels of corn that a busy combine tossed aside.

He points out a bare spot in one of his fields where a worker spilled a sack of fertilizer, and it burned a large hole in the field. Corn will not grow there now for a few seasons. He points out in another field where he found an Indian arrowhead. He says he has found three, or four since then. However, the first one was not chipped. It is complete. It now rests on his mantel above the fireplace.

Tapestry says, "Michigan's history is steeped in Native American Indian lore. This land was theirs. Indians used to hunt, make love, have meetings and cook venison in these woods. They used to hide from the French settlers like panicky rabbits. Those bold white men tromping through their land must have been frightening and maddening to the Indians.

"The only thing for us, in modern society, to be reminded of the Indians' legacy is the nameplates of a couple car lines: Pontiac and Cadillac.

"At the time of the Indians' annihilation, the white men's dogs meticulously tracked the Indians' hidden campsites. Those hasty foreigners, today's businessmen, drew their big guns and destroyed the "wild" men."

The agent says, "Guns still exist and kill."

The mayor also shows Kevin where his sister and brother live, both in the same farm complex, but in two distinct homes; both well-kept and strikingly large. One is made of old stones, cleared from the fields. The other is a long, flat white house with a long porch and green shutters. His brother lives in that one. He also owns Lyons' golf course. His sister owns the Antique Store.

"Mr. Tapestry, what's the one thing you want to see happen in this town? Your family seems to own everything. Why not sit back and retire? In spite of what you say about Derrick, he seems to have a good head on his shoulders. Why not let a little commerce into Lyons while you're at it? What would a few more homes with heated swimming pools do to the country? What would bringing in a McDonalds do to the Cafe?"

Mr. Tapestry says, "Let me put it to you this way. I hate Ted Turner with all my might. He's bought up half of Montana to have what I have—land. The idea of a person having their own piece of countryside is appealing to many people. Some for the right reasons, some for the wrong ones. Turner just wants to play farmer and raise bison on land he bought from money brought in by his damn TV stations.

"He doesn't know a lick about what it takes to be a farmer. You can buy all new tractors, the best chunks of land and a prized bull to start your own herd. But you can't buy the love it takes to make all of it work. When there's a drought, when your cattle come down with a disease, when it rains for a month straight during harvest time, it's your love of farming that gets you through those times.

"The other thing is if we create some damn bedroom community for Madison, the next thing you'll know we'll have a Wal-Mart, then a Texaco station, then a supermarket. It wouldn't stop. There's enough of that in Madison. I only go into that town to check on some buildings I own, and that's it.

"Farming is my life. There aren't too many of us left. In case you haven't read *Newsweek* lately, only one percent of Americans are farmers, the rest have moved into the cities and turned their backs on the land. If only they knew how hard their ancestors worked to carve out this land. It's sad to think our heritage is almost dead. Either that, or it's being bought up by Hollywood types who want recapture the spirit."

Kevin concurs, "You know you're right. I read in *People* that Michael J. Fox just bought a farm to raise his family on when he's not making movies."

Mr. Tapestry says, "They're all doing it, raising ostriches, emus, bison and God knows what else. They think the land is theirs to buy. They think buying a farm makes them farmers. Horseshit. It makes them rich people with a farm. That's it.

"Here's a fact: Beginning of this century, more than 50% of Americans lived in rural areas. Today, just 25% of Americans live in rural areas. Mechanization has made it possible to work larger farms with less labor, so families have moved to cities to find work. In a sense, farmers, like me, have sealed our fate through our own efficiency.

"The death of the small town was also based on a man named Ford, also a Michigander. His philosophy, "A car in every garage," kind of the technological equivalent of F.D.R.'s social welfare, made small towns easy to pass by. When farmers depended on animals for work and transportation, there was a town every six miles or so. But when automobiles replaced horses, farms got bigger, the number of farmers decreased, and small towns started shrinking."

Kevin says he understands.

"Sir, I have this question that I've been dying to ask someone, but I know it's going to sound stupid."

"Go on then. What is it?"

"Sir, what's cud?"

"That's not a stupid question. Cattle don't digest food like humans. They don't have the stomach acid to break down their food. So, after they've swallowed the silage the first time, it comes back up to be chewed a second time, which is cud. Cud then travels back down the cow's throat to be further broken down in the cow's three other stomachs.

"Kevin, I'll teach you anything you need to know about farming. Just ask. But you better hurry. In a few years, all this may be gone. Or, I may say to hell with it and retire to my cabin up north. And if Horton wins the election next month, all this may be gone sooner than that!"

Kevin is dropped off at his Contour by Mr. Tapestry.

"One more question, mayor."

"Yes?"

"What about Jerod McMurtry?"

"What about him?"

"Sheriff Sackett thinks that he could be the killer."

"Hogwash. Now, as I said when I first met you, I only care about this town. I don't like seeing its people murdered, or maimed, as I heard Abe was last night. Likewise, I don't like people being misjudged. Now, good luck and good day. And if you still have any questions about the McMurtry boy's guilt or innocence talk to his pa, Cliff. He and I have known each other our whole lives."

The gentleman farmer leaves the rookie at the silage pit. Tapestry's auburn Ford with a banged-up tailgate rattles away. The wintry driver meanders up the lane as if he does not have a care in the world.

Kevin takes a look at his car before getting in. Not only is it filthy, now the sides have been splattered with oil. He looks down at his leather loafers, blood dots his shoes. His once blue suit is covered in white corn dust. Kevin takes off his suit coat and rolls up his sleeves. The rookie exits the silage pit and drives up the lane to go to lunch.

Chapter 8

Traveling up the hill, the rookie spies a tractor about a half-mile away from him. He pulls up behind it. Mud flies off the tractor's big knobby tires. It is not a new, or an old tractor. It is a well-maintained machine that looks as if it has worked through countless seasons.

The driver is about 40-years-old and seems edgy, as if Kevin's car has invaded his space. The man is sunburned. He wears a blue-denim shirt, jeans and a big, brown leather belt. He has big ears and a kind face. As Kevin passes him, a large rock spins out from underneath the rear tractor tire and smashes into the Contour's windshield. Luckily, it only breaks the passenger's side.

"Damn."

Kevin passes the farmer. Looking in the rear view mirror, Kevin sees the farmer's broad shoulders relax and dip down. Kevin pushes on the accelerator and completes his drive to the compound. He exits the farm and drives back to Lyons. This time, Kevin does not notice the trees. He looks through them at the cornfields. Mr. Tapestry's combines cut paths through the miles of golden maize.

The agent passes the Truck Stop. Noticing more of the town's layout, he sees a small pond on the right, then the Grocery Store. Over the train tracks his vehicle rattles. He passes the Hardware Store, which is connected to the grain elevator. Finally, he stops at the intersection of North Lyons Road and Main Street. Kevin takes a right, for an early lunch at the Café.

At the Café, he orders a sliced turkey breast, Swiss cheese, cucumbers and mayonnaise on rye bread and a lemonade to go. He pays cash. He walks down Main Street to a small park next to The Library. He sits beside a circa-Civil War cannon under three maple trees. A rather steep medium-sized hill of sloping grass makes up one side of Crackerbarrel Hill Park, named after the barrels that workers used to roll down the hill. The hill made unloading the trains easier.

Kevin unwraps the wax paper from around the sandwich. He takes a big bite and rests against the cannon's cement-filled barrel. He eats in silence. He takes another bite of the sandwich and looks at his watch. It is almost 12:30 p.m. He concludes his lunch and walks back into town.

His belly happily filled, he saunters over to the Amoco Station. He walks up to the cash register and patiently waits for service. He hits the chrome bell. No one comes to his assistance. Kevin enters the dark bays where the mechanics toil.

Out-of-order cars float up high in air. Their dirty undersides face the stained concrete. Kevin walks through the doorway and sees a twenty-year-old and the outlines of two mechanics in the back, who are smoking cigarettes.

Kevin announces, "Good afternoon. I need some help."

The younger continues to spin-balance a tire, but slower.

Kevin waits for a response.

The only sound is the thumping of the young man's hands on the tire.

Thump-thump.

Kevin, realizing he's up against some hard nuts, demands, "Kid, stop spinning that goddamn thing and look at me."

The kid stops spinning the tire and looks back at the owner and the senior mechanic. Two lit cigarettes burn hotly near the back. Kevin cannot see the smokers, only their glowing instruments.

Kevin asks the glowing dots, "How long will it take to replace a Ford Contour's windshield?"

One of the glowing dots drops to answer, the senior mechanic responds, "Don't have one. Have to special order it. Could take a week."

Kevin yells, "A week!"

One of the dots burns brighter at Kevin's misfortune.

The other orange dot drops to the ground and an oily boot smothers it: "Yeah, do you want us to special order you one?"

"Let me think about it. Now, where do the McMurtrys live?"

"Who's asking?"

"Agent Sir."

The kid skeptically stammers, "Your... you're the agent?"

The kid steps toward Kevin.

"Yes."

"My ma and pa sayin' they're glad you helpin' us out."

"Did you know Doug Richards?"

Shaking his head no, he says, "I would see him in town, some. But, we weren't buddies, or nothin'. Doug was a real partier. Booze is the Devil's drink. I don't touch that stuff. No, sir, not me."

"I understand. Well?"

"Oh, the McMurtry farm is east of town, off Miner Road. Take North Lyons 'til Belleview. Go east until you hit Miner. Take a left. It's the farm on the right."

Kevin looks at the uncooperative shadows in the back.

Agent Sir barks at them, "On second thought, order me a windshield! I'm not sure how long I'll be here."

The owner steps forward into the light. His eyes narrow. He flicks his cigarette towards Kevin and walks back to his workbench. He picks up and bangs down his tools.

The kid, realizing he may have lost his job, makes a beeline back to the balancing machine.

Kevin walks out of the garage into the sunshine. He walks over to Dr. Fortune's office. The door is open and he walks into a very quiet office. He pokes his head in to give his condolences to Abe and his family, but the young farmer was transferred to Madison just before lunch to see if the doctors can re-attach his hand. The coffee room is empty. The funeral director picked Snipes a half an hour ago.

He walks down a short, carpetless hallway. To left is Dr. Barbara Fortune's personal office. The hallway deadends at a unisex bathroom. Kevin notices her personal office door is open just a crack. He quietly opens it. Blond hair falls on bent arms that are resting on her desk.

"Excuse me?"

The beautiful doctor raises her head. She hadn't been crying, but she was close. Her blue eyes resemble small mountain lakes. Her porcelain skin is flushed. She immediately stands up because she doesn't like people to think that she's weak.

Barbara Fortune is anything but weak. She finished top of her class at University of Michigan, where she also lettered in tennis. She also has completed two marathons. She was asked to pose for "Playboy," and even though she needed the money, the pictures would have killed her parents.

She worked for Kaiser Permenante for two years because she felt that H.M.O.s (Health Maintenance Organizations) were best for blue-collar people who rarely can afford health care. Then she discovered that her bonuses were tied to keeping people out of her office. She was paid extra not to refer patients to a specialist. This "gatekeeper-approach" was the exact opposite of why she became a physician.

Then she and two male partners created "HM-Not." A private doctors' office that tried to cater to the common person. But after only six months, this good cause turned belly-up. Then a year ago an opening came up for a country doctor. She would be paid a salary and be able to help out everyone. She's been in Lyons ever since, and loving it. Training for her first Hawaiian Ironman competition, cycling and running on Lyons' open country roads and swimming in Abe Jenkins' pond.

The female doctor straightens up and asks, "Yes, what may I do for you?"

Kevin introduces himself, "Agent Sir."

Barbara says politely, "Yes come in. Sheriff Sackett gave me your blood sample."

Kevin asks softly, "Did it match?"

She acknowledges, "Yes, Doug Richards was murdered there. Unfortunately, no one else's blood was found."

He asks considerately, "How's Abe?"

She lets out a long, overdue breath and says, "Better, looks like he may be able to keep his hand. His wife reacted quickly with a picnic basket and lots of ice."

Kevin sits down and says, "Look, I'm sorry I intruded."

Barbara sits down with him and reacts, "No. No. It's my fault. This one got a little personal. I know Abe because he lets me swim in his pond. He's a doll. But he's also pig-headed."

"How so?"

"We both know that Abe was shot because he talked to you. That was no combine accident."

"Yeah, I was afraid of that."

"What are you going to do?"

She brushes back a strand of hair from her mouth.

Kevin says, "Right now, I'm going out to see a young man named Jerod McMurtry. People say he's trouble. If he did shoot Abe, believe me, Jerod's going down."

He stands up and pumps out his chest.

A light bulb goes on in her head, she smiles and asks, "Hey, weren't you C.U.'s quarterback?"

"Yes."

"You won the National Championship that year."

"Yes."

"And you beat us with that Hail Mary pass with no time left on the clock."

"Yes."

"Son of bitch."

"Excuse me?"

She laughs and says, "Sorry, big Michigan alum."

Kevin laughs with her.

She asks, "Why not the pros?"

"Was drafted to Oakland. Second pre-season game, I was sacked and separated vertebrae in my neck. My physician said that if I get hit like that again, I could be paralyzed. Sat down with my parents and we decided that my health is too important. So, here I am."

"Do you miss it?"

"Do you miss tennis?"

"What?"

"I saw you in 'Sports Illustrated', too. So, I guess we're two washed up athletes."

"Speak for yourself, I'm entering my first Ironman next year."

"Good for you. OK, now, back to the case. Anything else you can tell about Doug Richards?"

"Yes, he had marijuana and a small amount of nicotine in his system."

"Well, I knew he smoked pot, but not cigarettes. Could he have inhaled second-hand smoke at Lou's bar?"

"Possibly."

"OK, doctor, you've been a big help. Thanks."

"No problem."

"See you at Palmer's harvest party this Friday?"

"Didn't know there was one. Maybe."

"I hope so. My boyfriend was a linebacker for Michigan and he'd love to meet you."

"Patrick Waters?"

"Yep!"

Making a sarcastic face, he says, "Great, your boyfriend made mince-meat of my ribs. He must of sacked me three times that game."

"Three and a half."

"Doctor will you do me a favor?"

"Of course, but call me Barbara."

"Here's my card. Please overnight your findings to the lab."

"Will do."

The agent smiles and says, "Thanks Barbara."

Kevin walks back into town. He passes in front of the Antique Store. Em's great aunt, Jude, is rearranging the front window. She carefully places large dolls onto small, wicker rockers. Kevin waves at the handsome, old woman. She politely nods.

The rookie gets into his increasingly no-longer-new automobile and follows the directions to the McMurtry farm. The farm is a nice medium-sized spread that has been in the family for three generations. Jerod is the fourth. The McMurtrys are one of this town's oldest families.

The main feature about the McMurtry farm is that every piece of wood is whitewashed, except for the dark green shutters on the house and the main barn; it's fire-engine red. The two-story house and its porch, the fence surrounding the three-acre horse pasture, the horse barn, the pump-house, the hay-stand, the pig barn, the low-lying chicken barn and even the rabbit cages are all white.

Kevin pulls into the driveway. On the left are the horse pasture, horse barn and pump-house, which is used to bring up well-water. On the right are tall pine trees and the residence. The driveway runs straight passed the residence and then circles around inside the farm. Now, Kevin is inside the farm. Ahead is the hay-stand, a structure that stands one-story high, has a roof to keep the hay dry and built with openings to keep the air circulating so that the hay doesn't rot.

The main, red barn stands four-stories high. Inside are a dozen head of cattle and a few milking cows. All the McMurtry's tools, feed and farm equipment are stored in here. To the right of the main barn is the pig barn, chicken barn and rabbit cages. Pine trees circle around the back of the farm. In the center of the driveway are flowerbeds, now plucked clean with the soil turned over, a naked pear tree and ill-used lover's swing.

Kevin circles inside the farm and stops at the main barn. He gets out and shouts for someone to come out, but no answer.

Inside the McMurtry house, a woman in her late fifties, making an apple pie, hears the agent and puts down her rolling pin. She wipes off some of the flour onto her smock. She exits the kitchen and walks into the back porch. Still a strong woman, she pushes open the outer door with one hand and yells back at the M.B.I. agent to come over to the house.

The agent waves to her and walks across the farm to her.

"Hello. Is Jerod here?"

"Yes, but he's ill today. Sleeping upstairs."

Mrs. McMurtry, a hard-working housewife, faithful and all-loving, will do anything to protect her family. She knows that her son Jerod isn't a saint, but it's just a phase that he's going through. He'll snap out of it. Then he'll find a sweet woman and settle down.

Jerod's upstairs sleeping, but not because he's sick, but because after he shot Abe, he was so disgusted with himself that he drank himself into a stupor. Jerod talks tough and has always been into scrapes, but he has never intentionally shot a man either in self-defense or to make some extra money. In the latter case, which is why Jerod accepted the challenge, he at first felt obligated because he accepted the money. Then he felt thrilled, the adrenaline pumping through his body, because he was standing over Abe and had complete control. Then he felt scared because of the possibility that Abe's wife could have written down his license plate number. Finally, he was sickened because he had purposely injured another man, a fellow farmer, for the three thousand dollars it will take him to pay off his truck.

"Mrs. McMurtry, it's important. May I see him?"

"No. But you can talk his pa. Cliff is in the garage. Take this path between the house and those rabbit cages. You'll walk under them pine trees. The garage is at the end of this here path. And Agent Sir…"

"Yes?"

"Believe me, Cliff won't be too happy to see you."

Jerod's mother firmly closes the door and returns to her pie.

Agent Sir walks forward. As he gets nearer to the garage, the darker it gets. The pine tree's thick boughs and generous needles block out the sun. The dead needles below him cushion his feet. At the end of the path, Kevin sees movement and scattered sources of light in a tall tin-covered building.

The rookie walks into the dark garage and mistakenly steps into a pool of oil. The rest of the dirt floor is glassy smooth from workmen's boots and the constant drip of oil. The room is very dark, but soon Kevin's eyes adjust. There are guts of engines scattered everywhere. The tool holders on the walls

are half-empty because Mr. McMurtry's sons and farmhands hold the rest of the tools in their black paws.

The men work with the help of caged light bulbs attached to orange extension cords. These workers huddle over one of the engines. There is an ancient air pump near one corner and an acetylene torch hooked up to some beaten up tanks in another corner. The air is a foul smelling mixture of gasoline, sweat and 30-weight oil.

Kevin asks the nearest worker, "Cliff McMurtry?"

The worker points an oily socket wrench into the farm owner's direction. Kevin spots Mr. McMurtry standing in the back, looking over a beat-up workbench. Kevin steps over a welder's mask and walks over to him. Mr. McMurtry's broad shoulders are to the rookie's face. His blue denim shirt is black with stains.

"Cliff McMurtry, I came over here to talk to your son, Jerod, about Doug Richards and, now, Abe Jenkins."

Cliff McMurtry turns around. The man is standing under one of the dangling, caged light bulbs. His round face is bright red, like a ripe tomato. His big ears are even redder, like hot jalapeno peppers. He stares at Kevin hard. The rookie intuitively backs up and readies himself for a fight.

The farm owner retches, "You did a bad thing yesterday. I can't talk to you. Get the hell out of here."

Stunned, Kevin looks him over for a sign that he is being made to say this. No gun to his head. No strings dangling from his arms, as if he is a marionette being manipulated by midget farmers from the rafters.

"You mean Snipes?"

Mr. Murtry turns away.

"Look, your brother killed himself. He would've done it whether I was there or not."

Cliff McMurtry turns back to face Kevin. The red is draining from his face and ears. Now, his face is just pink, as chicken meat nearest to the bone that invites salmonella.

Kevin, understanding of a grieving relative, says, "Look, I'm sorry about your brother. My friend's Dad committed suicide because he was going bankrupt. It happens. But, I was there because a kid was murdered in your brother's silo. Not to harass him."

The blood has all but left Cliff's face. He looks around the garage at what he's built. His two other boys, Stew and Marty, are still at his side. Cliff knows that he has worked his ass off to make this farm profitable. If he loses Jerod because of something he, a grown man, has done then so be it. The McMurtrys have done well in Lyons because they have always lived a fair and honest life.

Cliff McMurtry confesses, "Agent Sir, I don't believe that my boy, Jerod, is a killer. This thing with Abe, I'm not so sure about. My other boy says that now Jerod will be able to pay off his truck. Money like that just doesn't fall in your lap. You can talk to him tomorrow. I'll have him stop by the sheriff's office to set things straight. He's too hung over now to do anyone any good."

Cliff McMurtry's face is his normal, tanned color.

The farmer continues, "Sorry I got into a huff. Bad things happen to good people. Guess my brother got the brunt of a whole lot of people's misdeeds. He just kind of gave up. Need for you to understand that."

Kevin says he understands: "John Tapestry says you're to be trusted. Thanks for your help and sorry for your loss."

Kevin turns to leave.

Cliff taps him in on the shoulder.

Cliff McMurtry says solemnly and softly to the dirt, but loud enough for Kevin to hear, "Agent Sir, if my boy is mixed up in this, be tough on him. His mother won't agree, but it's time Jerod grew up."

Kevin acknowledges Cliff and walks back towards the pine trees.

Kevin feels the need to check in with his boss. He looks at his watch: 3:00 p.m. He makes the fifteen minute drive back into town, not in a great hurry, since he feels that he's running out of leads and because he won't be able to talk to Jerod until tomorrow, Wednesday morning.

He walks into the Sheriff's Office. On the Starla's desk sits a lovely bouquet of daisies.

"Very funny," she mocks.

"Oh, come on, even though I was making light of your help, these flowers really are a big thank you to you."

"Sure."

"Really!"

"Ok, what do you want now?"

"Your phone."

"John went home early after fixing the toilet in the cell. He's still shaken up about Abe. Go ahead and use his phone."

"Thanks."

Kevin walks into the sheriff's personal office and dials Jim Caretaker.

A gruff voice answers: "This is Sergeant Caretaker."

"Jim, it's Kevin."

"Good, what's up?"

"Well I have my first real suspect coming into tomorrow to be questioned. Both the sheriff and myself believe a man by the name of Jerod McMurtry is behind some of crimes around here."

"Son, I know you will not disappoint me. You are a promising agent and, hell, this is your first solo assignment. You know my credo: Keep asking people questions, and keep asking 'em until you get the answers you need.

"Just be mindful of the fact that when your asking questions, you're in a way, pointing your gun at them and saying, 'Come out with your hands up.'

"When you ask questions and come up against a real hard nut, just remember to stand your ground. You're there to do your job. You're there to protect the peace. Pretend that just as your words are bullets, so are his. Fight with your mouth. And if that doesn't work, use your fists and finally your gun."

"OK."

"Now, have you formed any alliances?"

"Just starting to. Last night I had dinner with a man named Dale Horton, a real hothead who wants a piece of this town. Today I had a long talk with the mayor. Both men are at odds with each other. Whether or this affected Doug Richards' shortened life I don't know."

"Kevin, if you need help, I will send in another man."

"No, I'll handle it."

"Good. That's what I want to hear."

"Sir, I won't let you down."

Both men relax and breathe out together.

Finally, Jim says, "Hey, I have an idea: Take a break for an hour or two. Go lift some weights. It'll put you back on track. Boost your confidence a little."

"Sure, but where?"

"Try the local high school. When I was on stake-out in a strange town, I could always count on the local gym to clear my head."

"Good point. I will. Thanks."

Jim hangs up his phone.

The rookie leaves John's office, wishes Starla a good day and walks outside. Kevin, feeling better about things, pulls out a piece of gum and starts to unwrap it. The gum's wintergreen smell is interrupted by an earthy odor of a person who has not showered in many days. The rookie's eyes roll from his hands down to black toes sticking out of a pair of Birkenstocks. Kevin slowly raises his head. The skinny man wears ripped jeans and a Grateful Dead T-shirt. His face is sunburned. Locals call him Sneakers, because they wish that he had a pair.

The hippie, not at all a part of Lyons' system, independently states, "So, you're the M.B.I. agent. What's it like defending corruptness, stepping out every day wearing a false badge and keeping rich people safe from frustrated poor people?"

"Listen, pal, I help everyone, poor people, the middle-class and, yes, rich people. I help whites, Asians, Latinos and blacks. I help Christians, Jews and atheists. Why? Because that's I what I've sworn in to do. It's what I have chosen to do. Now, if you'll excuse me..."

The agent pops the gum into his mouth, clamps down on it and warns, "...unless you have any information about Doug Richards' death."

"OK, you want some help, then I'll tell you who I think killed that kid. This town killed Doug Richards. These farmers are the murderers."

Kevin warns, "C'mon man, shove off."

Sneakers grabs the rookie's arms.

Kevin, knowing he could swat this guy across Main Street with no problem, doesn't fight Sneakers advances.

The seemingly mad man says, "No. As an environmentalist who supports the Green Revolution, I deem that the fields must hate the farmers for subjecting its soil to order. The fields, stretching out, ache as they raise seedlings to full-blown plants then food. The soil only wants to cradle bushes, deer feet, pine roots and old rotting logs and lie in the shade. The soil hates the sun. It detests the fertilizer and the pesticides that burn into its skin. It hates being plowed. Then naked and freezing, it must bear the harsh winters without so much as a mossy overcoat..."

Kevin tries to interrupt the hippie's mad confession, but that only inspires Sneakers to speak louder.

"...the soil in old growth forests is lucky. It feels healthy. It wiggles in excitement as a hardwood tree sprouts out another root. To the soil in old growth forests, those sprouting roots are similar to tiny penises penetrating deeply into her womb. However, the burnt-out soil in Michigan's fields are just being raped every year.

"Nature is wild. Farming is the destruction of the wild. As one who ardently recycles and cares about saving what is left of our polluted world, I have to hate farming. Mother Nature definitely hates farming. These simple-minded farmers are spitting in nature's face. These country bumpkins think they love nature when they feed animals' steroids and aerial spray for bugs. Meanwhile, chipmunks, squirrels and birds are dropping like flies.

"Farmers think they are being true to nature when they cut down more trees to make way for pigs and all their stinking manure. The world is full of enough shit, why should they make room for more? Farmers kill things all the time.

"What do you think about that?"

Kevin is numb.

Sneakers shakes him.

Sneakers reiterates, "Well, what do you think about that?"

Kevin realizing Sneakers is crazy, pushes aside the man's hands and calls his bluff, "What kind of proof do have that all these men ganged up to kill a defenseless kid?"

Sneakers smiles and says, "M.B.I. man, I know you. I know that you're young. Your life skills aren't yet developed. You know how to shoot, run and figure out textbook cases. But you haven't been taught to see the big picture and how each part contributes to or deters from a case's complexion.

"M.B.I. man you need to <u>listen</u> to everybody, even if you don't want to. If you weren't so keen about dismissing me, you could have gained a much quicker insight into the rift that has one side of Lyons wanting progress and the other side wanting their old-fashioned traditions kept in tact. Thus, the killer's motive. Too bad, man."

Kevin, now, thinking that Sneakers isn't so crazy, concurs, "Yeah, I know, it's the feud between Horton and Tapestry. I've already figured that out."

Sneakers' eyebrows shoot up, "Man, that's pretty good. Looks like you're on the right track."

Kevin growls, "Not bad for a new agent with no life skills."

"Hey, I was just worried that you'd be in over your head. Looks like I'm wrong."

The agent loosens up: "No sweat. If you have any more information, I'm staying at the Best Western. Room #105."

"I do."

"Yeah?"

"Well, just look at this place! Lyons is literally dead. What is left, stands temporarily in case one of inhabitants is too lazy to drive an extra ten miles into Madison for their goods and services. There's one man, Dale Horton, who wants to change all that. Later, man. Keep the faith, brother!"

Sneakers smiles at the awe-struck rookie and gets into his late model, maroon, Saab 9000 Turbo, which he bought with the proceeds of the last 500 pound shipment of marijuana he sent to Detroit. Sneakers has one of the most profitable, hydrophytic pot farms in the United States. A Yale Law School Graduate, even the M.B.I., including Kevin's friends and co-workers, Ted and Tim, hasn't been able to catch him. The bumper sticker on Sneakers' Saab reads: "Hang up and drive."

Kevin shrugs his shoulders in disbelief.

Seems like Lyons is filled with all kinds, just like Ann Arbor.

Two days ago Kevin was sure everyone who lived in a small town was normal.

Kevin drives to his motel room and dials up Lyons high school. He introduces himself as the M.B.I. agent in town and wonders if he could use the school's gym. The receptionist transfers him to the V.P. He says that the weight room is open and to please feel free to use it during school hours, or when they are having a special function, like tonight's football game. The vice principal gives the rookie directions to the school.

Kevin asks the V.P. if he knew Doug Richards. He says yes and that Kevin should talk to the principal about Doug's behavior prior to his dropping out of high school. Kevin asks to schedule an appointment. The V.P. says that tomorrow afternoon is a good time, around lunchtime, when the students have an hour off. Kevin thanks him and says that he'll make that meeting.

Kevin undresses and puts on gray, cotton shorts, white Nike tank top and running shoes. But before he goes, he dials up Peg to see if she received her bouquet.

"Peg?"

She squeals, "Kevin!"

"Hi."

"I miss you."

"I miss you, too. How'd your day go?"

She says, "Wonderful. For lunch, a friend and I went to Delamonicos. You know that dear French restaurant near campus? We had a few drinks and then a few more, and basically talked about how gorgeous our husbands are."

"Thanks. What are you doing tonight? Are going out again?"

"What do you mean?"

"I couldn't reach you last night."

Peg, having had a million sexual thoughts about guys in her office, waiters at the restaurant and men that she purposely brushed up against on the sidewalk since last night's very real affair, offhandedly lies, "Oh, last night. Went out for some ice cream. Tonight, though, Jennifer is having a small party. We'll probably play bridge and drink a lot of Chablis. As the British say, 'It will be all beer and skittles!'"

She asks, "How's the case coming? Did you come up with any leads?"

"Yes, a farmhand by the name of Jerod McMurtry."

"Good for you."

There is a pause when neither of them speaks.

Finally, Kevin says, "I love you."

"I love you, too. And honey…"

"Yes?"

"The flowers are beautiful. And your card was so thoughtful. Thank you."

"Well, I meant what I said. Every word."

"Be careful and good-bye. I have work to do."

"Yes, good-bye."

Kevin pulls the wet receiver from his mouth and hangs up the phone. He knows that Peg wants him to come home, now. They have not made love for forty hours. Peg is miserable. But, she is going to have to ride out this investigation. At least until Kevin can solve the case.

Chapter 9

Kevin hops into his state-issued car and drives to Lyons' high school's gym. He parks out in front of the big red brick high school, called Panther High, and locks the Contour. The light in the sky is starting to fade. Corners of campus are getting dark. Behind the high school, Kevin can hear the roar of Gus' football game.

Kevin asks a teenager rushing to the game for directions to the weight room. He says that the weight room is next to the basketball court just as you walk in. Kevin jogs into the near-empty school. He opens a thick metal door, takes a right and walks across the court's squeaky wooden floor. He enters the weight room.

He struts up to the mirror and looks at his body. Kevin is a big guy. But what makes him visually bigger than most guys his size are his long arms, huge hands and a large brow. This extra exposed flesh is what makes him stand out.

Kevin works on his chest. Veins in his arms become visible. His flesh covering his pectoral muscles chest becomes red. His lungs heave. Sweat flows. He wipes it away and rests back down on the bench. He does eight reps of 275 lbs. Three times. He works his way up to his max: 315 lbs.

He has always found solace in the gym. In here, Kevin's thoughts are clear. There is only iron and him. He does not need to solve a murder. Just the thought of picking up a 45 lbs. bar with weights on both ends to lift up and down, up and down, matters.

After his last set, he hops off of the flat bench and gets a drink of water. His hot mouth gladly accepts the water's cool relief. He walks over to the decline bench and puts on 205 lbs. His body lies almost upside down. His legs are locked into padded stirrups. The blood rushes to his head.

He wraps his hands around the bar and pushes the weight up towards the sky, as that tragic Greek figure in Hades—the immortal who must push a bolder up a mountain, only to have it roll down just as it reaches the apex. Up and down, up and down.

Existentialists say our lives are similar to Sisyphus' toil. However, Kevin only feels similar to him during this one exercise; possibly, on a bad day, such as fighting in a cornfield because he desperately wanted Keith's confession, a mistake that won't happen again.

His incline bench goes easily, as does flys. He does 100 sit-ups and then leaves. He jogs out of the weight room and basketball court and walks to the back of the school towards the lighted football field.

He passes through the back doors onto thick green grass. Even though it's early in the evening, dew has started to collect at the tips of the grass. Kevin's wet sneakers make their way past an iron gate and then onto the red crushed gravel of Panther High's track, the same one that Doug circled when he was on the track team.

The roar becomes louder. Panther High in the maroon and yellow jerseys are playing a Catholic school's team from Madison, wearing green and yellow. Kevin can pick out #30 in a maroon and yellow uniform streak down the sideline for a first down.

The crowd yells, "Go Gus Go!"

Kevin reaches the seating area and looks for a place to sit. He sees Dale and Gail Horton in the parents' section and he makes his way to them.

The proud parents of the star running back welcome Kevin with open arms. Every parent here is happy to embrace Kevin and to hear him tell to them about his own football successes. Kevin feels like he's a kid again, playin' it up in front of adoring parents, who smile ear to ear as they witness the creation of an all-American boy.

The Panthers win and Kevin leaves the happy parents to wait for their sons to get out of the showers.

Kevin plans to take his own quick shower back in the motel room. Then he will go to Lou's Place for a few beers and interview some more locals. If Doug had been a minister instead of a drunk then Kevin would investigate the church. However, Doug's calling was drinking; his God was Jack Daniels.

Kevin returns to his motel room, hops in the shower and turns on the hot water. He rinses off the sweat and gladly accepts the light pounding of the shower's water streams. He pulls back the curtain and wipes away the steam from the mirror. He combs his wet hair. Naked with water still dripping off him, he walks towards the refrigerator and pulls out a Coors.

The sunlight is completely gone. But from his unlit room, he can still make out the dark, empty field across the highway. The field's corn has been harvested; its stalks are cut within inches of the ground. The corn stubble look similar to the stubborn whiskers on an old man's grizzled visage. Kevin settles down on the bed. He raises the beer to his lips and slowly takes in the alcohol.

He finishes the Coors, walks over to the small open closet and pulls out a navy blue Ralph Lauren polo shirt, a pair of Levi's 501 jeans and an alligator belt. He puts on socks and shark-skin cowboy boots.

Kevin makes himself a Scotch and flicks on the local news. Lyons' news comes from Madison. The top story is about Doug Richards. Kevin is surprised to see a color photo of himself on TV. This case is important to the area's residents. Channel 9 caps all the highlights and insinuates how unsettling it is for a small town to experience the hate and suspicion that are associated with murder.

The news cuts to the weather. Kevin takes a sip of his Johnnie Walker. A man Kevin's age, sporting plastic hair and a permanent grin describes the danger of frost. Another robot-looking reporter gives the commodity reports. The prices per bushel of corn and soybeans are down, but porkbellies are up. He cautions that corn and soybeans could be even more vulnerable in future Dow Jones' reports.

Kevin shuts off the TV and takes another sip of Scotch. Resting back on a pillow, he tries to think about the case—"The Case of the Bloody Pitchfork," which Channel 9 coined. The newscast does have a good point: How can a fierce killer hide out in a town of only 900 people? Logically, crime, even though a tragedy, can be dissected, studied and destroyed. Crime is not a moral problem that will always be. It does not get to keep on corrupting, just because it can. It has weaknesses. It can be stopped.

Kevin wonders, who did kill Doug? He altogether rules out Mrs. Richards, or Norma, unless she has a pair of killer hummingbirds in her closet. Besides, she was very upset about Doug's substance abuse.

The rookie has not met Mr. Richards, but Kevin feels that the man is just a hard-working Joe who works as little as he can until it is Miller Time.

The statistics divulge that little sisters, like Doug's Naomi, usually kill big brothers with a small handgun, a kitchen knife, or some poison, not a pitchfork.

The killer is either a drug-dealing peer, like Keith, or as Jed suggested, the killer could be a feuding Horton, who felt threatened by Doug's dirty habits, and either did the job himself or outsourced it to Jerod.

Kevin concludes that his way of defeating crime in this situation will be—as Jim said—to unearth the unconvincing farmers who are helping to support the killer. These accomplices will then lead the rookie to the real devil behind the brutal slaying. If a whole "herd" of farmers killed Doug, then Kevin will lock up the whole town.

A couple drinks later and Kevin is ready to investigate Lyons' only bar—Lou's Place. Kevin gets into his car and drives to the bar. He pulls up to the disgusting roadhouse. Rusted trucks with fading paint litter the parking lot. One vehicle stands out, though—a cotton-candy-blue Mazda Miata.

Kevin walks up to the battered wooden door at Lou's Place. A crude handwritten sign reads "RU21?" Kevin opens the door. When he walks into the bar, Lou's Place, the bar becomes silent.

Kevin thinks, oh, great. Here we go, again.

The bigger guys in the bar, who never look at newcomers or at anything until there is some excitement, cannot help but turn their heads Kevin's way. The action of the men's heads turning—one by one—resemble "the wave" at a football game. When it is complete, the entire bar is staring at Kevin.

Lou's Place is the small cave where Lyons' warriors huddle to groan about the day's misadventures and plan for tomorrow's hunt. They grip their pool cues like clubs.

The lighting is nonexistent. The one window facing the street is thick with grease. The men recognize each other from the glow of lit cigarettes.

The booths' brown plastic covers are riddled with burn holes made from unsteady hands. The plastic plants are bare. Their leaves have been stripped from their stems.

On the littered tables rest golden aluminum ashtrays. They resemble baby tombstones beginning to take shape. There are big piles and little piles of ashes, depending on the degree of the smoker.

In the center of Lou's Place rests a prehistoric pool table. The table is trashed. The green felt is worn from where many players have slapped the white cue ball on the dot. The gray slate is actually visible in spots where the balls have created gray paths to the holes. The jukebox still plays 45s.

Kevin looks around, but no one seems to be doing anything illegal, such as selling dope. He walks up to the tarnished, brass rail for a Budweiser beer and a tequila shot.

A tall, skinny bartender with bloodshot eyes comes up and asks Kevin for his order. The bartender slaps down the beverages and nervously waits for Kevin to pay. The rookie pulls out a shiny, brown Coach wallet that Peg gave him and pays for the drinks.

No one moves. The only sound comes from a corner behind Kevin, as a patron exhales cigarette smoke.

Keith Spelling, the worker in cornfield, and his buddy walk up to Kevin.

Keith slurs, "Well, lookie here. It's the big city policeman dressed up as a rhinestone cowboy."

The rookie looks around. Everyone is listening.

"Keith, if you really want to fight, then let's go outside. Just you and me. But, it seems to me that, that old man in the field yesterday respects you. Even the mayor and sheriff think you're innocent. Fine. I'll leave you alone for now."

Keith grimaces and says, "Doug was my best friend. I never touched him. But I think I know who did. And I'm gonna kill him."

Keith and his buddy stumble out. The bar comes out of its trance. The crack of a new pool game erupts and the momentum for getting drunk begins, again.

The rookie slams the tequila shot and then pushes the empty, stub of a glass across the bar. It stops just before the edge. The bartender uninterestingly picks up the empty shot glass and drops it into a pool of gray dishwater.

Kevin lets the eighty-proof fluid burn its way down his throat, taking with it the bile that has been steadily rising since he walked through the beaten door of the bar.

The rookie looks across the bar. Drunk men wearing brown coats slouch over the rail. Their rounded, slumped shoulders resemble mounds of dirt.

Kevin takes a gulp of beer and stands back towards the center of the room. He looks at the men's stony backs and waits. They start to sway on their barstools, as if they know Kevin is anxious to speak to them. But no one turns around. Their backs remain in Kevin's face.

Kevin spins around.

In the back corner, he sees three youths with wet hair crowded in a table. Gus is one of them. Kevin walks over. His cowboy boots clunk on the wood floor.

The youths fumble for their beers.

"Gus, what are you doing here?"

"Hi, Agent Sir. We're, um, celebrating."

"Do you know the owner?"

"Yes, sir."

The kid nearest to the wall knocks over his beer. He scrambles for napkins in order to mop up the liquid that is cascading over the table into his crotch. The other two tense up their bodies and squeeze their mugs' handles for support, as if they were being jostled in a New York subway.

"You know, when I was your age, my friends and I would have to stand outside the liquor store and wait for an older guy to buy us beer. Looks as if you don't have that problem."

"No, sir."

"Look, I don't care about this. As long as your parents are OK with it."

They sit motionless.

Gus knows that if his Dad ever found out that he had been found drinking that he would be grounded for months. His Dad is still fuming from that other incident with Doug Richards.

There is a sound of beer hitting the rubber seat.

The biggest kid finishes his glass of beer and says, "Come on you guys. Let's get out of here."

The vinyl seats loudly creak as they rise. They put on their tinkling letter jackets and head for the door.

Gus looks back and says, "Agent Sir, please don't tell my Dad."

"OK. Be careful. And good game tonight. You ran well."

Kevin passes by the pool table. He watches an old man with gel in his hair and a deep cough beat his opponent. In between his shots, the old man puffs on Camel sawed-offs. Kevin shakes his wooden-feeling head and summons the energy to leave. Kevin finishes his beer and stumbles out to his car. The Miata is gone.

A voice from behind Kevin, says, "Hey, you."

Kevin turns around and sees it is Sneakers. He has the smile of a stoned man. Sneakers is puffing on a joint, sitting on a cement parking barricade.

Sneakers waxes romantic, "You know what makes this land great? We can

have hippies and Republicans living in the same town; atheists and Christians. Remember the '60s?"

Kevin laments, "Look Sneakers. I'm exhausted. Besides I could arrest right here for smoking that thing. Go home. Go to bed."

Sneakers challenges, "But you know what stinks about America? The minute one group of people starts to disregard the different subcultures that exist, thinking that their movement is better, snuffing out others' right to express themselves.

"That is why I moved out here. These hicks understand repression. They are becoming as much of a subculture as the hippies ever were. Times are a changin'.

"Country folk are becoming an oddity themselves. Guys dressed in bib-overalls and corncob pipes with their *Farmer's Almanacs* tucked underneath their arms are being replaced with suits having their masters degrees in biology and business. Rural America is dying, along with its phony, Norman Rockwellian ideals."

Kevin says, "Talk to you tomorrow Sneakers."

Kevin falls into his car and drives home. He rolls down the car's window. The raven sky is beautiful. It is not that sickly city-gray, caused by endless street lamps and kaleidoscopic neon signs. Tonight, he can actually see stars. The crescent moon peeks over the trees that line the street. A chilled wind fills the car.

The rookie drives out of town and hits the access road to the Best Western. The road runs parallel to the highway and it's a nice, quiet back way into his "home away from home." Starla told him about it when he first arrived. In his two days of taking this road, he has yet to see a car. So, he is surprised to see one approaching. It looks strange, too, traveling very low to the ground.

As the fast car zooms closer, it swerves into Kevin's lane. The car stays in Kevin's lane and speeds towards him. It is right in front of him, now. The night sky and its many stars vanish. Its small round lights blind him!

Kevin yanks the Contour to the right. His car's nose dives into a ditch and smacks against a tree. There is a small popping sound, and then a whoosh from the steering wheel. Kevin's head bounces off the headrest into a soft latex airbag. His seat belt tightens up and cradles his arms, chest and waist.

Kevin lets out a breath, which has been waiting to escape minutes ago. The airbag deflates around his lap. He rests his head back and says a small prayer.

The night country sky with its many wondrous stars comes back into view. In front of him, the wrinkled hood has scarred the tree, taking out a chunk of bark and leaving clean-looking, new wood.

All of a sudden, Kevin feels very tired, as how Abraham's great ancestor, Shem, in the Old Testament must of felt at the end of his 600 years of life. Kevin looks at the clock and it is past one a.m.

Kevin unlocks the seat belt and wipes away the limp air bag. He shuts off the car's lights. He exits the wreck. He tests his legs. They feel fine. He rolls his head

around his shoulders. His neck creaks and pops, but it has always done that. He shakes his arms. No pain.

He turns up the moonlit road, putting one foot in front of the other. It won't be a short walk to his motel in stiff cowboy boots. The crickets rub their wings together and make a noise similar to a garbage disposal whining with nothing in it.

Kevin wonders, what if that crazy driver comes back?

He pats his gun in his blue Patagonia fleece jacket and keeps walking. Far overhead, the inky sky enshrouds him. Closer to the ground, dying, autumn leaves lightly blankets him, as if the palm-shaped leaves are loosely-woven fibers in an Amish woman's flimsy shawl. A slight chill creeps through his fleece.

In the distance, the motel glows orange. Kevin picks up the pace. But, as he walks nearer, he realizes that the light is not the motel, but a blinking traffic light.

Ugh!

He still has a couple miles to go.

As he walks, he looks at the weeds in the ditches on both sides of the access road. Out here, weeds grow faster and thicker than corn. Maybe, the farmers here should harvest weeds instead of corn?

According to Ted and Tim, farmers did try to grow other things besides corn. It seems that a couple of struggling farmers grew hemp to supplement their meager earnings.

Kevin, in better spirits, laughs out loud, thinking of Ted telling the story.

They were somewhat ingenious in their methods. Growing corn in the perimeter of the fields, they nurtured marijuana in the center of their fields. So, any passerby would think these guys were just doing what every self-respecting farmer does. However, these pot farmers ran into problems and the law when they bundled it up, loaded it into a horse trailer and tried to transport it out of state.

According to Ted, they got caught by a highway patrolman when a bundle came undone. The marijuana flew out their horse trailer. The drug's distinctive smell drew many cars, whose rabid occupants followed the horse trailer.

The pot farmers created piles of accidents from people running across the highway to pick up whatever weed tottered to the ground. If the drug farmers were not so high themselves, they would have noticed a parade of cars following them. In the end, the two pot farmers only got a couples years in the State Prison in Madison.

Kevin passes underneath the blinking light and run faster into the relative safety of the shadows. Off in the distance, a semi chugs its load. Kevin's arms swing freely by his sides. His heels pound the pavement. Soon, he is in darkness, again.

At last, he jogs onto the motel's flat parking lot, passing a couple of resting cars. He slows down his pace and walks the remaining fifty feet towards his room. He leans against his motel room and lets out a sigh of relief.

He stabs a key into the door's lock. He walks in, turns on the lights and shuts the door.

He knows that he will wake Peg. However, if he does not call her, now, she will be furious if she ever learns that he was almost killed. He sits down on the made-up bed, fumbles with the receiver and punches the buttons.

The phone rings four times. She picks up her end.

Her voice, low and raspy, asks, "Hello?"

Kevin blurts out, "Hi honey, it's me. Don't talk, just listen. I got into an accident tonight, but I'm fine."

She yells, "Jesus, Kevin. What happened?"

"There was another car that got into my lane. He ran me off the road. I'd rather not talk about it. I just called to say I'm alright and I love you."

Peg scolds, "Oh my God, I'm glad you're not hurt. Kevin, this M.B.I. crap is getting old. In Detroit, you chased after armed drug dealers. Now, you are away for days and you almost get killed."

"It's my job, honey. Besides, I've only been gone two days. I don't rag on you about your job when you've had a bad day."

She says, starting to sound awake, "That's different. My job isn't like yours, and you know it."

"I'm tired. I just called to tell you what happened. I love you. I'll call you tomorrow when I know what to do. OK?"

She says, "I love you. Try and get some sleep. I know I won't, now!"

"I love you. I only called because I do love you. You know that."

"I know."

When Peg hangs up the phone, her newest companion rolls over and turns off the bedside light. Peg met him at Jennifer's party. They were bridge partners and, now, lovers.

Kevin calls the office. He knows it is closed, but he will leave a voice mail for Jim to let him know what has happened. During the day, Jim checks it every half hour.

When the answering machine at the M.B.I. office goes on, Kevin says, "Jim, it's Kevin. Someone ran me off the road tonight. I'm fine. Thank God for airbags! Oh, I called Peg and told her about the accident. I needed to tell her that I am fine. I hope that was OK."

Kevin hangs up, lays back on the stiff motel bed and falls immediately asleep with the lights on, his boots dangling over the side of the bed and fully clothed.

Wednesday morning comes hard. At 7 a.m., Kevin's phone shrieks. It sounds like a conglomeration of pots and pans banging, a baby crying at Wal-Mart and a riff from AC/DC's "Hell's Bells."

The sun streams into his room. Its blazing light and all the lamps on in Kevin's room make for more illumination than his eyes can absorb.

He puts the unbending pillow over his face, leaving a small hole to breathe through.

Grabbing the phone from its cradle, he pulls it down under the pillow to his dry mouth and says, "Hello."

Jim asks, "Kevin, you awake?"

"Ugh, yea. Good morning Jim. Sorry about the car. I'm not sure who did this to me, but I'll find out."

"Don't worry about the car. Now, what happened?"

Jim's low, gravelled voice sounds concerned.

"I was driving back from Lyons' only bar, Lou's Place, where I had a couple drinks. I was there because I have a feeling whomever killed Doug either hangs out there, or has friends who drink there. I am finding out Doug liked his beer and other things. Anyway, no leads. I went home. As I was driving back to the motel, a car came towards with its lights on..."

Jim interrupts, "What shape were the headlights?"

Kevin straightens up and sees where Jim's going: "They were round, so it was probably an older car right?"

Jim corrects, "Or a new car designed to look retro."

"The driver came at me in my lane and accelerated. I hit the brakes and continued to move forward. Finally, when I could tell the car 'wanted me off the road,' I went into the ditch and smashed the car into a tree."

"Well, I'm truly grateful you're fine. Don't worry about calling Peg, I'd do the same thing. Now, back to the crime scene. You say the car came at you. Was it a truck, a big car, or a small car?"

"It was small, but there was something unique about it. Before I was totally blinded, I could only see its windshield, no roof. There was sky behind it. I know, it was a convertible!"

Jim proudly exclaims, "Good. Now, if that car is an older model and it swerved to miss you before you went into the ditch, wouldn't there be traces of oil that spilled from its pan onto the pavement? If not, then it's a newer car. And what about skid marks from its tires? I want you to go back out there this morning and get some samples of the oil and measure the tire tracks. OK?"

"Yea, no problem. Thanks for the help."

"Aren't you scheduled to meet with Jerod today?"

"Yes."

"Good, let's wrap this investigation up. You know how hard the death of a child is on the parents. You've read in other agents' cases about the lengths that some parents go to exact revenge, or take their own lives. The result of kids getting killed is the parents always feel accountable. Call me this afternoon for an update."

Jim hangs up his phone.

Kevin says, "Bye," to a dial tone.

The rookie shakes out his brown hair and brushes his teeth. He puts back on his shorts, T-shirt and Nikes. He slides an empty evidence bag half-way underneath his shorts' waistband. He jogs out the door and locks it. The bright, yellow orb in the sky is piercing. He unlocks the door, goes back inside and grabs his orange Oakley wrap-arounds. He leaves his room, again, and begins to run across the parking lot.

The two cars that were in the parking lot last night have left. His feet strike the access road and he begins his five-mile run. Sweat forms on his brow and moisture collects in the pockets underneath his arms. He reaches the traffic light.

Kevin slows down his pace to a seven-minute mile. He looks into the ditches for clues, but only discovers beer cans and plastic wrappings. The only signs of human life out here are man's garbage. The trash that lines the ditches is in various forms: faded beer cans, candy wrappers and a crumpled up cigarette pack. The Cambridge cigarette pack is full.

Kevin stops.

Why would someone throw out a full pack of cigarettes?

The misshapen carton is also ripped.

Suddenly, he remembers what Gus said: His Dad smokes this brand and gives Gus his tabs. These cigarettes are Mr. Horton's. And that car last night was the Miata in Lou's parking lot. Gus ran Kevin off the road! But why?

So as not to smudge any fingerprints, Kevin picks up a maple leaf. With it, he gently retrieves the cigarette pack and places it into his samples bag. He stuffs into his shorts and jogs forward. After a few strides, he picks up the pace. His strong legs fall in front of him and his arms swing naturally.

Sweat streams down.

His heart pounds.

He feels good.

The trees droop over him; they are not proud-looking, as the ones on North Lyons Road. Kevin thinks that these trees must be too close to the highway. With the highway's steady supply of exhaust and round the clock engine noise, the trees cannot concentrate to grow tall, straight and strong. Last night, the darkness deceived him. This stretch is not healthy at all.

Plants, like people, respond well to proper care and consoling. Peg is always fussing over their ficus at home, and it is huge. She will be great with their kids—when Peg decides that she is ready.

Kevin thinks that he is ready, but Peg is determined to break the glass ceiling at her law firm. She has said that by year's end, she has been promised to be made a partner. So, Peg and Kevin will have wait a few more years. That will give her the time to plan for a maternity leave, without jeopardizing her career.

But what Kevin does not know is that Peg does not want her own children. The stretch marks marring her body would kill her.

Kevin stops running when he reaches the wrecked Contour. It does not look as bad as it did last night; its bumper is pushed in only slightly.

Kevin walks around its trunk and looks down at the rough pavement.

Sure enough, there is a good set of small black tire skids that circumnavigate the Contour's hulk. There are many small, dried ink-colored droplets scattered across the blacktop, which is not a good sign for retrieving simple oil samples.

The rookie gingerly steps in between the droplets. He pulls out the sample kit from his shorts. With the calibrated forceps, he measures the tire tracks, grooves and all. With a tape measure, he gauges the width between the two skids. Using a small glass container of acid, he pours some of the liquid on every droplet near the tire tracks. He waits three minutes and then with an eyedropper, he collects each droplet, squeezing it into its own glass container.

He opens the door of his car and throws the sample kit over onto the passenger seat. He pulls the keys out of his sock and tries the engine. It turns over. He places the drive into reverse and steps hard on the gas. The front bumper gives way, staying with the tree. The Contour chugs backwards out of the ditch. Kevin puts the car into drive and heads back to the motel for a hot shower and hotter coffee.

When Kevin gets into his motel room, he sees that his phone's red message indicator is blinking. He dials up his message and hears that he's to phone either Ted or Tim at the bureau.

Kevin rings up Ted at the M.B.I.'s office in Ann Arbor.

Ted, dragging on his omnipresent cigarette, sets down the cancer-stick and answers, "Agent Ted Smothers."

"Ted, what's up?"

Ted smiles. He taps the cigarette into his ask tray and takes a drag.

Exhaling the cigarette smoke, he jokes, "Hey, rookie, what happened to you last night?"

Kevin darts back, "This guy and I were playing a game of chicken, and I lost."

"So, what about your case? Jim said it's been rougher than you thought."

"The paranoia in this town is amazing. Everyone's afraid to open up about Doug Richards. Their demeanor—how they walk, how loud they talk, even how they eat—is oddly defensive. It's as if someone gave this town a good beating. Lyons is similar to a mistreated dog, cowering under the porch of civilization."

Tim consoles, "That bad, huh?"

"I can't figure it out. Here I am a state agent who's trying to help these people catch a killer, and they all look at me as if I'm the bad guy. What's up with that?"

"You can't take it personally. They just want to be left alone. They don't respect us because we stir up things. I bet, if Jim never sent you down here, Lyons would have eventually caught the killer. After a few months, some idiot would have gotten drunk in a bar. He would have let it slip out that he killed someone. And that would have been that.

"Small towns aren't unjust, just slow. It takes time for things to surface. I know because I grew up in one. Our town never let people get away with crime, but the perpetrators weren't caught over night, either."

In the bullpen, Ted motions for Tim to join in on the conference call.

Tim says, "I agree with Ted, don't take it personally. Just follow our modus operandi: keep asking questions. Talk to people like you do with Ted and me. Open up. You'll get faster results, and you won't have an ulcer by age..."

Tim halts, then asks, "...how old are you anyway?"

"25."

Ted retorts, "Jesus, 25. What are you out for? To be division chief by 30? Lighten up."

"Look you guys, I appreciate the help. I will try to lighten up."

Kevin asks, "Ted, if I send you some evidence, can you make sure our lab boys push it through? There are going to be tire measurements and oil samples. Also, see if you can match the fingerprints found on a cigarette pack with anyone on our network. Check the drivers license bureau, too. If anyone recently received, or renewed their license, we should have their prints on the computer."

A long stem of ashes that has been building on the end of his cigarette falls into his lap.

"Sure. Anything else, rookie?"

"No that's it. Thanks."

Ted says the lab should have the evidence analyzed by tomorrow morning and that they received the blood work from Dr. Fortune. She was right: The blood found in the silo was Doug Richards'. Ted hangs up.

Tim says, "Kevin, are you still there?"

"Yes."

"One more thing: it's about Peg."

"Yes?"

"Well, before work, I dropped off some Chicken Parmesan and a bottle of white wine, with a card that Sally and the kids put together. You know, to keep Peg's spirits up while you're away."

"Thanks, Tim. That was very nice."

"There's more."

"Go on."

"Next to Peg's car was another BMW. Not knowing whose it was and being the detective that I am, I waited for the guy to leave your condo. I also wrote down the plate number. Kevin?"

"Yes?"

"I think Peg's having an affair. I mean she kissed him at the door. He was half dressed when he left. And his hair was tussled. Sorry, my friend."

"Whose was it?"

"Checked the plate and the car belongs to Mr. Zack Ehnes."

"Shit, he's one of the partners at Peg's law firm."

"Yep. What are you going to do?"

"Don't know. I made a pact with myself that once I got married that I would be officially off the market. I would never sleep around. Looks like Peg never made that vow."

"Kevin, I know that it's none of my business, but if one in half of all marriages fail then maybe you got unlucky this time around. Or, you can bite the bullet and give her a second chance."

"I need to call Dad. Talk to you later Tim."

Kevin hangs up.

Chapter 10

Peg is cheating! Kevin slams his head back until it hits the pillow. His red eyes look up at the ceiling. Salty tears run down his face and collect at the curls of his mouth.

He says to himself, "Damn, she is sleeping around."

He uses his tongue to collect the tears resting on his lip. He wipes away the tears with his palm and squeezes out the remaining signs of his discontent with my forefinger and thumb.

What should he do?

He dials his father.

"Doctor Sir's office."

"Hey, Carol it's Kevin. Is Dad around. It's important."

"Sure hold on."

Dr. Sir, one of Gross Pointe's most loved pediatricians and having been prepped by Carol, jokes, "Hey kiddo. How's the first case?"

To Dr. William Sir, life is too short not to have fun.

"Dad, not good. I mean the case is fine. It's Peg."

Dr. Sir's voice lowers, "What's wrong?"

"Dad, she's having an affair."

"Son, I'm sorry."

"You and Mom were right."

"Your mother and I always liked her, we just never trusted her."

"I know."

"What are you going to do?"

"My gut instinct is to divorce her, this second. But I still love her. I'd be willing to work it out. I guess."

"Son, we'll support you. No matter what you do. However, be careful. Don't let her get away with it again. Set up some ground rules."

"Yea. How's your practice?"

"Fine."

"How's Mom?"

"She misses you. Come by the house after you get back from your case."

"OK."

"Kevin?"

"Yes?"

"Again, I'm sorry. Tell Peg we love her. That everyone makes mistakes. That no matter what she'll always be our daughter."

OK. Love you."

"Good bye, son."

Kevin disconnects from his Dad and tries Peg, but she's in court. He leaves a message for her to call him tonight at 6:00 p.m., telling her secretary that it's <u>extremely urgent</u>.

Like a drunk man, Kevin struggles to peel off his clothes, still numb from discovering his wife's infidelity. He carefully steps into the tub and takes a long, hot shower. The water pounds away at his face, shoulders, stomach and toes. He lathers up shampoo and scrubs. He uses the washcloth and washes away the sweat and smell. More than that, he feels as if he is getting rid of last night's accident and this morning's bad news.

He shaves, dries himself off and puts on a pair of clean underwear. He opens the outside door as far as the chain will allow to let in fresh air and draw out the steam. He puts on a pair of Gap khakis, a blue oxford and a subdued, brown and blue tie. Loafers and a blue sport coat complete the collegiate look.

He picks up the phone and calls Sheriff Sackett, struggling to remain focused on the case.

Starla answers and says that the sheriff has stepped out, but that they have Jerod McMurtry in the cell for questioning. He turned himself in earlier this morning. Kevin says good and that he'll be in within a half an hour. They hang up.

Kevin looks up the phone number for the Richards' residence and dials Mrs. Richards.

A woman answers, "Hello."

"Yes, Mrs. Richards. Agent Sir. How are you today?"

"I've been better. This morning I was doing a load of laundry and came across a pair of Doug's jeans. I thought I had packed all his things away!"

"I'm very sorry."

"Any news?"

Their dog barks.

"Well, maybe. I'll let you know."

"I'm sure you're doing your best."

Kevin knowingly asks, "Listen, Mrs. Richards. I was at Panther High yesterday and I have a thought. Did Doug go there?"

"Yes, all the kids in this area go there, even some from Madison. I was the first class to graduate from Panther High. Before they finished building it in 1955, everyone went to Lyons School."

"I am going to talk to the principle there today. He may give me some clues about your son's murder."

"Good idea. But why the high school? Do you think the killer was one of Doug's high school friends?"

"Maybe. One more question Mrs. Richards: 'Were Gus Horton and your son ever friends?'"

"Yes, but that was a long time ago. When we lived next door to each other in town, Gus and Doug played together all the time. But then we bought this farm and then the Hortons' business took off and they built their new place. As our boys grew older, they went their separate ways."

"Thank you."

Kevin hangs up and prepares to leave.

He opens the door to the parking lot and takes a look at his once-new car. The front bumper is gone. The windshield is dangerously bashed in. The sheet metal is dinged from numerous pebbles hitting it. Oil and mud cover the sides. Dead bugs lie on top of all the grime. When the rookie gets back to Ann Arbor, Sergeant Caretaker is going to take one look at the rookie's first state-issued car and want a refund taken out of Kevin's salary.

Ugh!

Kevin speeds to the Sheriff's Office.

Inside a commotion ensues. The sheriff is arguing with Cliff McMurtry. Starla is yelling at the mayor. And Jerod McMurtry is screaming at his mom. Kevin walks in and everyone stops to hear what the rookie will say.

Mayor Tapestry announces to Agent Sir, "Son, get over here. Jerod confessed to maiming Abe, but that's it. He denies killing Doug Richards. What should we do?"

Kevin says, "I don't care about Abe. I know Jason did it. What I want to know is why did you shoot Abe's hand off, Jerod?"

Jerod's parents look at their son.

Jerod says, "Can't tell you. I know I screwed up. But I can't tell you."

Kevin shouts, "Goddamn it, we're not talking about a slap on the hand and spending a few months in this cozy cell. We're talking about 5 years in the State Pen, a place where a good-looking man like yourself will soon be someone's girlfriend!"

Jerod gets up, grabs the bars with his strong hands and argues, "To hell with that. I'll beat those bastards black and blue."

"No you won't. I've seen 'em. Those men in prison are even bigger than you. That's all they do is lift weights. Hell, the only time they get excited is when a new fish, like you, gets sent in. Not only that, but they outnumber you. Once they find out that you're a short-timer, you're done. Most of the criminals in the State Pen will be imprisoned for life. What do they care if they get caught forcing you to have sex. Get the picture? You don't want to go there! Hell, last year, 17 men died in that hole, and all of them were short-timers!"

Mrs. McMurtry cries.

Mr. McMurtry sadly shakes his head.

Mayor Tapestry puts his arm around Starla.

Sheriff Sackett sits down.

Jerod, mutely stands there. His knuckles are white, trying to crush the steel bars as he hears the truth from Agent Sir.

Finally, Jerod bends, "Dammit, I know you're right. But I won't tell you who hired me. I'm not a snitch."

Kevin turns to Jerod's parents and says, "Folks, it sounds like you're going to have to get a good lawyer. And Mr. McMurtry…"

The farmer looks up and says, "Yes?"

"I know you and I had an agreement, but you don't want to follow through with it. Yes, it's important that your son knows that he's wrong and that because he's a man now, he's responsible for his actions, but not this way. Madison State Prison is a hellhole. Do your best to keep him out of it. There are others ways for Jerod to grow up."

"OK."

Mayor Tapestry pleads, "Jerod, my boy, are you sure you won't turn Judas on this son-of-a-bitch just this once? I understand that your word is your honor, but not when we're talking about ruining a man's livelihood. Even if Abe recovers, doctors say his hand is only going to be 25% effective. Imagine trying to lift bales of hay using mostly one hand. You've destroyed Abe's life."

"Sorry mayor, I won't."

Everyone adjourns to Main Street for some fresh air, leaving Jerod alone in his cell.

Kevin asks the group, "Who's he protecting?"

Mayor Tapestry says, "Don't know."

Kevin says to the McMurtry's, "Before Jerod goes to trial, see if he'll talk. If we can nail this guy, maybe the judge will let Jerod off on parole."

The sheriff tells the crowd that he needs to prepare Jerod's lunch. Starla silently follows him.

The mayor and the McMurtry's walk over to their cars for a solemn chat about Jerod's predicament.

Kevin looks around the otherwise quiet town for some solace. Not finding any, he instead taps into his anger at Jerod and his cheating wife for the energy he needs to carry on. His eyes focus on the insurance placard that advertises Horton's business.

He walks across Main Street and around a Lexus with a fish symbol on its trunk and through the front door of the insurance office. The office reeks of cigarettes.

Kevin says to the aging receptionist with tight skin and blue hair, "Agent Sir from Ann Arbor."

Her mouth, a slit, in her otherwise flat face opens, saying, "Good day. Please be seated."

"I'm in a hurry. May I have a word with Mr. Horton? It is very important."

She grimaces, shakes her blue bun yes and then buzzes her boss.

Buzzzzzzzz.

The electronic device shakes the office.

Horton comes out of his inner office.

Mr. Horton does not welcome Kevin; rather, he squints at the rookie through a curtain of smoke.

Kevin looks back at the receptionist. Her face is even tighter now, as if her epidermis is a thin film of Saran Wrap straining to cover a bowl of cherries.

"Mr. Horton we need to talk."

Mr. Horton dejectedly inquires, "Yep. I knew that. What can I do for you?"

Kevin looks over at Mr. Horton's receptionist. She hisses at the rookie, like a snake.

"Where'd you go last night after the game?"

His fat quivers, the waves working themselves up from his belly to his face. His jowls flap, wildly.

"My wife and I went to a dinner party at Judy and Frank Dunham's. You remember the couple who kept asking you about that Hail Mary pass?"

Cigarette smoke billows from the open furnace of his mouth.

The religious insurance salesman, in one seamless series of movements, crushes his old cigarette, pulls out his Cambridges from his shirt pocket and lights a new one. Mr. Horton begins to disappear behind, what was a curtain, is now a wall of smoke.

Kevin demands of the dark image being engulfed in the smoke, "Do you own a convertible?"

"Yes, a Miata. However, usually, I drive my Lexus. Just got off the phone with my boy. Looks like he and his friends were out celebrating last night and accidentally ran you off the road. How much do I owe ya?"

"I'll have the agency send you the invoice."

"Fair enough. I hope you weren't hurt."

"No. I'm fine."

"Will you press charges?"

"No."

"Thank you. That's very white of you."

"Excuse me?"

"Oh, nothing, just an expression. Thanks just the same. What else can I do for you?"

"That's it. Tell Gus, not to worry."

The receptionist takes a call and tells Dale that he needs to answer the phone. Dale retreats into his inner office. Kevin quickly leaves the smoky place and once outside sucks up as much fresh oxygen as his lungs will allow.

He looks at his watch and sees that it's 11:30 a.m. Time to meet Doug's principal. Kevin gets in his Contour, starts its raspy engine and drives to Panther High. He reaches the school in a few minutes and parks in the visitor's slot. He hops out and walks up the long pathway that leads to the large, maroon metal doors.

He gives one a yank, turns left and walks into the administrative offices.

He walks up to the front desk.

He pulls out his badge and says, "Hello, I'm Agent Sir. I have an appointment with your principal please."

The woman looks at the badge, then up at Kevin. She nods, gets up and walks to the back office. Out steps a medium height man. He has a kind round face and graying hair near his temples.

He steps up and says, "Hi, Principal, Hal Vernon. What may I do for you?"

"May I speak privately with you in your office?"

He shows Kevin the way.

"I need to speak to you about Doug Richards."

"Different kid, that Doug."

"How so?"

"Well, before he dropped out, he was a mixture of being both a talented student and a troublemaker. He loved the band, and from what I understand from his instructor, he was very good. His English teacher said that he could write very imaginative stories. He even ran track one year.

"But, he also hung out with the longhairs and then he started smoking, swearing and causing trouble in his other classes. Finally, he just dropped out."

"Tell me more about the longhairs."

"It is hard teaching our kids because of the longhairs. There are those students who want to learn, and there are those students who cause trouble— the longhairs. It takes all my teachers' energy to restrain the longhairs from disrupting class.

"One good thing, though, about Panther High School is there are not the city problems—teenage pregnancies, guns and gangs—to deal with here. Drugs and alcohol are the teachers' main concerns outside the classroom. Too many kids are escaping through these substances."

"How it is possible for your kids to get their hands on the substances?"

"I'm sure it is the longhairs around Lyons who supply the pot and booze."

"OK, then what about Gus Horton?"

"What about him?"

"I believe this case is about good vs. evil and that Gus Horton is the lynch pin."

"I don't see how Gus could be a part of your investigation. Gus and

Doug are so different."

"I can assure you sir that Gus is not a murder suspect. I really like Gus. He reminds me of myself when I was in school. However, Gus was driving his dad's Miata last night after the game and he ran me off the road. He had been drinking."

"How do you know?"

"Saw him at Lou's Place."

"Oh, yes. Was Gus with a really big kid?"

"Yes."

"That's Lou's son, Doug. Lou Seal sometimes lets the boys have a couple beers after they win. I wish Lou wouldn't do that. Everyone on the PTA has spoken to him about it. He says that boys will be boys. If they don't get their suds at his place, they'll find someplace to get their kicks."

Kevin says he understands. He thanks the principal for his time and lets him know that he can be reached at the Best Western, #105.

Hal Vernon tells Kevin no problem and to feel free to use his weight room anytime. His secretary told him that Kevin called yesterday.

Kevin leaves the office and thanks the secretary. He walks out into the hallway. The cafeteria is on the other side. The place is swarming with kids on break between classes. The rookie stands there for a minute surveying the room. As usual, just as when he was going to high school, the room is separated into different groups of teenagers who congregate at their own tables.

The jocks are nearest to the vending machines, muscling each other and laughing out loud. At the table nearest the stage of this cafeteria, which doubles as the auditorium, are the babes. They are squealing, and their eyes rove around, picking out the cutest jock of the week.

Closest to Kevin are the brains. They are diving into books while stabbing at their eyeglasses' nosepieces. The tables in between are the class clowns, the preppies, the wannabes and just your run of the mill students. Where are the longhairs, as Hal called them?

Kevin turns right to leave. He leans against the front door and pushes. But, the door hits something halfway.

Someone calls out, "Ouch."

Kevin squeezes through the opening. The next second, his eyes burn and his lungs fill with smoke. The door comes back at Kevin and catches him on the chin. Kevin takes the blow and finishes forcing his body out the door. He stands there for a few seconds while his senses come back.

Here, in front of him, are about thirty longhairs, all smoking cigarettes and making rude noises.

Kevin says, "Excuse me."

He walks through them coughing.

In the back ground, one says, "The dude didn't even say he was sorry. Dick head."

Halfway to Kevin's car, the air clears. He takes a couple of deep breaths. Kevin looks back and gives the crowd a fierce look. Darn longhairs!

Kevin gets into his car and slams on the accelerator and speeds to town. He approaches a truck pulling a horse trailer. He passes it, even though there are two solid yellow lines. A car travels towards him, dangerously close. He pushes his Contour faster, and he just makes it around the truck.

Kevin wipes his brow and tells himself to get a grip. Once in town, he parks in front of The Café. It's now 1 p.m. and Kevin's starved. He looks into the restaurant.

Is he physically hungry or spiritually hungry?

His parents, who love their church, always remind Kevin that no matter what, God will always love him, especially in the worst of times. The rookie adjusts his eyes to the right towards the Episcopal Church, St. John's.

Kevin gets out of his car, skips lunch and walks over to the church to feed his soul.

He will talk to the minister about his marriage. Maybe, he can help. The rookie does not know where else to turn. His Dad helped, but not enough.

He walks up to the large wooden doors and sits down in an empty pew near the back. He pulls down the kneeling pad and rests his elbows on the wooden pew in front of him. He pushes his face into cupped hands.

"Dear Lord, thank you for everything. Thank you for my wife, my parents, my job and my health. Please direct me to do good works. I love you and want you to take care of everyone dear to me. I know I fall way short of your ideas about how I should live. Please forgive me. Please, please forgive me. Also, help Peg and I keep our marriage together. If you do, I promise that I will come to church more."

Kevin raises his head, looking into the stained glass windows above the altar. Jesus' torn body droops over a rough-looking cross. The mid-afternoon sun beams through and fills the church with sunlight colored by the stained glass. Dark reds, blues and yellows bounce across the room.

Kevin thinks that he should pray more often. It feels good.

Reverand Maynard Baynes, a small, white-haired gentleman with glasses and who takes a shower two or three times a week, walks up to Kevin. His followers love him because he is soft-spoken and kind. His sermons are never loud; this old priest trusts that he does not have to scream out in order to get his congregation to believe him. He ambles over to the rookie, who has finished praying.

Kevin stands before the priest and asks, "Could you spend a few minutes with me in private?"

"Yes. Meet me at the small, white house just before Chestnut Hills Farm in about ten minutes. It's on the right-hand side. You'll notice our sun-porch from the road."

"You mean at your home?"

"Yes. I do all my counseling there."

"OK. I'll see you in ten minutes."

Kevin climbs into his car and heads down North Lyons Road towards the priest's home. Just before the hill that leads to Tapestry's farm, there is a smaller house with an all-season sun porch on the right. Kevin pulls into its driveway. Higher on the hill, above the priest's small house is a large, white house, similar in size to Derrick and Em's. The two homes share the same driveway. A large white barn separates these two proud homes.

Kevin shuts off the car and walks towards the small, white house. In front is a little, black boy statue holding a lantern. Kevin walks up some cobbled steps towards the house. He knocks on a thin, screen white-washed door. In a few moments a handsome, old woman opens the inside door.

She welcomes, "Hello."

Her chiseled face has some sags, but her white hair is perfectly coiffured. She has on pearls, a boiled wool vest, a cream silk blouse and khakis.

Without hesitating, she lets Kevin inside. Kevin walks into their home. It smells of a mixture of mothballs and Ben Gay.

She asks, "Would you like a cocktail?"

"No thanks. Some coffee, perhaps?"

She retires to the kitchen. Kevin follows her.

"I met your husband this afternoon. He asked me to meet him here. I'm not a member of your church, I just need someone to talk to. It's about my wife."

She smiles and says, "Oh, Maynard, well, he can help. But, you'll have to bear with him, though."

"Thanks, but I don't understand."

"You'll discover that my husband is somewhat of an iconoclast. He believes in all the tenets of Christianity, and he gives a good show, but he's always willing to break the bounds for something. I'm much more conservative."

Kevin looks out their kitchen window and see a small, beautiful garden filled herbs, flowers and vegetables. In the center, a stone cherub spits out water.

Outside on their driveway comes the sound of crushed gravel. The old woman straightens up her old back. She rushes toward the door. Kevin follows her. Together they see a silver Honda Accord slowly pull up to the home.

Out steps the priest, who somewhat resembles Albert Einstein, but with tidier hair. He bumbles up the cobbled steps with a glazed look. His wife opens the door for him. He cracks an elfish grin.

While taking off his tan overcoat, he says, "Good day Martha. Who do we have here?"

"My name's Kevin Sir, the M.B.I. agent from Ann Arbor, I was praying in your church. I asked to talk with you in private."

He smiles again and says, "Oh, that's right. Martha, Kevin and I will be on the sun porch."

They walk through a tiny living room with many antiques and oriental throw rugs covering the floor and furniture. There is a small black and white TV on a plastic stand with a coat hanger and some tinfoil for an antenna. A simple silver cross hangs above the TV. Kevin follows the old man onto his porch. It is much different than the rookie expected. It is very warm.

Some apple and pine trees tower above the all-glass room. The branches have been trimmed near the top. Plenty of sunshine streams in from the sky. Oriental throw rugs cover the furniture. There is a large bookcase next to the wall that separates the house from the porch. Kevin sits down on a green, twill loveseat with his back to the driveway.

Maynard sits in a calico chair. His body slips into the upholstery, perfectly. Maynard's chair faces his colorful bookcase, not a thirty-two-inch

TV set. Where his remote control would be, lies a worn black leather Bible with many pieces of paper sticking out of it.

Kevin lets out a sigh, knowing he could relax in here all day with a good book and some hot chocolate. In the distance, he can barely hear Martha getting the coffee ready. They are a quiet couple. Kevin does not smell the Ben Gay any more.

Maynard lifts his bushy eyebrows and asks, "So, young man, you're going to deliver this town from evil?"

"No, you do that. I'm only here to bring Doug Richard's killer to justice."

He looks at the rookie with milky eyes.

"What you are doing is a fine thing. Don't you forget that. Doing the right thing is like making love to a beautiful woman; it just feels divine. Right Martha?"

In comes Martha with a silver coffee pot and two ivory cups. She shakes her head at Maynard's suggestion, as if she has heard it all before, and yet she cannot help from taking pleasure in his off-beat and erotic allegories. She sets the items on a wicker table.

She says, "Maynard please, you're embarrassing young Kevin."

"Heh, heh," Maynard laughs.

Kevin smiles and pours a cup of coffee for Maynard.

He politely takes it, fills the rest of the cup with Drambuie and continues, "Yes, this is a wonderful town. Everyone here, well, except that Snipes fellow, is a good person."

Kevin almost spits out his coffee as Maynard mentions Snipes.

Kevin agrees, saying, "Oh, Mr. Snipes was mean-spirited..."

Maynard cuts Kevin off and says, "I don't wish him ill. It's just that the Devil will have a special place for old Snipes, that's all."

Maynard goes on for a while about how good the town is and which women he finds attractive. It is fun chatter, but after two more cups of coffee, Kevin is beginning to feel restless.

Finally, Kevin butts in and says, "Maynard, I need to get something off my chest. I agreed to come over here because I'm having problems with my wife. I don't usually go to church, but I don't know who else to turn to. Can you help me?"

"Well, why didn't you stop me sooner young man. Of course, I'll help.

First, how's your sex life?"

"Um, it's fine."

"How often do you do it?"

"Is this a normal question from a priest?"

He nods yes.

"Well, um, when I'm home and not on assignment, almost every night!"

"Good boy. Now, when did you start having problems with your wife?"

"Last night. When I called to tell her that I had been in a car accident, she complained that I'm never home."

"There you go. It's sex. She wants you home for that one reason."

"Forgive me Maynard, but for a priest you're awfully hung up on sex. I mean you're probably right. But how would you know?"

His eyes twinkle, saying, "Look son, next to God and Jesus, my wife is the most important thing in my life. I love God. I love Jesus. Every minute of my life, I try to make love to them, either publicly on the altar or privately through prayer and reading the Bible. It's a moral union between souls.

"But God also wants us to enjoy each other on earth, especially with our lifelong mate. To me, Martha is the kindest, most beautiful person in the world. I show her my love by making love to her as often as I can. Of course as you get older, well... Anyway, sex is a gift from God.

"Being that a priest is also a marriage counselor, I've found that the amount of sex a couple has is directly related to their happiness. If a couple is acting like two rabbits then counseling only takes a one or two sessions. Usually, their argument was over something stupid, such as the husband forgot to enter a check in the checkbook and they're overdrawn, etc. However, if a couple has sex just to have kids, or to please the other then counseling takes years at best. Usually, I can't fix their relationship. Do you get my drift?"

He bends over and whispers, "And besides, who says priests can't have some fun under the sheets."

Nervously, Kevin laughs. Is this guy crazy, or is he the most sane person Kevin has ever met?

"Maynard, thank you for your opinion. I'm sure sex is part of the problem. Peg and I will talk about it."

The two men conclude that Kevin's next task is to talk to Peg about their sex life. If Peg truly just needs a man by her side every night, then Kevin can make some sort of arrangement in that area.

Kevin gets up and shakes Maynard's hand.

He turns to go, feeling somewhat relieved.

Then a thought takes over him, one having to do with Dale Horton, who must be one of Maynard's biggest supporters.

"Sir, I need to ask you one more thing before I go: What can you tell me about my investigation? I mean people here trust you. Has someone told you anything about the case that would lead to Doug's killer being put behind bars?"

Maynard grabs his Bible and flips to a passage marked by a red strip of cloth.

He reads, "Exodus 20:13 reads, 'You shall not murder.' That's it. That's all I know. Whoever killed Doug broke God's law. The murderer will be punished by God. I may have heard rumors about Doug's killer, but I'm not going to implicate anyone based on gossip. Sorry. It's terrible what happened. I wish you luck."

Kevin thinks, all of a sudden this once dainty man who spoke passionately about life has turned into a little coward who is ducking behind the cross.

"Maynard, please, it's important you help me."

He shakes his head no.

"Sir, Lyons trusts you. You must know something about this case."

Even though Kevin does not feel that he has threatened him, Maynard looks scared. His wife standing under the doorway between the sun-porch and living room approaches her graying husband and puts her arm around him.

She says, "Please tell Mr. Sir what you know. You know it's right."

Maynard gets up and leaves the room, backing away from his wife's suggestion.

His wife stands there for nearly ten minutes, hoping Agent Sir will leave before she breaks down. Agent Sir doesn't budge.

She finally breaks the silence: "He's a very good man. He just doesn't want to get in the middle of things. What we know is that Doug, rest his soul, was being picked on a lot by Keith Spelling and his friends. Things must have gotten out of control."

She concludes by whispering, "It seems from all the scuttlebutt that Keith

Spelling must have done it, or at least knows who did it."

"Martha, thank you for your honesty. You and your husband can breathe easy."

She leads Kevin to the door. The rookie walks out into fresh, autumn air. He zips up his fleece coat and walks to his wreck of a car. The clock in his car reads: 4 p.m. Enough time to change and workout before confronting his wife.

Chapter 11

Kevin stops by his motel and picks up his gym clothes. The red light is blinking on his phone. The message is from Sergeant Caretaker. The rookie dials his boss.

"Sergeant Caretaker."

"Sir, It's Kevin."

"Kevin how'd the interview with that McMurtry fellow go?"

"Good and bad. He confessed to roughing up one of my sources, but denied killing Doug Richards."

"Anything else going on?"

"What do you mean?"

"Kevin, Tim told me about Peg."

"Oh."

"You've done a hell of a job getting people to open up. The first few days are always the worst. Mayor Tapestry is glad you're helping Lyons out."

"Yeah, the mayor is a very decent man."

"Do you think that you can truly concentrate one hundred and ten per- cent on the case knowing what Tim said he saw this morning?"

"I don't know. Haven't talked to Peg, yet. She was in court all day to- day."

"Son, I think you need a second man there to help."

"Yes, sir. If that's what you think. Fine."

"Good. Tim will arrive first thing tomorrow morning."

"Thanks."

"Hang in there."

Kevin drives to Panther High's gym. He arrives at the high school's large parking lot. He studies the near empty lot with all of its hundreds of marked, empty parking spaces. He wonders, why should he park in a designated spot when he could park in any spot he wants to, taking up as many as three spots, or maybe even taking up a handicapped spot? What if he broke the law? Doug's killer did. So, does that mean Doug's killer has more guts than Kevin does? Doesn't it take spunk to kill, rob and rape?

If the killer was born in another time when mayhem was more accepted, say, in Medieval times, wouldn't Doug's killer be a local hero, instead of a fugitive? Wouldn't Kevin have been nothing more than a knight, blindly serving a pompous king and fulfilling his fleeting wishes, a king who would have had many concubines? He is sure Peg's great, great, great, great, great grandmother was one of the king's best.

Kevin parks legally, gets out of the car and slams the door shut. He stomps up the wide concrete sidewalk to the entranceway. There are four large steel doors. He tries one of them and yanks it. It gives a centimeter and then resists his pull.

Darn, it is locked.

Out of frustration, Kevin begins banging on it, hoping a janitor will hear him and let him into the weight room. He pounds on the door for a few minutes, and, finally, a kid dragging a mop comes to the door.

Kevin curtly thanks him.

Once inside the weight room Kevin lets out a long sigh. His muscles tense up, but his mind relaxes. Today, he must work on his biceps and shoulders. He walks over to the squat rack and lowers the guides to shoulder height. He places a forty-five-pound weight on both sides of the forty-five-pound bar and strap on the locks. He sits down and begins to lift. He lowers the weight to his trapezius muscles located behind his neck and lifts up towards the ceiling.

His cells burst with energy. His blood rushes to his brain. When his brain cannot take the pressure any more, the blood circulates to the other areas of his body. His whole body becomes red and alive. He does eight reps three times. He accomplishes other routines to build his shoulders in about thirty minutes.

He takes a sip of cool water and then sets up the preacher's bench for his biceps workout. He puts on a forty-five-pound weight on each end of the twenty-five-pound curling bar. He pushes up his T-shirt to reveal his biceps. Facing the mirror, he curls the weight. The iron tears away at his muscles. Kevin grunts and groans. Sweat trickles down his nose and the sides of his face.

After he does two other sets of eight reps, he does two other exercises to build his biceps: dumbell curls and straight-bar curls. He looks up at the clock, and he has been here an hour. Exhausted, he stumbles over to the drinking fountain and gulps down water, half breathing hard and half inhaling the precious juice. His shirt is soaked with sweat.

Kevin drives back to his room. Once inside the motel, he strips and takes a shower. He dries off and gets dressed. He sits on the made-up bed and takes in a beer. He gets up and looks out of the picture window, taking in the Coors. The field is orange with the setting October sun.

Ring!

Kevin sets down the beer and answers, "Hello?"

In the background, Kevin can hear Roxy Music playing.

Peg says, "Honey, what's wrong."

"I miss you. We haven't seen each other for a few days…"

With each word, the tone of Kevin's voice rises. At his last word, he is shouting.

Kevin demands, "And I'm getting sick of it! Not only that, but I hear you have a boyfriend, one of the partners at your firm, named Ehnes! Tim saw him leaving this morning still buttoning his pants."

She pulls back the receiver from her ear. Her face feels red.

She pleads, "I love you with all my heart, but I was lonely."

"Peg, I can't take this arrangement. It's not fair. We really need to talk."

Her heart rises up into her throat.

"OK, let's talk."

"My work will sometimes take me out of town. I need to know that I can trust you."

"You can."

"Then why this Ehnes guy?"

"I don't know. I'm sorry."

"Peg, if you do it again, we're history."

"OK."

They hang up.

Peg drops her wineglass and cries.

Kevin throws his beer at an inexpensive oil painting of some Aspen trees and falls onto the bed.

In their marriage, Kevin has always succumbed to her will. He has had to rearrange his thoughts to suit her. There are givers and takers. Peg is a taker. Kevin is the giver. In their marriage, he has always gone down to his knees and prayed to her in order that his words might keep them together. Kevin was sure that this trade-off is common in any relationship.

But this! What was she thinking?

Peg is the love of his life. She is similar to a maple tree on North Lyons

Road. She is firm, strong and beautiful. She gives him the feeling that when he stands under her, life can get no better. As the leaves that fall ever so gently to the ground, her hands caress him. Her roots run deep under him. He loves her. He does not want to lose Peg. So, he's willing to work with her one last time.

He pulls out his wallet and looks at a picture of beautiful Peg.

Love is such a bizarre mixture of possession, loss and recovery. The times he really loves Peg are the ones when he cannot be with her, when they are away from each another either physically as with he being on assignment or emotionally as their fighting over money. And then when they see one another for the first time or suddenly make up, an incredible transformation takes place in his heart.

During this span of change, his heart quickly sheds its feeling of loss. His heart becomes lighter, as if it had been encased in lead and the fires of love have melted away the deprivation. The lead drips. His heart rises up, floating into its natural spot. His body shivers. He will never feel any better.

Kevin's heart is heavy right now. He cannot make it rise up, only Peg can do that. For now, he will just have to live with this terrible feeling. For now, he will just have to get through this minute and all the minutes to come before he makes up with Peg. Meanwhile, he will be tripping over his heart because it has sunk to his feet.

He throws his wallet across the room. He feels trapped.

Life is nothing more than a series of cages that he must climb into and out of, possibly graduating onto the next level. First, he is stuck in a metal-reinforced trap with a guy named Jim. His boss gives Kevin cheese if he does things right in the cage called law enforcement. Second, he is entrapped behind bamboo bars with a girl named Peg. If he says the right things and acts as if he loves her, she gives him water. Third, he is serving time in a country called America that expects him to pay taxes, in part for his salary, but more importantly to help run a country that spends more on nuclear missles and submarines than on schools, hospitals and low-income housing combined. Fourth, he cannot move to another country to make his life better because other countries are in worse shape. Cage after cage after cage.

No human can say they are truly free. Criminals may say they were destined to go behind bars because of their upbringing. Kevin thinks, we are all behind bars because we are human. This world has devised more cages and more little traps than Alcatraz. We are all prisoners. It just depends how big, or how small a person wants to make their own prison. Some elect a five-by-nine cell, others hold out for a home in the suburbs. It is all the same.

Jim has Kevin by the balls because if he does not solve this case, he will be forever trying to make it up to the bureau. Peg definitely has him by the nuts because if he does not try to love and forgive her, he will be forever wondering why he let the girl of his dreams walk on by him. America has him by the gonads because the politicians know they are leading the most productive nation in the world, so they can mess up and say, "Hey, big deal. Live with it."

The really odd thing is he is trying to capture a killer to put behind steel rods when he feels as if he is already doing time. The choices he has been given, truly gives him no real freedom.

He awakens from his thoughts, the ceiling above him comes back into view. He gets up and retrieves a glass of water, undresses and falls back into bed. He shuts off the lights and fitfully drifts off to sleep.

Tonight he has a very strange dream: He and Peg are on a school bus. They are both very young. All the guys on the bus are trying to flirt with her. Kevin is sitting next to her in the same seat.

His friends have tied him up with a big thick rope. Tape is place over his mouth. He sits there paralyzed while the other boys tell Peg dirty jokes and touch her. She laughs with them and lifts up her skirt. Every now and then, when Kevin thinks that he is going to bust with jealousy, Peg will stroke his hair, touch his cheek, or kiss him.

Thursday morning Kevin sleeps to 7 a.m. When the alarm rings, the rookie gets up. He takes a shower, gets dressed and drives to the Cafe for breakfast. He's famished from skipping all of yesterday's allotment of three square meals. He orders a Denver omelet, sausages, pancakes, hash browns, coffee, no-fat milk and the biggest glass of orange juice in the place. Kevin finishes his breakfast, pays and then walks outside. Kevin's watch reads 8:30 a.m.

Kevin drives back to his motel room. Parked in the lot is another Ford Contour with special state plates. Good, the other agent, Tim Maxwell, is here.

Kevin gets out of his car and knocks on the other Contour's driver's side window. Tim looks up from the sports page and nods his head in acknowledgement. The smaller agent gets out of the car and the two men shake hands.

Kevin asks, "What did the lab come up with from those samples?"

"The tire tracks were made by very small Michelins. The smallest on the road, today, in fact. We cross-referenced the width of the car's skid marks with some measurements from the state's automobile data bank. Since, you and Jim deduced that the car that ran you off the road is a convertible, and based on the evidence you collected and we sorted out, the car has to a Mazda Miata. No question about it. The key to the discovery is the width between the two skid marks. The measurement gave us the width of the chassis, and no other car on the road has the Miata's specifics."

"Good. Now, what about the liquid samples and the cigarettes?"

"The liquid samples are a bust. They are standard transmission fluids from half a dozen cars. Besides, the Miata is too new to be dripping oil or to have cracked seals. In terms of the full pack of cigarettes, it had two different sets of fingerprints, but neither one showed up in the computer. Sorry."

"Tim thanks for your help. Dale Horton, the owner of the vehicle, already told me that his son Gus was driving the Miata. But it's nice that our lab agrees."

"Well, it seems you need a break in this case and together Jim thinks we can pull it off. Are you ready to hit the streets? Whose car should we take? Yours or mine?"

Tim glances over at Kevin's beat-up car and whistles in disbelief.

"What in the hell happened to your car?"

"Farm life doesn't agree with my driving. I guess."

"Shit, looks like we're taking mine."

They drive down North Lyons Road. It is a splendid autumn day. There are a few clouds, but there is still plenty of blue sky. The leaves on the trees are almost gone. Their car plows through all the fallen leaves and they swirl up behind them.

Tim says, "You know, I wouldn't mind living out here. It's quiet. Look at that farm over there. My kids would love it. We'd get a horse and some pigs and chickens. We'd have a big garden. I think I'd enjoy farming.

"No people, just my family and all the land I could farm. I think that's why I go up to our cabin every chance I can because I want to get away from it all."

"Yea, I think I know what you mean."

The pair reaches the crime scene. Kevin shows Tim the spot where Doug was killed. Tim recoils at the musty silo and the large stain of dried blood on the dirt floor. Kevin tells Tim how Doug was killed and Tim grows sad, as if his illusion about farm life has been interrupted by big city crime.

In the dark silo, Tim places his hand on Kevin's shoulder.

Tim communicates, "Kevin, let me drive you back to the motel. You fill me in and then we'll separate after lunch to see what each of us can unearth."

"Yeah, sounds good."

Agents Maxwell and Sir retire to room 105 at the Best Western to develop a game plan. Inside the motel room, while the two M.B.I. agents are getting their notes together, there is a knock at their door. Donna comes into their room with a fresh pot of coffee, fruit and her homemade brownies.

She lays them on the corner table and says, "Here you guys go. I know that you've got your work cut out for you. Here's something to keep up your strength."

Tim and Kevin thank the kind manager.

Donna smiles and leaves.

Tim asks, "OK, who are main players?"

"Sheriff Sackett, but he doesn't do anything but hand out speeding tickets."

"What do you mean?"

"He's similar to a new bag of potato chips you buy at the grocery store: On the outside he has all the markings of a full-fledged cop—uniform, title and badge—but once you open him up, you find out he's half the man you thought.

"I don't know how he got to be a cop, but I think he's just mooching off his tax payers to pay his mortgage and buy his wife chocolates while she watches *Days of Our Lonely Lives*."

"OK then, who's next?"

"Starla, Sackett's assistant, is nice, efficient and totally infatuated with me."

"Who else?"

"Dr. Fortune, the local physician, loves her patients; hates bureaucracy. Then there is Mrs. Richards, the victim's mom. She's confused, upset and close to a break down."

"What about Mr. Richards?"

"Doubt it. Mrs. Richards says that there is no love lost between the two men."

"Go on."

"Then there's Jerod McMurtry. He's guilty of maiming Abe Jenkins, a small time farmer who was filling me in about Lyons, but denies killing Doug Richards."

Tim writes Jerod's name down and asks Kevin to continue.

"Derrick and Em Palmer, a wonderful couple who are the heirs to the town's biggest farm, seem to me to be utterly clueless about the murder and completely in the dark, except for the fact that Derrick does employ Keith Spelling, one of my suspects, and did employ Doug Richards, the victim. Finally, there is Mayor John Tapestry, a legend around here who may lose his bid for re-election next month to Dale Horton, Lyons' local insurance agent."

"So who do you think did it?"

"Could be Keith Spelling, Jerod McMurtry or someone else like Dale Horton."

"Why Dale Horton?"

"Dale is so certain about his code of ethics that he could have done something criminal, but think it was righteous. In Dale's world, he's relishing the fact that he really hates certain types of people—liberals, druggies and boozers. But he's always had to tone down that stance. He's known that while society will back him up, as your run-of-the-mill citizen supports MADD, it won't tolerate some loon with a grudge who preaches on a soap box about how wonderful the day will be when all Joe Sixpacks are burned in hell.

"It's not your classic cover-up. Over the years, I'm sure he's learned to camouflage his rhetoric. I think he's done such a good job to the people of Lyons that he's grown lazy. He kind of let down his poker face Monday night. As an outsider, I thought I could see through his ruse."

"So how does that fit in with killing Doug Richards?"

"That's the crux of the case. I don't have a link between Doug's death and Dale's involvement. The only one I can come up with is Dale's son, Gus. But, according to Mrs. Richards and Panther High's Principal, Hal Vernon, Doug and Gus haven't been friends in a long time."

"Why do you think Doug was murdered?"

"He was a longhair who got caught selling drugs."

"What's a longhair?"

"Oh, they're just people who party too much. I guess. The whole town can't stand 'em."

"Well, maybe Dale found out that his son was buying drugs from Doug and decided to do something about it."

"That makes sense. You should have heard Dale talk the other night. He's got this Christianity thing all mixed up with his own personal vendetta against drugs and alcohol. He's like that guy you and Ted busted last year."

"I remember reading from your report that the killer had a fetish for matchbooks. He had to collect all different kinds, the more the better. But you busted him because you connected him to a guy from his workplace who wouldn't give up his matchbook.

"In one of my classes at the academy, I learned kooks kill because they've divested themselves from reality. They justify their crimes based on some dysfunctional, yet highly elaborate, set of rules they've developed and grown comfortable with. We all play mind games with ourselves, but it's the killers who go one step further and actually penalize those who don't play along."

Tim smiles and says, "Exactly, I concur. Dale killed Doug because he didn't fit into Dale's world. In fact, Doug was threatening Dale's world by selling drugs to Gus. Dale snapped."

"Exactly."

"So, Agent Sir, let me ask you a question, what mind games do you play? I mean, you said everyone does it."

"Tim, I just want everyone to be safe and happy. Really, I hate what money does to people. If it weren't the wackos like Dale, the matchbook man and all those Detroit gang bangers, I'd think that money is the only thing that destroys people. Obviously, though, there are ideologies that get into the way, too. Politics causes us problems. However, I think money/greed is our main problem. Our nation is turning into one big corporation instead of one big community. We've gone from being a democracy to the world's greatest monopoly."

Tim asks, "One more question: what happened between you and Peg?"

"I'm giving her one more shot. She and I will have a lot of talking to do when I get back."

"Sorry I found out."

"Ah, don't worry about it. Better you than me. If I had seen the bastard, I'd have killed him."

"The sergeant wouldn't have liked that."

"I know. That's why I'm glad you found out."

Tim pats Kevin on the shoulder.

Tim looks over at the clock and it reads: 12:00 p.m.

"Let's go grab a bite."

Tim and Kevin leave the motel room and drive separately to the Café. Inside the swamped dinette are sweaty farmers. Men talk about the harvest, whether or not this winter will be a cold one and the unlikely confession of Jerod McMurtry. Tim and Kevin sit at an unoccupied table. Soon, a plump waitress comes up and takes their order. Kevin has a salad with ham strips, and Tim gets a cheeseburger and fries.

The agents are halfway into their meal when a large man stomps up to the table. His overalls are covered with corn dust. The stranger places his hands on the table, staring Kevin right in the eyes. The rookie looks down at the man's hands, there are some fingers missing.

He shouts, "How could you suspect Jerod?"

Kevin retorts, "Hey pal, I didn't know I had to clear things with you. I was just doing my job. Now excuse me, my partner and I want to finish our lunch."

He looks at Kevin's plate and says, "Rabbit food, just what I thought a spineless, city boy eats."

Kevin jumps up and his blood's pumping fast.

"What's your problem?"

"Look mister, Jerod couldn't have killed Doug. That night, he was up by my house. We were all playin' poker. That's all. If you want your man, take a look at some of the suits in this town, the ones who think that they're holier than thou."

Tim asks, "Like who, for instance?"

The farmer calms down and says, "I don't want to get involved."

"Well, OK, then let me finish my lunch."

The farmer lowers his head and walks away.

Kevin sits down and stabs at his salad, shoving the greens and ham into his mouth.

Tim asks, "Is this what you saying on the phone yesterday? You can tell he's protective of Jerod."

"It seems that way."

Kevin and Tim walk out of the Café.

Kevin asks, "OK, so, where you off to?"

"Panther High to interview Gus. If he's the lynch pin to this case then it's time for him to sing. What about you?"

"Well, if Dale Horton is our man, than there's one man, a man of the cloth, who'll be able to help us—Reverend Maynard Baynes. But first, you'd better introduce yourself to mayor. He doesn't like surprises, and he didn't invite you. You'll like him a lot. But as he said, Lyons is his town."

"Fine, let's get it over with."

The agents get back into their cars and drive to the Chestnut Hills Farm. Kevin remembers someone saying that Mr. Tapestry lives in the small white house on the other side of the silos. They drive into the worker's entrance. Kevin looks over at the Palmer Mansion. There are three, large carved pumpkins with childlike grimaces resting on the green painted planks of their porch. They look similar to orange soccer balls having found their way past the goalie and into the home's gothical goalposts.

The yard is half raked—one part shows off green grass and the other shrouded under broken, brown leaves. The yellow and white awnings are packed away, leaving the porch bald-looking. The pool is covered.

The agents drive to the small house and park next to Mr. Tapestry's auburn Ford truck. They walk up the sidewalk to the door. Kevin knocks on the door. In a few minutes, Mr. Tapestry opens it. He is wearing nothing, but boxer shorts. The tall, handsome man shifts in the doorframe. His gray hair is neatly combed. His old body still has many muscles left to show off.

He shouts, "Howdy boys, come on in."

Kevin says, "Well, we don't want to interrupt. My partner Tim, here, wanted to meet you, plus I came to give you a status report on the case."

Behind him on a polished cherry hallway stand is a silver framed photo of a gorgeous woman.

He says, "I've come down with some bug. But, I'll be fine tomorrow. Do you want a drink?"

No thanks they say.

"Mr. Tapestry, this is Agent Tim Maxwell."

They shake hands.

Tim, pointing to the photo, asks, "Was that your wife? Lovely, woman."

Mr. Tapestry launches into a eulogy: "Marion, beautiful, fair Marion got breast cancer when she was 40. Emily was away at college. The whole thing happened so fast. First, Marion was my wife, then she was dead. She was an actress on Broadway before I met her. She looked like Vanna Whitehead, but with black hair. I've been without her for more than 30 years."

He sadly smiles.

Tim says, "That must be hard."

Mr. Tapestry says yes.

The old man asks, "So, do you boys have any new leads?"

Kevin says, "Yes we do. We think Dale Horton is involved."

Mr. Tapestry says, "I gotta tell you. I'm real impressed with your boss Sergeant Caretaker. I'm glad you're here Agent Maxwell. Agent Sir's been doing a bang up job. But I'm glad the M.B.I. is taking us country folk seriously."

Kevin reiterates, "Sir, I just told you who we think killed the Richards' boy."

Mr. Tapestry sits down and waves his hand at the rookie to be quiet.

He says, "Damn, what's this world coming to? That no good insurance salesman. I should have known. He's always made a killing off my insurance premiums. So, why shouldn't he make a killing some other way, like stabbing Doug Richards? Why do you think he did it?"

"We think he's upset about Doug selling drugs to his son, Gus. His religious beliefs are clouding his judgement. So, he played God and punished Doug."

Mr. Tapestry says, "I'll never understand Dale's type."

"How so?"

He says, "One day a week, he goes to church. The other six days a week, he's off stealing people blind and causing trouble."

Kevin corrects Mr. Tapestry and says, "He goes to church more than that. He also attends a Christian Men's Group at Mr. Johnson's house."

Mr. Tapestry gets up and challenges, "Ha! Johnson, he's another one. He cheats on his wife, he cheats people out of their homes, and he calls himself a Christian. Boys, the end doesn't justify the means. They may hope to go to heaven by calling themselves Christians, but when you treat people as they do, they aren't any better. In fact, I think they're worse."

"Well, you could be right. I didn't know Mr. Johnson was an adulterer. But, I see your point about being hypocritical. I'm going to one of their meetings tonight. Maybe, I can shake things up a little."

Mr. Tapestry says good luck and to come by the place tomorrow night because they're having their annual harvest party, complete with a roasted pig.

The two agents wish him well and say they'll be glad to attend. They walk back to the Contour.

Kevin says, "Getting old is rough. What's there for us to look forward to when we reach Mr. Tapestry's age?"

"For me it'll be a lot of fishing and hunting."

"Tim, after you get done with Gus, meet me back at the motel. OK?"

"Sure."

Kevin gives Tim directions to Panther High.

Kevin gets in his car and drives up the road to Reverend Maynard Baynes. Kevin reaches the little house a few minutes and knocks at the door. No one seems to be inside.

Then from around the back, a faint voice cries, "I'm in the garden."

Kevin walks around back, past a cement birdbath with a sundial. He walks through a small wooden gate. Martha is stooped over some dying tomato plants, covering the ground with straw to ward off the cold nights.

Kevin says, "Hello Martha. It's nice to see you again. Is Maynard home? I need to talk with him."

The small woman slowly straightens her back. She is wearing a flowered smock, leather gloves, jeans, boots and pearls. Her hair is bundled up with a lavender, silk bow. She walks past the agent. The pair makes its way back to the front door.

A youngster, who looks familiar to Kevin, is racking leaves in the other yard across the driveway. The rookie waves to him. He seems discouraged. Kevin looks at his progress. He will be raking for some time. A thick blanket of leaves covers the huge yard. As soon as the boy clears some leaves away, others come spinning down from the tall trees above him.

Kevin says to Martha, "I don't envy that kid. He looks familiar, though."

She says, "He's a good boy. He's Derrick's oldest, trying to make some extra money. If we don't get those leaves up before winter, they're a mess in the spring. Ever try raking up wet leaves? It's three times the work."

"What do you mean 'we,' are you related to those people in the big house?"

"Yes, my daughter and her family live there."

"Well, why doesn't one of your daughter's kids do the work, instead of making Derrick's son sweat it out?"

She winks at Kevin and says, "Because they're lazy. Both of her sons don't do anything but play baseball, buy video games and watch TV. She spoils them, and their father is too busy working as a lawyer in Madison to care for them. It's kind of sad."

Kevin and Martha walk into the warm cottage.

Maynard yells, "Martha, honey, did you get the tomatoes covered? I can feel winter coming. It'd be terrible if we didn't save the last of those tomatoes."

She shouts, "Yes. Yes. Now be quiet, we have company."

She whispers to Kevin, "You know where to find him, on the sun porch. I'll go into the kitchen and fix you some apple cider."

Kevin walks back through the cozy home. The old man is sitting in his chair reading the Bible and sipping on a Scotch. He nervously smiles when the rookie enters. He sits down on the calico covered sofa.

In a minute, Martha comes back with fresh apple cider. Kevin takes the cool glass and raises the dark, brown liquid to his mouth. It is sour and sweet at the same time.

Kevin asks, "Did you get this from Orchard Farm?"

She smiles and says, "Isn't it delicious?"

"This is great."

Martha says, "I'm glad you like it. They make the best cider. And this is the best time of year to get it. Fresh from the press."

Kevin looks over at Maynard. He is working hard to put a dent in his Scotch.

Kevin thinks that maybe he should give him some more time before he launches into his investigation.

Kevin asks Martha, "How long have you lived in Lyons?"

She looks up at the sky and moves her lips as if she is counting the years.

She says, "Fifty-one years. I met Maynard at my childhood church in Kansas. He was a handsome, young preacher, and I was a dull farm girl. We moved east when Maynard received his first church. I've been Mrs. Baynes ever since. And we've never left Lyons."

Maynard speaks up, "Dull? Ha, you were and are the most beautiful woman I've ever met."

Kevin guesses it is time.

Kevin asks, "Sir, what can you tell me about Dale Horton?"

Maynard looks as if he has just seen Beelzebub rise up from hell. He grabs his decanter and pours in more Scotch. He swirls the buttercup-colored alcohol with his forefinger so that the ice will melt faster. His eyes follow the swirling ice cubes, but no answer comes from his mouth.

Kevin prods, "Come on, Maynard, what do you think of Dale. He goes to your church doesn't he?"

The old man shakes his head yes.

Martha protests, "Please leave my husband alone."

"Madame, the last time I left him alone, you told me a lie about Keith. That boy could have gone to jail because I left your husband alone. I don't want to upset you; I only want the truth. Please."

Maynard sips his Scotch, remaining silent.

Kevin thinks, what would Maynard have to gain by keeping his mouth shut? Maybe, if the rookie pretends to know the truth, the priest will break down.

Kevin bitterly says, "Our good priest, Maynard, doesn't want to give up the Hortons and their kind because of all the church donations he'll miss! Isn't that so? Stop fiddling with your drink and answer."

Maynard's big eyes look up at Kevin. The priest shakes his head yes.

Kevin continues with his fake wrath: "And so, you and your wife decided to point me towards a poor kid, who knew Doug, to keep me away from Dale, the real murderer. Why, that's despicable. How could a priest and his wife lie?"

His low voice moans, "Dale and his friends are my best worshippers. I heard rumors they were mixed up in that ghastly killing. But, Keith and his friends scare us. They're like wild animals. If they didn't kill Doug, then find something else to arrest them on."

"Sir, I'm sorry, but I can't go arresting people just because you, your wife and your well-mannered friends don't like Keith's kind. To be honest, I'm not too fond of Keith, either, but I have to deal with it. So must you. Good day."

Chapter 12

Kevin gets up and walks out into the cool Michigan air. The boy across the yard has made a few piles of leaves since the agent went into talk with Maynard. Kevin drives back to the motel. He calls Mrs. Johnson for directions to their house so that he can attend tonight's Men's Group.

She says that he will have to go up South Lyons Road about a mile. She gives to him their house number. She also invites the agent for supper. Kevin, thinking that the more he knows about Dale's friends the better, says that he will be happy to come.

Tim knocks on Kevin's door.

"Tim, come in. What happened?"

Tim pulls out his notebook and says, "I recorded Gus' confession. His father did catch him buying drugs from Doug Richards."

"Great, tell me Gus' exact words."

Tim says, "OK. First, Principal Vernon had Gus come by between classes. I met with Gus in private. I told the boy that I was your partner and that he was in big trouble. I didn't say why. I just let Gus come to his own conclusions."

The rookie says, "That's smart. Then what?"

"The boy said that he was very sorry that he wrecked your car. He said that he and some friends were out cruising because his parents went into Madison to a friend's dinner party. The Panthers had won the game and he and Doug Seal were out celebrating with LiLynn and Suzy. Anyway, he wasn't paying attention to the road, probably because he had a few beers, first at Lou's Place, then in some cornfield.

"Anyway, he was driving along, when he saw his father's cigarettes on the console. He picked them up and was concentrating on tearing off the tab for his workout suit. He said that he wasn't watching the road. Finally, he got the tab off and threw the cigarettes into the ditch. That was when he saw you. He didn't want to stop because he didn't want to get in trouble.

"Gus then let out a big sigh. That was when I told him that, that wasn't the reason I was interviewing him. I told Gus that the bureau already knew the car that ran Agent Sir off the road was a Miata. That was when Gus started to get nervous. He rubbed his palms across his pants.

"I asked him about Doug Richards. Stressing that if he didn't tell the truth, we were going to arrest him for drunk driving. He confessed that this past summer, he had been grounded because he had been caught with Doug Richards, smoking pot and drinking beer. Gus said that his dad was furious.

"I said, well, can't your dad understand what it's like being a kid, especially in Lyons?

"Gus said no because his dad is a devout Christian."

Tim closes his notebook and smiles at Kevin.

Agent Tim Maxwell says, "We're getting close."

"Good job. That's great."

"Hey, Kevin, you told Mr. Tapestry that you're off to the Men's Group tonight. What's that?"

"They're a Christian organization. Dale's the leader. He invited me to come. The meeting should be a good opportunity to see how these men really act. I'm going to go over to the Johnson's a little early for supper."

"Sounds like a plan, but be careful."

"They're Christians!"

"Tell that to Doug Richards."

Kevin drives up to a nice, long one-story home that looks as if it was built about five years ago. There are some large oak trees in the front. They still have all their green leaves attached to the branches.

Mrs. Johnson ushers Kevin into her modern home. She says that her husband is outside putting the cover on their swimming pool. She leads Kevin through a series of rooms. They walk out to the pool's long concrete deck. Mr. Johnson is leaning over, struggling with a large piece of blue canvas.

Kevin asks, "Hello Mr. Johnson. May I give you a hand with your pool cover?"

His tan face broadly grins, revealing a genuine smile.

"You betcha! I've been fighting this damn tarp all afternoon. I swear it shrinks a little every season. Either that, or I'm getting older!"

Kevin helps Mr. Johnson tack down the covering. In a half an hour, they are finished. They are both a little sweaty. Mr. Johnson asks Kevin to come into the kitchen for some ice tea. Kevin gratefully accepts. The short host waddles his way through the glass doors. The agent follows him into his home.

He yells, "Honey, where's the ice tea?"

She rushes in and says, "You know where, in the fridge."

He looks back at the agent and laughs, "Oh yeah. Of course."

Mr. Johnson is a good-looking man. He has got a full-head of black hair with streaks of gray. His face looks as if it is just waiting to laugh out loud. His bulbous stomach looks unafraid to welcome a large piece of cheesecake whenever one is in the neighborhood. Even though it is the day before Halloween, he is wearing madras shorts. His tanned calves are huge.

Kevin drains the ice tea from his glass and sets it down. He is now ready to bait Mr. Johnson.

"Mmmm, that was good, almost as good as Horton's coffee."

Mr. Johnson smiles and says, "He sure makes a good pot of coffee."

"Yes, when I was over for dinner, I must have had four, or five cups. And Gail's pot roast was divine."

Mr. Johnson smiles.

He says, "Well, right now we're having spaghetti."

"Sounds good."

The three adults sit down and enjoy an authentic Italian meal, complete with non-alcoholic grape juice.

Mrs. Johnson asks, "Agent Sir, may I ask you a personal question?"

"Of course."

"Do you enjoy your job?"

Kevin lies, "It's hard to be a Christian when you have to deal with crime and the filth on a daily basis. Part of my job is dealing with the druggies and drunkards. They're a sad bunch."

Mr. Johnson says, "You sound a lot like Dale. He can't stand them, either. None of us can. They're a disgrace. They don't work. They raise hell. They're not good for the community image."

"I know what you're saying, Brother. I mean, here I had Keith dead to rights. And Mr. Tapestry practically lets him go. Your mayor let a boozehound, a dope addict, and God knows what else, walk out the door!"

Mr. Johnson says, "Keith isn't like you and me. You and I know that being a man means abstaining from booze, working hard, building a family, and going to church. You can't just do some of those things and neglect the rest. Being a man means sacrifice. Tonight, you'll see who makes up the real backbone of Lyons."

Supper is over and one by one a well-dressed man walks into Mr. Johnson's home. Mr. Johnson gets up to meet his guests. Agent Sir excuses himself and heads to the bathroom to collect his thoughts.

After a few minutes of splashing water on his face, he dries off and opens the bathroom door. He follows the sound of men's voices and laughter down to Mr. Johnson's den.

The rookie walks down the basement stairs into a richly furnished room and is immediately greeted by all the men. He cannot believe how nice everyone is at the moment. He is handed some coffee and told by the group that he is always welcome here.

Kevin thinks that this collection of men is similar to a gas fireplace—all looks, no real warmth.

Dale calls the meeting to order. They have a prayer and then every man goes around the room telling his woes and getting encouragement from the group. When it comes to Kevin, he reiterates to the group what he told Mr. Johnson, about his disgust of drug dealers. The crowd applauds. The agent thanks them for their hospitality. The meeting comes to a close with another prayer.

The Men's Group breaks up for the night and the men get up to go. One member Derrick Palmer remains seated, praying to God for the strength to manage three farms and for the courage to keep silent about Dale's crime.

Agent Sir walks up to Derrick and pats him on the shoulder.

The rookie says, "You know that we need to talk."

Derrick opens his eyes, looks up at the M.B.I. agent and shakes his head yes.

The successful, young farmer says, "Meet me in the field behind Chestnut II. Tomorrow we'll be cutting down corn back there."

Derrick gets up, thanks Mr. Johnson and Dale and leaves.

Kevin does likewise and goes out to his car. He drives back to the motel.

Kevin knocks on Tim's door, #107.

Tim is watching football on ESPN and drinking a soda.

"Tim, do you want to go to Lou's Place for a few beers? I need to wash down my disgust for those so-called Christians in a big way."

"Sure, I thought you'd never ask."

Kevin and Tim go to the bar and order a couple pitchers of beer.

After a few glasses of beer, Kevin asks, "Tim, you've never told me. What's your religious stance?"

"Agnostic, with a capital 'A'. What about you?"

"I am more of a believer. I believe a Supreme Being exists. I just wish He'd show up more often and give me more guidance. So, what do you think? Do you think the Men's Group did it?"

"Sure sounds like it. I don't understand how they can call themselves Christians when they can't turn the other cheek to a minor problem like drugs. Do they think they're doing the world a favor by murdering them. This is why I am so confused about religion."

Tim asks, "Kevin, are you going to call Peg tonight?"

"Maybe."

Kevin takes a sip of beer.

Tim rubs his hand across the dirty table and says, "I've thought a lot about what you said concerning money corrupting people."

"Yes?"

"Well, it makes sense. And do you know who is at fault?"

"Who?"

"Advertising agencies. Advertising fuels society's decay. Advertising creates an abnormally high level of demand. It goads consumers into desiring more products and services than they truly need or can afford. Does not advertising plants seeds of greed, telling people that they are unfulfilled unless they buy, buy, buy? And what if a person cannot buy, buy, buy?"

Kevin jokes, "That's what credit cards are for."

"Very funny. No, these frustrated consumers take it upon themselves to break the law. They become criminals so that they can illegally obtain the money to buy, buy, buy.

"Greed destroys those on the edge who are too weak to abandon thoughts of caviar when they can only afford Wonder Bread."

"Well put. But, let's go. We have a big day tomorrow."

Tim and Kevin leave Lou's and drive back to their motel rooms for a solid night's sleep. Inside the rookie's room his message is blinking. He retrieves his message from Peg. It's a simple one that sounds very remorseful. Kevin picks up the phone to call Peg then sets it back down on its cradle. He's too upset and ashamed to call her back.

Friday morning comes and both agents awake around 6 a.m. Each one trying to best the other decides to go for a run before the day begins. Tim's short legs struggle to match Kevin's long stride, but Agent Maxwell's big heart more than compensates for Kevin's superior athletic ability. They race across the parking lot at the end of their seven-mile run. Kevin beats Tim by a few steps. Sweating and smiling, they go into their respective rooms for showers.

Tim gets dressed and walks over to Kevin's room. Kevin finishes dressing into a pair of Levis, a white Ralph Loren Polo shirt and his favorite Sperry boat shoes.

Tim says, "Time to check in with the boss."

"Yes."

Kevin dials the M.B.I. office.

There is a series of clicks, and then Jim says, "Hello, Sergeant Caretaker."

"Sir, it's Kevin."

"Agent, what's up?"

"Tim and I think we got our man. It's Dale Horton. Local businessman. He's a Christian, who lynched a kid because the kid broke one of Dale's commandments."

Jim says, "From what I understand about Christianity, you're supposed to forgive people, not kill them because of what they don't believe."

"Exactly, but Dale Horton's gospel is twisted. He judges non-believers and coerces them into submission. If they don't yield, he murders them. He caught his son Gus entering into the world of drugs. Then Dale killed Gus' supplier—Doug Richards, who was really just a user himself, occasionally selling a dime bag for pocket change. The whole thing is a waste."

"Well son, you had a lot of balls figuring this one out. Good job."

"Sergeant Caretaker?"

"Yes?"

"The Academy never taught me how to do this."

"Son, my job is to retrain you and to teach you the lessons of the street. Kevin think of yourself as a "hot shot," firefighters who skydive into the middle of blazing forest fires. When a wall of fire is bearing down on them, the first thing they do is to start a bunch of little brush fires. That way, the main fire has nothing to consume. When you, as a M.B.I. agent, go into a strange situation, like Lyons, by yourself, you need to show people that you're capable of a little violence, so that the bigger violence is thwarted.

"Lyons is like the town I grew up in Southern Georgia. The law couldn't do anything about crime unless they pulled out their batons and started breakin' heads.

"Kevin, you've tapped into your Cimmerian side."

"My what side?"

"Your dark side.

"You see Kevin, when you're working a case by yourself, you have to rely on different parts of your psyche to get the job done. You're mentally playing badminton between your good and bad sides. Only you can determine which side wins depending upon the situation.

"I think you've proved your mettle. Tell Agent Maxwell to hurry and wrap this case up. We've got a lot more crimes to solve."

"Yes sir."

Jim hangs up.

Kevin releases the phone and looks back towards Tim.

Tim asks, "How'd it go."

"Good. Sergeant Caretaker is a smart guy, isn't he?"

"Very."

Tim and Kevin get into Tim's car and drive out to talk with Derrick Palmer. They turn into the Chestnut II's driveway.

Kevin sees a red pickup truck down by the last barn before the huge empty field. He drives towards it. He parks and gets out of the car. There is a strong manure smell in the air. Pigs squeal inside the low-lying barn. Kevin walks to the side entrance with Tim in tow.

There is a narrow walkway covered with manure. A thick wooden plank juts out of the doorway leading up to a manure spreader, a machine that farmers tow behind their tractors across their fields to effectively dispose of animal waste. A man with a blond beard and stained teeth swears as he hauls a load of manure-soaked straw in a wheelbarrow up the plank and dumps it into the machine. He turns Kevin's way and then grins.

He chucks the empty wheelbarrow off into the weeds and hops down into the manure and mud in front of Kevin, splashing the goo over the rookie's pants and shoes. Kevin looks down at the mess he has just created. The pig-man does not seem to care because his whole body is covered with the stuff.

Kevin gruffly asks, "Where can I find Derrick?"

The man turns around and goes into the building. Kevin and Tim follow him into the stinky barn. The ammonia-like smell shoots up their nostrils as they enter.

Even though it is late fall, when all the bugs should be dead, or dying, there are thousands of plump black flies buzzing about. The sound of the pigs' squealing is deafening. A dirty radio blares Ozzy Osbourne. The man goes over to it and turns it down. He lights a cigarette and stands back as if to say, "If you want to ask me a question then do it in my home, even if it is a Superfund Cleanup Site."

Kevin asks again, "Where is Derrick?"

"In the back."

"How can I get there?"

He says, pointing a smelly finger at Kevin, "Take the road through the compound then along side North Lyons Road. It'll cut straight through the field. Take it to the woods. You'll probably have to wait until they're done making a pass."

As he finishes, a loud squeal comes from one of the pens. The men walk over and see that a sow has stepped through one of her piglets, crushing the baby with her hoof. The pig-man picks it up and examines the tiny beast. Then he walks over to the door and pitches the dead piglet into the manure spreader.

Kevin and Tim walk out and take in deep breaths. Tim looks at Kevin as if to say, "Let's get the hell out of here."

They walk towards their car and drive off, following the pig-man's instructions. The ride is very bumpy, but everything he said is right. In about fifteen minutes, they are at the point in the field where the corn stubble and the standing corn meet.

In front of them is a muddy semi with long trailer behind it. Behind the two agents is the farm from where they just came. It looks very small. The shiny, steel silos look similar to a woman's sewing thimbles. Kevin cannot make out North Lyons Road.

Down the cornrow, a combine is munching the standing corn and spewing out kernels into a dump truck. Corn dust hovers over the two machines and moves with them, as if it is the same dust cloud that follows Pigpen in the *Peanuts* comic strip. Kevin sits on the hood of Tim's car, waiting for Derrick to materialize.

The combine chugs closer.

Kevin can make out the blades in front of the machine. They pull the corn stalks inside. The machine cuts the plants close to the ground. Inside the machine, the stalks are shucked and the corn is stripped from the corn-cobs.

The loud and angry looking machine eats its way closer and closer. The blades come within feet of Kevin. The machine goes into neutral. The blades stop, but the machine continues to run. Kevin waves up at the driver to come down.

Derrick steps out. His head and eyebrows are covered in white corn dust.

Kevin looks up at the windshield of the dump truck. Keith is driving. Derrick motions for Kevin to come up into the combine's cab.

Kevin jumps up the metal ladder, climbs in and shuts the door. They take off and start harvesting another row of corn. Derrick reaches up to the stereo overhead and turns down a Barbra Streisand tune.

Derrick concentrates on going straight while saying, "The Men's Group is taking the law into its own hands. Someone's got to stop this drug epidemic before it reaches a new generation of kids, like mine."

The rookie prods, "So, you condone violence?"

"Yes, in a way."

"What about Doug Richards? Did Dale do it?"

"Yes."

"Derrick, you're a real son of a bitch. I don't get it. Your precious Men's Group says they do good, but they don't. It's similar to this whole Christianity circus: Christians beat each other up during the week then say their peace on Sunday for forgiveness so that they won't feel guilty. What about the guy with a fish symbol on the bumper of his car who cuts you off in traffic? What about the nice, Christian guy who says that you're his friend then undermines you to your boss in order to get your job? What about the ministers who sleep with boys? It's all the same."

Derrick stops the combine and screams, "It's not. Jesus accepts everyone the way they are: sinners. We have to believe in Him for redemption. In Jesus' eyes, you're no better than a Dale who murdered 1,000 Doug Richards. Until you come off your high horse and stop trying to figure everything out with your brain, Jesus won't accept you. Dale screwed up. But if he says to Jesus, 'Jesus, I screwed up, please forgive me,' then Jesus will. But he won't even lift an eyelash for you in spite of all your good works because you don't love Him. That's the real crime here—your lost soul."

"So that's how you really feel. Derrick I can't see how your religion can make me a better person. And I certainly don't see how your religion is going to save Dale Horton from going to prison. Good bye."

Kevin fumbles for the latch and opens the door.

Derrick yells, "It's better to spend twenty years in prison here on earth then to spend an eternity in hell."

Derrick slams the door.

Kevin jumps to the ground and runs back to his car.

Tim is kicking at the corn stubble.

Tim knowingly asks, "Things didn't go well between you and Derrick, did they?"

"No."

The two men get into Tim's car.

The rookie says to the seasoned veteran, "Derrick just said that Dale did it."

"Good, now all we have to do is squeeze Dale at tonight's party."

"Exactly."

"Say, did you ever call Peg?"

"No. I guess I'm still upset. Besides I'm sure we'll be out of this town soon."

"Where to now?"

"What time is it?"

"10 a.m."

"Let's go talk to Gus Horton one last time."

The two agents drive to Panther High and pull Gus out of Algebra II. They take him outside. The three of them walk to the back and sit on the bleachers facing the football field.

"Gus, do you know why we're here?"

"Yea. I had a feeling you'd figure it out."

"Can you tell me what happened?"

"Everything I've told you before is true. Doug did sell me some pot, and Dad did find out. He was so angry. He kept saying he'd get Doug and his no good friends. I became suspicious of him when I got back from a scary movie, 'Fun House,' in Madison. He was sitting on the couch and sweating, as if he had just worked out, or something, which was weird because dad never exercises.

"I said goodnight. I was hanging my coat up there in the foyer when I

noticed a lot of mud on Dad's wingtips. There was a piece of vine hanging from one heel with ivy leaves on it. I could think of only one place where ivy grows around here, back by the old graveyard a half a mile away.

"I told my buddies about it. So, after football practice we went back there and found the bloody pitchfork in some weeds. It wasn't hard to find because of all the broken vegetation around the site. I made the guys promise not to say anything. We brought it home. It's in the garage, in my sports' chest."

Tim asks, "May we have it?"

Gus nods yes.

The men get up and walk down the bleachers. They get into Tim's Contour and drive to the Horton's household. Luckily, Gail is off shopping. Gus unlocks the security gate and then the ornate wooden door. He turns off the alarm system.

They walk through the kitchen and through a door leading to the garage. Gus rummages through a large wooden box, tossing hockey sticks, aluminum bats and frisbees to the floor. At the bottom is the pitchfork. He hands it to Kevin.

In the dark garage, Kevin places his hand on Gus' shoulder and asks, "What else?"

The darkness seems to ease Gus' confession. He begins to cry.

Through his sobs he says, "Shortly after our discovery, I asked dad if he'd

ever kill anyone for doing drugs? And he looked me in the eyes and without blinking said that he already had. But that Jesus would protect him and me.

"He said, 'It's time for normal people to protect their families and communities from the druggies.' At first, I was dazed. But then it made sense.

"I mean, I've always hated the longhairs at Panther High, they're worthless, and they always disrupt class. Then, you showed up. I got to thinking again that what dad did was wrong. I want to do what's right, like you do. I love my father, but what he did was wrong."

Tim asks, "Son, will you do us a favor?"

"Of course."

"We still need to confront your father. Will you promise not to say anything to anybody until our case is over?"

"Yes, of course."

"Do you want us to drive you back to school?"

"Yeah, I don't want to miss football practice today. We're scrimmaging."

The agents wrap the pitchfork in plastic garbage bags and put it in their trunk. Then they drive back to Panther High and drop Gus off. The agents drive into Lyons for a quick bite and to talk with Jerod. Starla and the sheriff are anxious to hear what Jerod said, but the agents tell them that they just wanted to clear up some details.

They then drive to Dr. Fortune's and give her their special plastic-wrapped package and hold a secret meeting with her in the coffee room. She agrees to help. The three of them coordinate their lab findings with the M.B.I.'s laboratory in Ann Arbor. The afternoon wanes and it's time to go to Chestnut Hill Farm's annual harvest party.

Chapter 13

Kevin and Tim go back to their respective motel rooms to clean up. Each agent showers and puts on new clothes. The air having become cooler this day, Kevin puts on his warm, chocolate corduroys, a cream Irish wool fisherman's sweater and Gore-Tex leather Timberline walking shoes.

The agents get back into Tim's car and drive to Chestnut Hill Farm. When they crest the hill just after Maynard's home, Kevin sees hundreds of people milling in front of the Palmer Mansion.

Seeing that the residence driveway is filled to capacity with pickup trucks, Kevin pulls into the worker's entrance. He drives along side the whitewashed fence and finds a place to park the car near the feed lot, next to a small building with a mammoth metal scale used to weigh cattle.

Kevin and Tim hurriedly get out and lock the doors. They walk across the compound to the sound of mooing cows.

Usually, Kevin smells cowshit in this compound, but the late-afternoon breeze is keeping down the stench. The men have cleaned up the compound. All of Mr. Tapestry's tractors are neatly lined up. The messy tool shed is even straightened. Someone has taken a weed-eater to all the weeds growing near the buildings.

Kevin walks in front of a pen of sheep. A new pitchfork rests next to the gate. The biggest animal steps up to him. He puts out his hand. Its teeth nibble at his fingers. Then Kevin pats the animal's head, stroking the wool down its back. Kevin pulls back his hand because the animal's fleece is coated with something. Of course, lanolin, the stuff they put into moisturizing cream. Kevin wipes it on his corduroys.

He looks down at the gravel road and walks by the bushes and fountains. Firmly, he and Tim stride by the residence and past clumps of people who are socializing. They pass the garage, patio and the house and take a right onto the front lawn. As they turn the corner, a wonderful smell fills their nose. It is a mixture of smoke and roasting pig covered in spicy sauce. They look over, unable to resist the temptation to see how the beast is being cooked.

A blackened oil drum has been cut in half, long ways. It has had hinges welded onto it. Spinning in its metal guts, a burnt pig horizontally pirouettes. The beast has been skewered with a long spike. It was driven into its mouth down through its hindquarters. Next to the pit is a large man, Arlo, who ushered Tapestry's cattle into his semi for a quick trip to Baum's, in overalls thickly spreading red sauce on the animal with a crusty paintbrush.

After he is done, he steps back and takes a gulp of lemonade—spiked with Jack Daniels—from a jelly glass. He looks at his friends, whom are similarly large, resembling human hogs standing on two hooves. They all laugh, snort, talk and drink.

There are three, large, convention-sized tables pushed together next to the barbecue pit. On them is a sea of Tupperware bowls filled with yellow and green coleslaw. Fat women drape over the containers and peel away plastic wrap.

Kevin and Tim walk back towards the garage. Across the driveway and about a quarter of mile away is a huge stack of wood. Some men are setting down brown paper bags filled with candles to mark a path from the house to the site of the bonfire.

Kevin and Tim walk up the patio steps into the kitchen.

Kevin sees Em.

She smiles and halts—The plate of deviled eggs she is carrying almost comes out of her hands. Her soft, black hair is tightly pulled back off her forehead. She is wearing a white turtleneck, a dark blue vest and checkered wool slacks. A long string of pearls falls down to her bosom.

She looks down at his large hands and says, "You don't have a drink."

Kevin asks, "You're right. Do you have a beer?"

"Of course, that's one of my Dad's biggest stipulations. The Chestnut Hill's harvest party must have martinis, and plenty of them! There's also beer. The keg is out by the pool, next to the wet bar. I'll join you in a minute. And Kevin…"

"Yes?"

"Derrick is sorry for having lost his temper today. He's waiting outside to talk to you."

"Thanks. Em?"

"Yes?"

"This is Agent Tim Maxwell. He came in from Ann Arbor yesterday to help. Would you mind if he asks you some questions?"

"No, not at all."

Tim and Kevin split up.

Tim goes with Em; Kevin walks outside.

Tim smiles at his beautiful, country host.

Tim says, "You have a very nice home. I think we could fit three of our homes in here."

Em pushes back a strand of black hair and asks, "Would you like to see it?"

Not wanting to be rude, Tim says, "Sure."

He hopes, though, that Em gives him the "Reader's Digest" version of a home tour. Being polite is one thing; being incompetent is quite another.

Em laughs and says, "Don't worry I won't keep you long."

They pass the sink, the stove, the phone and a huge chunk of wood on four legs.

"What's this?"

"It's a butcher's block. Derrick and I bought it from an old farmer who had us over for dinner. It was sitting in his barn; covered with red paint. Derrick striped the paint off and stained it. We use it for decoration, but a long time ago they used it for cutting apart chickens, flanks of beef and pork ribs. Derrick and I had one heck of a time getting it in here. It must weigh 300 lbs."

Tim says, "Huh."

From the kitchen, they go left, past the wet bar.

"This is our dining room. The oriental rug was sent to us from my parents when they visited China while travelling around the world. Every piece in here is an antique. This table is lovely, isn't it?"

Tim agrees. The dining room belongs in *Homes & Gardens*. It is that perfect. Wood walls circle the oval room. From the mural painted on the ceiling, angels with long, brass horns bless Em and Derrick's dinner guests. Burgundy velvet curtains drape between the room's many windows.

Tim states, "This room has a lot of arched windows."

Em smiles and says, "That's correct. The dining room has more windows than any other room in our house because it had to capture as much evening light as possible back when gas light and wax candles were terribly expensive, even for the gentry."

She quickly changes the subject and asks, "Are you married?"

The agent raises his hand and shows off a simple gold band around his ring finger.

She asks, "That's wonderful. Do you have children?"

"Yes, every time I come home from assignment it seems another child has popped up. I can't even keep count anymore."

Em laughs and says, "You and Derrick have a lot in common. He loves kids."

They walk through the dinning room into the living room, which is also accessible from the kitchen.

Em says, "We're particularly proud of this room because Derrick had to re-plaster the walls. Unlike dry wall that you just hammer into wood studs, plaster takes a careful hand to set into place. It took Derrick months to do."

Again, as Tim looks around, there are many expensive antiques adorning the room, such as their one-of-a-kind, green horse-hair couch from Spain.

He asks, "Em, where did you get all these old furnishings? They're exquisite."

Em says, "My great aunt, my Father's sister, owns the finest antique store in the area. You have probably seen her shop in town. It's nestled between the Cafe and Farmers Insurance. People come from all over to Lyons, just to shop at her store. She has been giving me antiques since I was a little girl. Some are on loan."

"Where does your aunt find them?"

"Our family has lived in this area for hundreds of years. She has many old friends that have either died, or move to places like Orlando. When they do, Aunt Jude buys them. She's the first one there, so she gets the best."

Em continues, "This whole countryside is very special to me. Besides attending the University of Michigan for four years and teaching kindergarten in Chicago for two years, I've lived in Lyons my whole life. I love it. This house is over 200 hundred years old. Sometime, Derrick should show you the basement. This place is built on beams that must be four-feet in diameter."

She shows the veteran agent the playroom with a large TV and video games, the downstairs' bathroom and Derrick's library. Derrick's library has a large, turn-of-the-century, French mahogany desk facing the front yard. The room is painted dark green. On the far wall is a built-in bookcase filled with many novels from the authors Hugo, Shakespeare and Benjamin Franklin, etc.

In the middle of the bookcase next to some bottles of Scotch and crystal glasses is a spot for a small, brown book. Above the book, a brass light illuminates the piece of work. The title reads *The Cracklebarrel.*

"What's this?"

Em says, "That is Derrick's history book about this area. He and a few other local authors penned it to preserve the area's past. It's full of fascinating tidbits. Would you like a copy?"

Stunned about Derrick having written a book while still managing the time to farm and rebuild the house, Tim says, "Derrick is an amazing man. I can't wait to meet him."

Em stands underneath the doorframe. She looks divine. She tosses her head back and laughs.

Em says, "I know, Derrick is quite the gentleman farmer. He's also on the school board. The county elected him last year. He's got one year left. And he's also on our church's vestry."

"Yes, I'd like a copy."

Em walks to the desk and pulls Derrick's book out of a box. She hands it to Tim.

"Thank you."

"Would you like to see the upstairs?"

Not wanting to seem impolite, the agent says, "Of course!"

They exit the study and immediately turn right. They climb up the long, narrow staircase.

Em says, "This is Scott's room."

It is filled with quilts and stuffed animals. They walk down the hallway into the master bedroom. On the rust painted floor are images of abstract flowers.

"What are these?"

Em says, "I painted them. Well, actually I stencilled them."

The pattern goes around the room about a foot from the floorboard. It is very quaint. On the dresser nearest to Tim is a photo of Em framed in silver. It is her wedding-day picture. It is very elegant. Em's hair is pushed up and her face and neck are very white. Tim looks away.

Off the master bedroom is a small washroom with a toilet and sink. On the far side of the room is a large, dark dresser, which must be Derrick's. They walk past the bed, which is covered with an intricate cotton spread. They walk into the next hallway. On the walls are various framed photos of the family skiing in Vail, on the beach in Oahu and in front of the Eiffel

Tower in Paris.

Em says, "This is Steven's room. He's our oldest."

There are many finely built airplane models hanging on fish wire from the ceiling. The bed is made. There is a gerbil cage near the window. They walk across the hall.

Em says, "This PJ's room."

The room is bigger than Steven's. There is a huge sleigh bed in the middle. There is a poster of John Elway, the Bronco's quarterback, on the wall.

They head down another narrow staircase. At the landing, they take a short left, stepping down a few more steps. Em opens the door and soon they are back in the kitchen.

Clutching Derrick's history book, Tim says, "Thank you. You have a very, very nice home."

Em broadly smiles.

As Tim is taking a tour of the Palmer Mansion, Kevin heads towards the bar. He silently closes the screen door and looks out at the social scene. There are many people here, all of whom he does not recognize. All the shrubs are neatly trimmed. Geraniums in red clay pots are everywhere.

Twelve kegs of beer are stacked up near the one that is in ice. People are filling their cups. Close by is a young man dressed in a white coat and bow tie. He is standing behind a long table with a white linen draped over it. He is busy pouring drinks into crystal-looking plastic cups.

This whole scene is something Kevin would expect in Ann Arbor, at one of Peg's friend's homes. Somehow, Derrick, Em and Mr. Tapestry have transported a bit of the city into Lyons.

Kevin walks over to the keg for a cup of beer. He downs it and walks back to the bar for a Scotch to sip on while he talks to people. Kevin walks around the pool. He bumps into Sheriff Sackett. The man's hair well-groomed and his eyeglasses are spotless. He is law and order's window dressing. Kevin holds out his hand and shakes his soft, white palm.

The rookie says, "I had a talk with Derrick. I will need you soon to help bring in Doug's killer. Are you up to it?"

The sheriff nods his head yes.

Kevin asks, "So, who are you here with?"

He quickly responds, "My wife Sue."

"Where is the better half?"

He points towards a small group of fat women dressed in flowered tents for shirts and brown rayon slacks.

John relaxes a little and says, "She's over there. I'll introduce you."

He walks ahead of Kevin in a jumpy sort of way. As the two peace officers approach the crowd, the women hush up. The sheriff stands next to a nondescript lump of clay—his wife. Kevin nods to her, politely.

Kevin addresses everyone: "Hello ladies. Nice party."

A long pause goes by unanswered.

Finally, John's wife speaks up: "Yes, it's quite a highfalutin affair. I guess Derrick and Em are the lucky ones, with the pool and big party. They're very nice to invite everyone. Must have cost a lot, though."

Kevin looks at Sue as if she has just "broken the ice" with a sledgehammer.

Kevin thinks that, that was an ungrateful thing to say.

He takes a gulp of Scotch.

The sheriff says, "Agent Sir, this is Mrs. Sackett. You can call her Sue."

Sue smells like Charmin toilet paper.

Kevin tries breathing in his Scotch to knock out her powdery odor.

Sue says, "John says you're here to get the Richards' killer."

Her fat face is smooth like butter. Her black hair is done up in a cone shape.

She continues, "You know, my boys never did drugs like the Richards' boy did."

Kevin looks around at the other women cows, and they all nod in agreement.

She continues, "That's right, my boys are all good athletes, and they don't too bad at school neither. We work hard for our house and all the things we got. I'm proud of my family."

She looks at John, and they exchange smiles.

Someone shouts, "Kevin!"

Kevin looks around.

Derrick trots up to Sue's circle. He is grinning from ear to ear.

He says, "Hey buddy, I'm glad you made it."

Kevin leaves the ladies and John staring at their ice teas.

Kevin says, "Hey, nice party."

Derrick, "Have you tried the barbecue yet?"

"In a second."

"Listen, Kevin about this afternoon…"

"Look, forget it. My folks feel the same way as you. They're always pressuring me to take religion more seriously. I just don't get it at this point in my life. I mean I try and communicate with God, but I never get an answer. It's like when Peg takes me to a museum and she asks me to tell her about what I see in some abstract painting. To me, it just looks like a bunch of colors randomly smeared on an otherwise good piece of canvas. It just doesn't speak to me. Sorry."

Derrick broadly smiles as if he's heard it all before, saying, "Don't worry, your time will come. Now, what about Dale?"

"Well, I know he's your friend, but Tim and I have to arrest him. The sooner the better. After some dinner, we'll move in. Agent Tim Maxwell is in talking to your wife right now. You know, Sue Sackett isn't too keen about this party."

Derrick frowns, and bluntly says, "Oh, to hell with her. Sue and her kind think that because they've lived in this town for centuries, they can make Em and I miserable. I think they're full of shit. Em and Sue hate one another. They grew up together. Sue really gave Em hell while she was growing up, too. Now, Sue is telling everyone in Lyons that I'm nothing but a gold digger for marrying the daughter of the largest landowner in Michigan."

"Sackett's secretary, Starla, mentioned that this place was the state's biggest."

Derrick shakes his head yes and says, "We're the biggest independent farm in Michigan; close to the biggest in the eastern Midwest. Sure, there are much bigger spreads around, but they're all owned by shareholders in New York, or bought up by Canadian and Dutch conglomerates."

"Do ever miss the city?"

"Let me put it this way: My life has been like the Bible. When I lived in the city I was acting as someone in the Old Testament: judgmental and unforgiving. Then, I moved out here to live in the country. Now, I'm acting as a man in the New Testament: full of love and forgiving. I guess you could say that my personal Jesus has been farming. I enjoy the simplicity of plowing acres and acres of soil. Besides I wasn't the greatest businessman in the world. I know I needed more out of life than pleasing clients."

"You said earlier that you were in advertising. With whom?"

"After I graduated from Michigan State, I went to work at Leo Barney, largest advertising agency in the U.S., as an account executive for Tropical Orange Juice and Unite Us Airlines."

"How'd you meet Em?"

"Couple years after college, I met Em at our local hangout—the Red Cricket, a fun piano bar. That was when I was still drinking. She and I got married and started a family. But then I got tired of the rat race, traveling eight months out of the year and meetings up the wazoo. I was drinking a lot back then, too: On the plane; the bar car on the train; in hotels, and three martini lunches.

"One Christmas vacation, Em's father offered me a job managing his land. I took it. I've been completely sober ever since.

"Besides we take enough trips to Madison to get our fill. Also, for the past few years, Em and I have taken the kids on the train to Chicago right after Thanksgiving. The crop is in and things have settled down enough to where we can spend a week, or so shopping, exploring the museums and dining out.

"Em loves the Chicago Institute of Art and all the impressionist works. The kids love the Museum of Natural History with the toy train and the dinosaurs, oh, and of course F.A.O. Schwartz. I just love watching all the businesspeople rush past me on their way to the Board of Options, or to some other high stressed, high-rise job and realizing that the corn is harvested, Christmas is around the corner and I don't have to please a manager whose main function is never to be pleased so that he can extract more out of me!

"You want to hear a funny story? Back when I was drinking, my best friend, Ron, and I were coming back one night from The Gaslight. That day, I had bought some new penny loafers from Marshall Fields. We were walking through the park to our apartment. I told Ron, I'd catch up and wanted to sit down on the bench and listen to the waves of Lake Michigan. Well, I passed out and someone ran off with my new shoes. The next morning, I walked home with a headache and bare feet. Ron hasn't let me forget that."

Kevin finishes his drink.

Tim and Em come jogging up. She puts her arms around her husband. They whisper to one another, and Derrick gets up to leave. He trots over to the bar and tells the bartender he will get more ice. Em comes over to Kevin and smiles.

She says, "Derrick works so hard, even on his off days. He's done a great job. My father is very proud of him."

Kevin's stomach rumbles.

Em smiles and says, "I know what you're thinking. Larry and Duke make some mighty fine barbecue. You and Tim go fill up your plates. We'll talk later."

The agents thank their host and walk through the crowd to the cholesterol-saturated buffet line. As surfers who paddle out to sea, the two men crash through small waves of people. They walk past the screen porch and through the entrance of the fence. They momentary stop when they round the corner—an enormous crowd is gathered. The pig is half gone.

Kevin and Tim quickly walk to the back of the food line. There is a fraught, pale mother in front of Kevin, similar to a gloomy babushka in a long line outside a sparse Moscow grocery store. A dirty baby in her weak grip struggles to break free. For support, the baby rests on her paunch. Five children of various sizes carelessly

run in and out of the line, buzzing about as big, black flies. One of her kids tumbles

in front of Kevin and knocks his legs back.

The urchin stops rolling on the ground when he sees Kevin's red face. The kid runs over and clutches his mother's dress. She turns around and, with the sad eyes of an old golden retriever, she soundlessly apologizes to Kevin.

Kevin asks Tim, "So, did you get any new information from Em?"

"No, she's totally in the dark. Derrick hasn't filled her in about Dale. The Palmer's have a lovely home, though."

As Kevin and Tim discuss the case, a group of longhairs behind the agents are trading verbal blows with slurred words. Kevin turns around.

It is Keith Spelling.

He is drunk.

Keith says, "It's the troublemaker from 'Anne Arber.' I bet if you didn't carry a gun, you wouldn't be so tough."

Kevin says, "Go away. You have had enough to drink."

"No, I won't. This is my town, my farm. Mr. Tapestry told me that he's on my side. You don't have a suspect no more. Do ya?!"

Kevin lies, "No, I guess I don't."

"Well, aren't you goin' to 'pologize to me. I'm waitin'."

"Look, I'm sorry that you lost your friend. But I'm not sorry for doing my job. I had to question everybody. I even questioned Doug's Mom."

"'Pologize, city slicker."

"OK. I'm sorry."

Kevin turns to face the food line, hoping he calmed the longhair.

A hand lands on Kevin's shoulder and it tries to turn the M.B.I. agent around.

Keith says, "'Pologize to me nicer."

Kevin grabs Keith's hand, spins it behind the attacker, wrenching the bent hand against his back. With a swift kick, Kevin cuts Keith's legs out from underneath him. Keith lands on the ground, hard. Kevin balls up his hand into a fist and slams it into Keith's nose.

Everyone at the party stops eating and looks their way.

Kevin gets down on one knee.

Kevin is breathing hard, but he manages to softly say, "Look, until I go back to Ann Arbor with Doug's killer, I'm going to be this town's personal pain in the butt. Do you understand?"

With blood gushing from his nose, Keith laments, "This town is screwed. No one gives a darn about our kind."

Kevin looks around the party. Some people keep their heads down, rather than to look him in the eye. Others look at him with a mixture of awe and mistrust. Kevin gets up and walks back to the food line. He waves to the crowd as a sign that everything's all right.

About fifteen minutes later, Kevin and Tim arrive at the food table. Kevin picks up a thin paper plate. On the long table are bowls of coleslaw, potato salad and baked beans. Some are topped with paprika, others have relish mixed into the country dishes.

Kevin takes a healthy helping of each and some green salad. He walks up to the barbecue pit and asks for some meat. The big guy in overalls solemnly nods and puts down a few thick slabs of delicious smelling roast on his plate.

Kevin and Tim hug the big maple tree next to the pit, looking for a place to sit. Everyone seems nervous about their standing here. Then a voice breaks out from one of the tables.

The voice hollars, "Agent Sir, please join us."

Mr. Horton sitting with a bunch of well-dressed folks asks Kevin to eat with him. Kevin flashes a brief smile Mr. Horton's way and walks over to his table.

Mr. Horton gloats, "Friends, as you know, this gentleman is from the M.B.I. He's going to help our fine town resolve that ghastly murder. Here, Agent Sir, sit next to me."

"Thanks. Everyone, this is Agent Tim Maxwell. He's just been assigned to the case just yesterday."

Everyone welcomes the new agent.

Kevin takes a place next to the insurance salesman. The rookie looks around the table. Every man and woman beams at him.

Mr. Horton crows, "Hey, great shot at Keith. He deserved it. He's always drunk, or high. Always trying to start something. They all are. What does my boy call 'em? Oh, yea... 'Long-hairs.' Looks like your case is on the right track. It's obvious Keith and his hoodlums are the ones. God bless America. And God bless the M.B.I.!"

Everyone around the table vigorously nods in agreement.

One lady says, "Yes, I try to keep a blind's eye towards those boys. They're nothing but trouble."

Another lady says, "I tell my boys. Look at them, that's what drugs do to you. They make you mean."

A man breaks in and says, "They don't go to college. They get drunk all the time. They're a disgrace."

Kevin thinks that he must agree with these people, mildly. These "suits" are proud of their lives, their kids and the fruits of their hard work: new cars, clean homes and money in their bank accounts. Kevin is sworn to protect their kind.

On the other hand, Kevin does not like how this group talks down to Keith and his friends. It is as if this table of people are better. Just as Sneakers warned. Kevin cannot condone Doug and Keith's lifestyle, but he still must protect their lives.

Dale preaches, "I hate these druggies. Do you know that Doug Richards even brought that filth into my home?"

Kevin says, "Is that right? You never told me."

"That's right, Doug Richards made Gus take some drugs. Gus was scared to death that Doug would stick a needle in his arm and introduce him to the Devil. The world is a better place without Doug Richards. I pray that Keith is next!"

An old, harsh voice interrupts Dale's tirade. Everyone looks up. It is Mr. Tapestry. The table falls silent.

The gentleman farmer says, "Kevin, don't believe these lucky farts. If it weren't for the Keiths of the world, these people would have to really work for a living.

"Horton, you should be ashamed of yourself for filling this M.B.I. agent here full of sunshine. You know, as well as I do, that Keith and his pals are the real citizens of Lyons. They've chosen to work the land, just as their fathers did.

"They pick rock, bale hay, slop pigs and break their backs every day. They haven't turned their backs on their heritage. You people make me sick."

With that, the Mr. Tapestry slams down his drink on the table.

He parts, by saying under his breath, "Goddamn insurance salesmen. Bunch of bankers in cheap suits."

Tapestry's large frame is propelled by long legs. They take him towards the house.

One of the ladies says, "Don't worry Dale, he's been drinking."

Horton shoots an evil look at her. Dale abruptly gets up, sliding the bench and Kevin back with him. He walks over to the pit and strikes up a heated conversation with the fat guy carving the meat. Kevin looks back at the table's occupants; they are in various states of dismay.

Mr. Johnson says, "Our mayor is somewhat right. Keith and his family are the reason this town is alive. We're a farm community. We shouldn't forget that, or else we'll become the next Madison. I live here because I can still walk out of my home and see fields and woods.

"However, this town is on the brink of becoming a success. The really big farms are in Iowa and Illinois, not Michigan. We're kidding ourselves about this heritage thing. That old man is sitting on a gold mine. He owns the whole town."

Tim asks, "And what do you do?"

He straightens his shoulders and says, "Name's Johnson. I'm in real estate. I'll wager that in five years, this town goes from a hick town to a bedroom community for Madison. People want to buy homes with lots of land to raise their kids. When they come to me with their questions, I tell them the commute is worth it. Tapestry is sitting on a fortune of property. But, he continues to farm. Lyons is bigger than a bunch of cornfields. It could house tracts of safe suburbs and a pool in every backyard."

Kevin looks down at his plate. He has barely touched his food in all the turmoil. He'd love to dive into the meal, but he feels that now is the time to put some heat on Dale, while he's still upset with Tapestry. Maybe the agent can push Dale over the edge. Kevin whispers into Tim's ear his plan. Tim nods in agreement. The rookie excuses himself.

Kevin lies, "Well, excuse me. In all this excitement, I seem to have misplaced my iced tea. I'll be right back."

Tim asks the table, "Why does the old man and Horton hate one another?"

The first outspoken woman says, "Well, it's because Dale wants to be the next mayor."

The table of diners cheers for Dale's side.

While Kevin's putting the heat on Dale, Tim diverts his table of followers with small talk.

Kevin moves in for the kill.

The agent yells, "Dale, may I have a word with you?"

The insurance agent, having lost is politeness, instigates, "Yea, yea what do you want?"

Kevin walks up to him. The agent has a good two inches on Dale.

Kevin leans down and whispers into Dale's ear: "I know you did it."

Dale clears his throat and says, "I don't like your accusation."

"I'm going all the way with this. We have witnesses who'll testify. We have a motive. And most important of all, we have the murder weapon. Tomorrow morning, as soon as our lab determines that Doug's blood was all over the weapon's tines and that we have a match of your fingerprints from a cigarette pack that Gus through out of your Miata to the ones on pitchfork's handle, I'll be over to your office in a snap with a warrant for your arrest. How do you feel about that?"

"I knew you were a no good liberal. And one more thing…"

"Yes?"

"See if Doug Richards can ever spread his filth again."

Dale turns his back to the rookie. Then he heads over to a group of large men to discuss tonight's beating of two M.B.I. agents.

Kevin walks back to get Tim. Together they walk towards the portable wet bar. The young bartender nods his head in agreement and pours Kevin another Scotch. Tim gets another beer.

The daylight is almost gone.

The large maple trees in the yard stand almost bare. There are large pockets in the trees with no leaves. The branches with leaves hold tightly onto their remaining golden offspring.

Kevin says, "Well, the cat's out of the bag."

"Yep. I saw Dale talking a mile a minute with those men over there."

"Are they his henchmen?"

"Yep. I'd get ready to rumble, as they say."

Kevin sheepishly asks, "Tim, do trees dream of spring right now, or do they relish winter?"

"They probably experience the latter. During December, they have released their burden of foliage. The trees are left alone. The winter's cold discourages curious kids from using their limbs as imaginary masts on a pirate ship. The snow has driven off squawking birds and buried annoying insects. The trees are officially closed for business. The trees cease being trees. Instead, they are large black columns hiding out inside their bark.

"The trees see the first snow as my father did when the Sunday paper arrived: Do not bother him, now. My dad stopped being dad when the Sunday paper arrived. He had become another anonymous reader hiding out in the newsprint; taking in the enormity of extraordinary, distant events that made his life seem safe."

Derrick comes over and says, "You look OK for someone who just leveled one of this town's biggest guys."

Kevin slowly nods yes.

Derrick asks, "What's wrong?"

"Looks like Dale is planning our demise."

"I heard about that. Stay cool. I'll help you two out if I can. I'll talk to you later. I've got a bonfire to prepare."

Kevin and Tim take in the approaching night. They have a couple more drinks and talk about the office and Tim's family. The air becomes colder. Then in the distance, bagpipes begin to play. Kevin lets out a sigh.

The party noise has lessened, almost in reverence for the night, the end of the harvest, the approaching winter, the hopes of a better start next spring, their thanks for this season's bounty, friendship and the quirky, yet, solemn sounds coming from the checkered bagpipes.

Kevin and Tim follow the crowd now walking towards the bon fire on the other side of the mansion. The burning fire in the middle of the field remains supreme, shooting sparks into the chilled Michigan air.

Kevin stands way back, taking in the scene, as if it is some past ritual that we humans have not been able to better, be it through religion, or technology. Fire and music are alive by themselves. Humans cannot add to their effects. We just must watch and listen. It does not captivate us so much as it catapults us into their worlds of light and sound.

Kevin walks up the lane lit by candles covered in brown paper bags. The crowd, like their cattle, shift side to side in unison. No one is breaking out to be an oddity, for this is a time to be one with everyone. The fire burns and the people stare. The music plays on and the people listen. Then, it stops.

Kevin stops, halfway up the lane. Derrick comes forward towards the crowd that is shaped like a crescent moon.

He says, "Friends, this is a time for us to be grateful. Lyons has a proud line of families and, more important, a deep commitment to the land. My family is blessed with many acres of fine, fertile soil and healthy livestock. We will always be farmers—nay, artists who create life out of nothing.

"A long time ago, the French came here and made a pact with Chief Pontiac about co-existence between the French and the Indians. I suggest we start making pacts between the factions that are destroying our community. This town is a great place to raise the Doug Richards of the world. So, we must fight this intrusion of violence. I will because this is the place that I've chosen to raise my family."

The people collectively mutter yes.

The weather has turned noticeably colder.

The crowd gathers itself to pack up and go home.

Derrick's men douse the bon fire.

Derrick tells everyone to be safe driving home. He thanks everyone for coming. Then he and Em head back up to the Palmer Mansion to begin cleaning up.

Chapter 14

The Chestnut Hills Farm annual harvest party is officially over. Kevin and Tim walk up the gravel driveway back towards their car. They talk about their plans for tomorrow's capture of Dale Horton.

Suddenly, from behind the cattle scale a half dozen men form around the two agents. They scream profanities in their direction. They are wearing bandannas over their faces.

Kevin looks at Tim and says, "Damn."

One of the attackers growls, "This is a message for you to stay away from some certain businessmen. I guess you could say it's a black and blue message."

He steps forward and takes a swing. Kevin ducks and hits him twice in the face. The agent then runs over to a smaller guy and puts him down. Soon, there are guys all around Kevin. But, he fights like a whirlwind, kicking and punching in a series of circles.

Kevin looks over at Tim. He is not doing as well. He is being overpowered by a couple of angry guys. They are on top of him. Tim's knees buckle. He is forced to lie of the pavement, while they kick and beat him. Tim's bloody face grimaces as a knife comes out of the boot of an attacker and into the agent's back. The blade ruptures his a life-sustaining organ.

Kevin screams as his friend and co-worker lies dying.

The leader of Dale's attackers curses at the assailant for killing him, but it's too late.

The leader, knowing that murder wasn't on the agenda, strikes at Kevin with all the anger he has. He realizes that he must end Kevin's life to save his own from going to prison, or worse.

Then an old truck roars through the compound, backfiring and smoking. The truck plows through the fight and separates Kevin from the angry mob.

A man inside yells, "Kevin hop in."

Kevin hops into the back of the pickup.

"Go!"

The truck's engine stops for a second, it backfires, then it roars to life. They take off, with the madmen running towards their vehicles. The chase has begun.

Kevin's driver takes a right. They take another right onto Belleview. The driver kills the headlights and they drive into Chestnut II. There is enough moonlight to make out the road cutting through the trees. The driver pulls into a barn and gets out. It is Derrick.

He says, "Quick, follow me into the house."

They crouch down and scoot out of the barn into the cold night air. They half run to the large, dark house. Derrick fumbles for the keys and opens the porch door. Then, he unlocks the inner door. The men step inside. Derrick locks the door.

He says, "Over here, in this room. There are no windows and you will be safe."

He grabs Kevin's shoulder. They fumble forward through the dark, empty house. The sound of their footsteps and heavy breathing echo throughout the unfurnished home. They finally get into the room and Derrick closes the door, shuffles with something and turns on the lights.

Kevin's blinded for a few seconds. The single bulb hanging from the ceiling comes into focus. The agent looks around and sees an empty book-case, some chairs and a folding table. There is a cot near the far wall.

"Derrick, what is this place?"

"This is where I'd come to get loaded, back when I drank a lot. I'd tell Em I had some work to do, and then I'd sneak in here. You can't tell from the road that there's anyone in here.

"I installed a darkroom curtain over the door so that no light escapes. I guess drunks will do anything to get their fix. Anyway, you'll be safe here. This house has been abandoned since Tapestry bought the farm a few years ago. Where's the other guy?"

"Tim's dead."

"Derrick lowers his handsome head and says to the ground, "Damn."

Then the farmer looks over at the wall and says, "I think there's a bottle of Scotch left over from my drinking days in that cupboard below the book-case."

Kevin finds it and opens it. He takes a big chug. He walks over and sits on the cot.

At last Kevin asks, "Derrick, why do you think people want to hurt other people?"

"Politics. People want power. When they can't get it legitimately, or fast enough, they lash out. Money is just an extension of their power. It even happens with animals. I saw this documentary about apes. The strongest one, the ape that wielded the most power, got his choice of women. Look at that book *Lord of the Flies*. Kids on an island, killing each other to establish the rank and file. Kevin, don't let it get you down. You're OK. You're safe."

Kevin leans back his head and lets it rest on the cracked windowsill. He takes another slug of Scotch and lets the warm liquid burn its way down his throat. He looks up at the high, white ceiling. He closes his eyes for a few minutes and lets the night's excitement exit his body, as if he is letting go a toy boat into a small pond. It is time for his mind to drift and relax."

"Well it looks like you've had it for the night."

"Yes, one more thing: Do you know where those guys went?"

"No. Give me your keys. I'll grab your car and park it in the barn behind this house. That way you can take off tomorrow and end this madness."

"Thanks."

"Do you need anything else?"

"No."

The wind outside pushes the boughs against the sides of the house. Some of the floor boards creak.

Derrick says, "I used to love drinking in this old house. It's always so peaceful."

"Sure you don't want a drink now?"

"No. I got to go and see if Em is all right. Don't worry, we'll get your car. Take care. Good night."

Derrick leaves. The wind gets stronger.

Kevin chugs the Scotch. He grabs a blanket. The wind is howling. The agent falls asleep clutching the wool blanket.

Morning comes. Kevin gets out of bed. His mouth feels similar to the inside of a dirty tube sock. His head rings a little. He stumbles up.

Kevin opens the curtain and door. He leaves his sanctuary into the bare living room. He looks out through one of the windows of the empty house. The wind has died down a little, but the trees still claw away at the wood siding. Big black clouds have moved into Lyons.

Kevin walks into the refrigerator-less kitchen and turns on the faucet for some water to kill his burning throat. The faucet sputters, some water comes out mixed with air. Soon the water is streaming. Kevin pushes his cupped hands into the cold water and slurps at it. He splashes some on his face.

Kevin finds Tim's car in the barn. Kevin walks across stale straw and past some dirty, old bales. A mouse darts by his feet. Kevin finds the keys under the floor mat and drives to the motel. Inside his room he jumps into the shower, shaves and brushes his teeth.

After he finishes dressing, the phone rings. It is Sheriff Sackett. He says that Tim's body has been found.

Kevin rushes out the door. He gets inside and puts the keys into the ignition. A snowflake hits the windshield. Winter has come.

Mr. Tapestry said that the Indians preached that the first snow always brought death. Kevin watches in amazement at the flakes coming down faster, melting into small droplets as they finally rest upon the windshield.

Kevin starts the car and slams the transmission into reverse, stepping as hard as he can on the accelerator. Then he throws the car into forward. He is heading towards Mrs. Richards because Sackett said Tim's body was thrown into the swamp. Kevin races through town and flies down North Lyons Road. The bare cornfields fly by him. In a few minutes, he is at the scene.

Kevin gets out behind some cars and trucks stuck in traffic because of the accident. He walks past the motorists towards a Madison Ambulance and Sackett's police car.

"Where is he?"

The sheriff looks at the ground and points to the occupied ambulance.

"Your buddy's in there."

Kevin walks up to Tim's body. It's all covered in blood, except for his bright blond hair. Kevin remembers the photo of the Maxwell family sitting on Tim's desk. They were vacationing on Mackinaw Island. It was a summer day. They were all having fun. And every Maxwell in the picture smiled beneath golden locks of bright blonde hair.

Kevin walks over to the side of road and plants himself on top of some wet weeds. He shoves his head into his hands and cries. The snow continues to fall, collecting on the top of Kevin's bent head and sliding down his neck.

No where in his job description does it read that he must witness the effects of a murdered friend. It is implied, as a native would say to me that Florida is hot in August. However, until a person climbs out of their air-conditioned car into the 110 degree heat with humidity visibly dripping from crocus plants, they do not truly realize how awful it is.

News has spread fast through Lyons that Kevin's partner has been killed.

There is a giddy crowd gathered around the bends in the road watching the scene. They view this calamity with a sense of "I'm glad it's not me."

It angers Kevin to think that they are here to get a piece of Tim when they did not even know him. Kevin knew him very well. He shared things with Tim. He told Tim things he has never told anyone. Tim told Kevin things he probably never told anyone. Their spirits meshed. A part of Kevin has died with Tim. He doesn't feel whole.

What about Peg? She and Kevin have spent much more time together than Tim and Kevin ever shared. Now, that she has cheated on him, Kevin's first thought was getting a divorce. In fact, he's still considering it, maybe that's why he hasn't called her back. Her infidelity has left him with another huge hole in himself. What happens to all these holes as life progresses? Do they get filled in by other relationships? Kevin does not think so. He thinks his spirit becomes Swiss cheese.

When he was born, he was just pure mother's milk, nothing artificial, all natural. As he got older, his parents, kindergarten teachers and society hardened him into cheese. He made friends and began to trust people. Then after a while, those people betrayed Kevin, putting holes into his spirit. He had become Swiss cheese. He had no real choice in this. It just happened, as it does to everyone.

How many holes can a person take before the remaining cheese just collapses in on itself and a man stops trying? This is the secret to life: No one knows how many holes a man has, or is capable of sustaining and withstanding. To Mr. Snipes, it is probably just a few. To a man of Mr. Tapestry's character, it is many. To Kevin, he does not know, yet.

The snow has stopped.

Enough self-pity.

Kevin jumps up and orders, "Sackett, follow me in your patrol car. I'm going to get Dale Horton."

Kevin turns around and walks past the crowd. He has an urge to push a few gawkers into the icy swamp and see how they like it. Kevin gets into his car, backs up and does a u-turn. He screams at the people in the road to move. At first, they do slowly. However, as Kevin begins to pick up speed, people are jumping out of his way as fast as they can. The road is a little wet. The snow did not stick.

The two lawmen drive into town to arrest Dale. The Miata is parked in front of the insurance store. Kevin and the sheriff get out. Kevin draws his Auto Mag and the Sheriff cocks his shotgun.

Dale's secretary sees the guns, but remains unfazed. She says Kevin and the sheriff will have to wait a moment until her boss gets off the phone.

The next moment, big Dale comes bursting from his inner office and runs past Kevin and the sheriff, knocking them back. Dale jumps into his sportster and peels away. Kevin and the sheriff look at each other as "Darn, he's fast for an overweight insurance guy."

Kevin and the sheriff rush to their cars and chase Dale through town. The little car is far ahead. Kevin sets his sights on it and speeds forward. The chase takes them through the countryside.

Dale, at one point, seems lost. He drives down the road leading to Baum's Slaughterhouse. His little car slides into the turn and crashes into a ditch, taking out some wooden posts that keep in the cattle that about to be butchered.

The posts badly damage his car.

Dale gets out and tosses a spent cigarette towards Kevin. The insurance agent runs towards the slaughterhouse in the wet field with the doomed animals. Kevin pulls into the driveway and races up the road. Dale is pushing the cattle aside.

His gray slacks become splattered with mud and manure. He stumbles and falls into a pool of black water. The grime covers his face. He is trying to get to the opening at the side of the barn, where the cattle get killed. He does not know about the two-ton weight.

Kevin jumps out of the car and into the muddy field and follows in Dale's wake. He has cleared a path through the cattle.

Kevin thinks that these animals are so huge close up.

Their brown bulk waits for Kevin to run past them. Then the animals close the gap, depriving Kevin of any sort of retreat. The rookie runs faster. He, too, slips in the mud and manure and does a face plant into the smelly earth. He splashes around trying to get up on his feet.

Kevin yells, "Dale, you son-of-a-bitch. You're under arrest."

The cries from the cattle ring loud. Moo. Moo. Moo. They drown out Kevin's screams. The cattle's nostrils shoot out water vapor. The cold air near the beasts turns to steam. Kevin can barely see. The path between the cattle is closing.

Cows' hooves step down and cut into his cowboy boots. Dale is just a few cows away.

"Dale, I know you killed Doug, and you killed my partner. You're history."

Dale looks back. His puffy face is splattered with mud.

Dale coughs, then he shouts, "Get away from me you maniac. Only Jesus can judge me, not man."

Dale is right.

Jesus is sentencing Dale to death.

Jesus is fogging Dale's mind with anger. There is no remorse coming from Dale. The anger pushes Dale further towards the lethal lead weight. Dale does not know it, but he has just past through the bovine's version of death row. In a moment, he will get justice.

The insurance salesman enters his death chamber.

Kevin stops.

Dale smiles back at Kevin as if to say, "I'm free."

Then, like God's mighty fist, the weight screams down from the sky. It crashes down on top of him. Dale's head is crushed.

Kevin kneels down in the mud.

In the distance, a police siren screams.

Sheriff Sackett helps Kevin up and takes him back to his motel room.

Kevin showers again and packs to go home.

He calls Peg to tell her that he will be there in an hour.

Kevin calls Sergeant Caretaker.

Jim reassures the rookie over the phone that he is behind him 100% and that he wants him back A.S.A.P. Jim says he will co-ordinate Tim's retrieval with the Madison hospital, as well as break the news to the Maxwell family.

Before Kevin leaves, he drives out to see Mr. Tapestry to say good-bye.

Kevin knocks on the door.

The gentleman farmer comes to the door. He is dressed in clean blue jeans and a blue denim shirt. His gray hair is slicked back. His broad face has some color in it.

"Hello Kevin. Come in. Do you want a drink?"

"Does everyone around here drink cocktails right after lunch?"

"No, just us old folks."

"Yes, please."

He mixes up Kevin a martini, with just a splash of vermouth and three plump olives. They walk through the tidy kitchen and sit in his living room. There are many antiques and oil paintings of settlers, or farmers as society now calls them. The two men talk about farming some more and Mr. Tapestry even gives Kevin that arrowhead he so loves.

"Sir, why do you love to farm so much? It seems to be more of a lost cause than a lost art?"

"A long time ago, people moved to Michigan to raise their families; but most of all, to raise their own food and to love their own land. I guess farming is in my blood, more than God is, or money or politics. I just enjoy every fall and spring as something new. I'm amazed at the cycle of death and life.

"Soon, I'm going to die. My grave will remain bare for a few months but then some weeds—definitely weeds—will grow on top of me, then hopefully some flowers. It doesn't mean anything. It's just something that happens. Farming is something I have to do."

A few martinis later, Kevin leaves.

He drives past the deserted fields and the woods in between the fields.

He thinks about being an M.B.I. agent. In an odd way, he is nothing more than a farmer who reaps in criminals during the autumn of their sorry lives.

Kevin puts in the Grateful Dead's *Workingman's Dead* tape. The drive back to Ann Arbor is pleasant, but he notices—like never before—how the space along side the road collapses under man's development.

Space is a premium. Less and less of it goes unused the closer Kevin gets to Ann Arbor. From the acres of fields around Lyons, to the block-long gaps near Madison, to alley-wide breaks in the city of Ann Arbor, he travels into an increasingly more compact society.

In Ann Arbor, neighborhoods sprout "For Sale" signs, not corn and tomatoes. If the residents are lucky, they may know their neighbors after a few years, only to see them move away.

Kevin anxiously shifts in his seat, as if the city's buildings are becoming bars in a prison. He rolls down the window, expecting the wind to relieve him of his discomfort, but he is rudely greeted by stale, cold air.

He reaches Ann Arbor. He exits the highway. Along side the busy main road are restaurants and strip malls jammed together. This is his neighborhood.

Before he left, this all seemed normal. Now it seems fake, as if he is seeing Christmas decorations go up at Target right after Labor Day. There are cars everywhere, even at six o' clock. The city's lights blind him.

Kevin cranks the stereo to the Dead's song "Uncle John's Band" and tries to block out this commercial scene. It does not work. There are lighted signs trying to capture his attention, his business, his money. The fluorescent overhead lights all converge to create a low-lying glow that makes it impossible to see the stars in the sky. He rushes past this scene towards his suburb.

He pulls into it, and drives past pleasant $300,000 homes. The condos are at the end of this suburb. It is perfect for the two of them. They do not have to mow the lawn, shovel the snow, or rake the leaves. Their little lawn and the grass look healthy. However, compared to Derrick's huge lawn, Kevin's patch is only a suburban ornament. The sprinkler system waters it every night during the summer at around nine o' clock.

Kevin pulls into their driveway and honks.

Peg, beautiful Peg, comes running out of the condo. A calico, silk scarf wraps around her neck, and it is tucked inside a rich brown cardigan stretched around her chest. She is wearing white, wool slacks. Her big, blue eyes and long black eyelashes pop into the window of Kevin's car. He smiles, shuts off the car and gets out. Her perfumed body clutches him hard. Her fingernails dig into his back.

She whispers in his ear a long, "I'm sorry."

"C'mon let's go inside."

They walk up the concrete steps, passing a small concrete rabbit with dried flowers wrapped around its neck.

Inside, Peg grabs her glass of wine, turns around and asks, "So, what do you want to do now, play bridge?"

"No, we need to talk."

The young couple sits down.

"Peg, do you remember how we met?"

"Of course, at a Grateful Dead concert in Washington, D.C. You and I danced all night. We had the best summer together I've ever had."

"Peg, don't you see? When we're together, everything's great. It's our careers that are messing everything up. If we didn't have to work so hard all the time, we could spend more time together. Peg, I love you."

"I love you, too."

Kevin continues, "Honey, my point is that when we were in Washington, D.C. we used to do tons of things that didn't require money. We'd go to those free outdoor symphonies, walk along the Mall, go to political discussions and drink cheap beer on our Georgetown stoop. Why can't we do that again?"

"Because, one of us would have to quit their job."

"Let's flip a coin."

"Forget it. Honey you're talking crazy."

She moves over to him and kneels down, resting her hands on his knees.

She says, "Kevin, look, I screwed up. I'm sorry. I missed you and I lashed out. I tried to undermine our marriage. I'm not good with men you know that. I don't trust them. Give me, give us, another shot. Let's both keep working. And maybe seeing a marriage counselor would help, too. What do you say?"

Kevin leans over and tenderly kisses her forehead.

He says, "OK, you're the boss."

Peg mischievously asks, "Now, bridge?"

"No, bed."

"That's what I meant."

Epilogue

Thanks for the taking the time to read my first novel, "Man Harvesting Man." As you've just read, religion, or the lack of it, is a central theme. Religion to me has always played a strong role in my development, thus there will always be religious aspects in my writing. From the time of <u>having</u> to go to church <u>every</u> Sunday, attending a private, Christian high school, Lumen Christi, being approached by my parents' best friends, priests, and having my littlest brother himself just graduate from Denver Seminary with his Master's in Divinity so that he can be a priest, it seems that I could sweat Holy water and bleed red wine.

So, my publisher, Dr. Marcus Barccani and his editors, suggested that I address the religious stance of the novel, not only because of the brevity of my first undertaking, but also because of its anti-clerical tone. Let me set the record straight: I'm not anti-clerical per se, but very clerical to the point that I'm hyper critical of the hypocrisy that exists in almost every churchgoer who proudly takes a couple hours out of their week to sing and pray and then spends the other 100 or so of their waking hours subtlety screwing each other over!

The point is that like it or not, in America, we have to deal with religion every day. Our country was built on Biblical statutes. Our Constitution reads likes the Ten Commandments. Yes, we've attempted to take out the words God and Jesus and used such language as "the separation of Church and State" but much of the United States' morality comes straight from the Good Book. So, either you follow this righteous path of "Love Thy Neighbor As Thyself," or you move on. Jail is still another option.

I'm not anti-America either, but it just seems that the more successful one is in our country, the holier they assume to become. We, the heathen, look at successful people and say to ourselves, "Boy, they really must be living the clean life. They must have been very good boys and girls." Bullshit!

Every one of us commits crimes all the time. We push ourselves. We push the envelope. We push the system. Just to eek out a little more. Just to attain a little more gold dust. The successful ones, I believe, have just developed really good blinders, like the ones racehorses wear at the Kentucky Derby. They know that they're committing little sins throughout the day, but so what, because they know that they're not breaking major laws and besides there are 10 more racehorses all around them thundering towards the finish line. And finally the successful ones know that ultimately, when the work-week is over, they can fall into the all-loving, all-forgiving arms of religion. The blinders fall to the floor as God's bright light beams through arched, candy-colored windows.

Christians in my book are not automatically antagonists because they're Christians. I just wanted to create a little insurrection about the personalities that I've personally witnessed, people who have prayed one minute and then consciously went out of their way to hurt someone the next minute. Even if you're not overly religious, or are not a part of a religious family to witness this hypocrisy, think of the times a Lexus with a fish symbol screwed to its trunk knowingly cuts you off in traffic. Nine times out of ten that Lexus is driven by a realtor on their way to a house closing who can't wait to cash their 7% commission check. Meanwhile, you, the mild-mannered atheist, almost had a heart attack!

Thus, the story of, antagonist, Dale Horton's rise and fall. In the book, Dale is a self-made man. He's followed the American dream of working hard, having a family and building his dream house. He's over-weight because he's either busy calling clients at his desk or eating nice meals with family and friends. And of course, every church function would be remiss without its share of cookies, cake and hot coffee. His large stomach gives to others the impression that he's a communal anchor. He's solid. You can always lean on Dale Horton for help. I made him a smoker because it's visible sin in our non-smoking society, and I felt Dale needed one bad trait that he was conscious of and not ashamed to purport.

Obviously, Dale's other great sin, though not as visible at first, is murder. Dale's belief system, nurtured in the Bible-belt of the Midwest, becomes twisted with the help of rural isolationism, where people respect each other's solitude. This buffer allows his religious beliefs to "ferment" into a type of Christianity that punishes, not forgives those who break God's laws. Dale reverts back to the Old Testament, a Christ-less void, where sinners were turned into pillars of salt and corrupt cities were pummeled with balls of fire.

In the setting of a house here and a house there, only after a few miles, Dale's belief system blossom's into a poisonous weed that wants to choke the life out of the town's sinners. When Doug Richards invades and pen-etrates Dale's fortress of twisted beliefs by selling pot to Dale's son, the worst happens to the town: a young man is murdered, a son loses his father, a dying town gets more bad news and a M.B.I. agent is bludgeoned to death. All because Dale believes right makes might. Wrong!

Religion is no more a shield than it's a sword. You can't hide behind the Bible while you consciously hurt people. Likewise you can't hurt people in the name of the Bible. Dale does both. He punishes then he hides.

I felt that as long as I was addressing the hypocrisy of religious believ-ers, to be fair, I needed to state my take on religion. Using protagonist, Kevin Sir, a naive young man who's an adolescent in the maturation process of discovering religion, I voice my concern by continuously posing the ques-tion: What's wrong with just being good, as opposed to being a good Chris-tian? To Kevin, there's nothing wrong with not believing that Jesus is the Son of God, as long as he is a good person. But what Kevin fails to realize is that to Christians, his good heart—without Jesus—gets him an eternity's stay in Hell.

I still have a beef with Christians about this. Why is it that a Christian who lies, cheats and steals is better off than an atheist who doesn't? Because, their answer is, that Christians know they're human and thus corruptible, but they're also saved because they believe in Jesus.

I just don't get it.

You see, when I was growing up in a Christian household, I tried very hard to be a good Christian. I prayed, followed the Christian tenets and even took turns in a teenager's prayer group. But one thing was missing: an an-swer. No one was at the other end of the phone. God or Jesus never answered me. There was not even a heavenly message machine. I felt foolish for pray-ing for so long to a mute entity.

Now, let me say that I still strongly believe in the concept of the Ten Commandments; such as, "Love Thy Neighbor As Thyself," etc., but when it comes to there being a higher power, I'm just not sure. I mean, when I was praying, I was praying for unselfish things. I wasn't praying for a new bike or an A on my next Latin test, I was praying for my Mom and Dad's health; my two brothers' happiness and goodwill toward men. You know, the big stuff.

I prayed for these all the time. After praying, I'd sit back, fold up the kneeler board and sit back on my pew, content that my job was done. I did this through high school. Then it hit me, I never really felt content. I was just happy that my Mom and Dad were happy that I just prayed.

So then I really tried to communicate with God. Nothing happened. So I thought, you know, I really shouldn't pressure him. God's got the U.S. and Russia pointing world-ending nuclear weapons at each other, famine in Africa, the Jim Jones thing, oh and Madonna. I'll come back later when God's not so tied up.

But God's always tied up! So I went back to the drawing board. I pleaded with him to just answer me. I just wanted to hear him say, "I hear you brother. I feel your pain, or I'm glad you're happy. But as long as you're on Earth, I really can't dabble in your affairs. There's this free will thing going. But I'm glad you called. Have a nice life. I'll see you on the flip side."

My littlest brother, the minister-to-be, says that all those words are as close as picking up the Bible and that God slash Jesus rarely singles us humans out to have a chat about day to day events. So read the Bible, he says. But have you ever truly read the Bible? When I was little, I could imagine Noah's Ark, hell, I still believed in Santa Claus. But later when I discovered that the adults in my life went out of their way to trick me, I could also no longer believe in other incredible stories: Jesus healing the blind and crippled with the touch of his hand; Shem living to 700 years old; Adam and Eve getting kicked out of the Garden of Eden; and, the biggie, Jesus' resurrection. It all seemed fantastic. So with all of these unbelievable stories and the fact that no one was listening to my most intimate confessions, I said to religion, "You know what, I need a timeout."

This is where I am today—in limbo. I still occasionally go to St. John's Cathedral or the Episcopal Church where my brother works, but every time I pray, nothing happens. I'm not mad, just sad because I don't get it. And so I'm not saved. I'm also a little scared: Remember that being good—without Jesus—means that when I die I could be in nice, warm, tropical-kind-of-place, where every meal is barbequed and my horned patron will forever prick me with a stick-like thing. Ouch.

The Author

John Waters, like many of Colorado's transplants, came to ski and never left. He graduated from the University of Colorado at Boulder with a degree in English. He's a registered financial planner, who really enjoys the gyrations of the stock market. He teaches financial classes for Denver Public Schools and writes a financial column for D'Zine, a leisure magazine.

A Virtual Publishing Group Edition
2000